MEN
DON'T
CRY

PART 2

GOD BLESS CANADA!

Chris Ross

Note for Librarians: A cataloguing record for this book is available from Library and Archives Canada at www.collectionscanada.ca/amicus/index-e.html

ISBN 1-4120-9927-7

Printed in Victoria, BC, Canada. Printed on paper with minimum 30% recycled fibre.
Trafford's print shop runs on "green energy" from solar, wind and other environmentally-friendly power sources.

TRAFFORD™
PUBLISHING™

Offices in Canada, USA, Ireland and UK

Book sales for North America and international:
Trafford Publishing, 6E–2333 Government St.,
Victoria, BC V8T 4P4 CANADA
phone 250 383 6864 (toll-free 1 888 232 4444)
fax 250 383 6804; email to orders@trafford.com

Book sales in Europe:
Trafford Publishing (UK) Limited, 9 Park End Street, 2nd Floor
Oxford, UK OX1 1HH UNITED KINGDOM
phone +44 (0)1865 722 113 (local rate 0845 230 9601)
facsimile +44 (0)1865 722 868; info.uk@trafford.com

Order online at:
trafford.com/06-1684

10   9   8   7   6   5   4

Brett,

God be with you,

always!

Chris Ross

PART 2

John Thomas 2nd
1801 – 1874.

INDEX

ILLUSTRATIONS

SYNOPSIS

John Thomas was born in a coal mining town in Wales. He worked in the mine a few years and hated it, so decided to leave against his father's wishes. He sailed to America arriving in Pennsylvania about 1798. He met a beautiful girl named Mary, whose parents had emigrated from Holland to America the year before. Her parents were aristocratic and would not consider the likes of John – a common laborer – marrying their daughter. John and Mary married anyway and sailed to Vermont where John got work making flag poles. The final words of Mary's father would ring in their ears all their lives. "Don't you ever bring dat man or his children home to our farm."

Mary and John had two sons. When the boys were about ten and twelve years old, their father was killed on the job. Unable to support the boys, Mary apprenticed them to a clothes dryer for seven years, to learn a trade. She then left to go back to her parent's home. The man the boys were to work for appeared to have a surly disposition.

CHAPTER 1

FREEDOM BECKONS

The Thomas brothers – John soon to be nineteen and Hosea, now seventeen, lay face down quivering and groaning on their bed. Their thin and bony backs were red and swollen from the angry bruises that almost broke the skin. John ran his fingers through his blond curly hair and clenched his fists. His blue eyes were squinted almost closed.

The year was 1820, and things had not gone well for the two boys under the care and tutorship of Mr. Johnson. Tears were filling Hosea's hazel eyes and running down his face into the bedding. He brushed his dark brown wavy hair back from his face and looked at John, anger and pain written all over his countenance.

"I can't take any more of this treatment," Hosea cried, as his thin body shook the bed. "I'd like to smash Mr. Johnson's whipping stick into kindling wood."

"Hush," John whispered, "These walls have ears remember? We don't want to get another beating, do we?"

"There was nothing wrong with Mrs. Mayfield's clothing." Hosea clenched his fists. "I hate being apprenticed to a clothes dryer. I want to be a farmer who lives in the country and has freedom." Hosea was whispering very quietly now, recalling the consequences of aggravating Mr. Johnson any more. Both boys lay quietly for a time thinking about the events that had taken place.

"Mrs. Mayfield could have paid for the work," John remarked. "Her clothes looked pretty good. Doing them over again didn't make any improvement that I could see."

Another silence followed. Hosea was restless, and finally turned his face to John. "I can't stand any more of this so-called training," he whimpered. "It is getting worse the closer we get to the end of our seven year apprenticeship." Speaking more resolutely, he continued, "I'm not going to stay for another year and a half of this. *I'm going to run away!*"

John's broad shoulders tensed, and his large bony frame suddenly came off the bed. In the dusk of evening, he was standing over Hosea and had his brother's arm in a vice-like grip in his large hands.

"*Don't do it*," he whispered urgently, desperately, so quiet Hosea could hardly hear him. "*You know they'll catch you, and the law says they have every right to hang you.* Lay low until our backs are healed up some, and I can think of a plan we both can take part in." John ran his fingers through his hair again, giving it an anguished tug. "Don't do anything foolish. *Please Hosea, keep your head about you.*"

"Father would never be able to sleep if he knew he came from Wales to provide this kind of death for us." Hosea blew his nose.

"Mother would be broken hearted too, if she knew." John lay down again. Desperately trying to console Hosea, he continued, "They both thought Vermont was a great place to make a living and raise a family." He paused thoughtfully. "It would have been too, if father hadn't been killed. She did what she had to Hosea." John's eyes softened at the mention of his mother.

Closing his eyes, he lay thoughtful for several minutes. When he opened them he turned to face Hosea in the darkness. "Give me time to plan something so that we both have a chance to escape alive," he pleaded in desperate whispers.

"I wish father had never died. We wouldn't be in this mess if he had lived." Hosea was heeding John's advice and softening his angry outbursts.

"Things change, Hosea. What happened to father was not anybody's wish or plan. We shook hands on this deal thinking it was going to be hard here before we moved in. We just didn't think Mr. Johnson would be so heartless." Grimacing as he turned onto his side, he continued, "We must think ahead to move on. I want desperately to leave here, too, so keep your head. I want to live so I can tell my kids about it, just don't do anything foolish." John couldn't conceal the desperate urgency in his voice. "If they catch and hang you, they will hunt until they find me and will beat me until I would wish I were dead, too. *Do you get it?!*"

"Yeh, I get it John. I'll keep my head."

✳   ✳   ✳

Four days later John put his hand on Hosea's back. Hosea flinched and gasped. They were going to bed, and as John pulled the thin covers up over the two of them, he turned to Hosea. "Do you think you are good enough to run for two or three days without stopping?"

"What do you mean?" Hosea couldn't conceal his rising excitement.

John clapped his hand over Hosea's mouth to remind him to keep quiet. "*I've got a plan*," John whispered so quietly Hosea had difficulty hearing him. "Tomorrow, don't do anything different than usual. Do a good job for Mr.

Johnson, and make sure you don't get another beating, understand?"

Hosea nodded his head in the darkness, and John took his hand off of his mouth. "Then what?"

"Do you understand the importance of not raising suspicions?" John was beginning to feel desperate. Hosea was taking the whole plan too lightly and could cause things to blow up in their faces.

"*Hosea. Do you understand?*" he whispered hoarsely.

"Yes. I want to live too, you know. What's your plan?" Hosea demanded, "Tell me what you have planned."

Again John hesitated.

"Come on John, tell me," Hosea insisted.

"Well, alright," John relented. "North of Woodstock there is a large oak tree not far from the bank of the Bernard Brook. After we have completed our deliveries tomorrow evening, we will circle around town and then go to that tree. The first one there will climb up into its branches and wait until the other one arrives. There will be no time to waste, so don't fool around. From there we will make our plans of travel."

"What if one of us gets caught and can't get there?" Hosea worried.

"The first one there will wait an hour, which should be more than enough time." John continued, "If the other doesn't show up by then, the first one must go on alone. There is no need for the both of us getting killed if one of us can get away."

"I like it. I'll be there." Hosea spoke quietly, but with excitement and enthusiasm.

"Don't forget to act absolutely normal tomorrow, or you will be suspected of being up to something," John warned. "We will be in trouble before we do our deliveries if anyone suspects. *Now remember that.*"

"I get it. I get it. I'll remember," Hosea promised, but John was still worried.

✳   ✳   ✳

The following day things went well enough. Hosea got scolded for leaving a shed door open, otherwise things went as planned. When evening came and it was time to make the deliveries, Hosea picked up his bundles and headed out. John put his orders together then gathering them up, headed out to do his deliveries. When he was finished delivering, he went out the end of the street and into the trees there. He circled around town, picking up speed as he went and reached the designated tree. Hosea had not yet arrived.

John climbed up into the massive tree and sat down on a large limb to wait.

CHAPTER 2

ESCAPE!

To the east John could hear the Bernard Brook bubbling over the stones and around the rocks in its bed. To the west and north he could hear coyotes howling to each other, planning their nights hunting trip. To the south of him the town was quiet. Everyone would be indoors having their evening meals. *If only Hosea would hurry up!*

The Bernard Brook traveled out of heavy bush from the north, past Woodstock to join the Ottau-Quechee River to the south. John was thinking that to go along the Bernard Brook to the tree cover would be a good way to go. The trees would afford them cover while they traveled, and the various red, yellow and green colors of them would be a good camouflage to conceal their whereabouts.

"Hosea, come on. What's keeping you?" he whispered to himself. "Please God, keep Hosea safe."

At that moment he heard Sheriff Polson's hound dog Hooter baying. A chill ran down his back. John knew Hooter was a good tracker and had assisted Sheriff Polson in capturing many elusive escapees.

"Time's up Hosea," he said. "I've got to go."

With a heavy heart he clambered out of the tree and headed south-east to the stream. He was almost to the creek when he thought he heard men shouting from town. Not stopping to listen, he broke into a run to the creek's edge. Stopping to take off his shoes and socks, he stuffed the socks inside the shoes, tied the laces together, and flung them around his neck. He splashed into the cold water, and continued going in a south-east direction until he was in the water up to his knees.

"Follow this scent Ol' Hooter," he said as he turned around and headed in the northerly direction of the stream, staying in the water at knee depth. Unable to go very fast in this depth of water, he went as fast as he could, thinking, *Must hurry. Got to hurry.*

An hour later, still in the water following the stream's twisting and turning course, he thought, *It might be safe now to get up on land where I can make better time.*

The sun was going down and its hot rays gave everything an unrealistic appearance of being golden. With his shoes and socks on, he started running through the trees and gradually curved his direction to the west. He hadn't gone far when he came to a faint trail that was going in the direction he wanted to go. He gladly followed it and although it was getting dark he was able to distinguish it by the opening of the trees against the backdrop of the evening sky. He could feel the ground sloping up and knew he was getting into the mountains. Behind, he heard the distinct sound of Hooter baying.

"Sounds like they might be at the place where I went into the water," he said with fear in his heart. "Hooter will figure it out in a while. I just hope I can fool him again."

He started running even though he was exhausted, and still going up hill. His heart pounding with fear, plus the exertion of the rough hilly terrain littered with deadwood that he kept tripping over, caused his breath to come in gasps.

"Can't stop now," he said aloud. "That ol' dog will keep going all night. So must I."

It was pitch black dark without a moon in the sky, but he kept going, not sure of which direction, but watching the Big Dipper and the North Star, and hoping he was heading north-west. Mosquitoes were a problem. He found that as long as he kept moving, he could only swat his face and arms. His back was their banquet hall.

✳   ✳   ✳

Much later he felt he had to rest. His knees were bruised from falling over the deadwood, and his legs were numb. The air was much cooler, so the mosquitoes were no longer bothering him. He sat down under a large tree, and leaning up against it, gasped for air until he was able to breathe comfortably. He then dozed off to sleep, unable to stay awake any longer.

"John." He woke up with a start.

"Who is calling me?" There was no answer. He looked around and listened, but still no sign or sound of anyone. Fear gripped him, and a chill ran down his spine with the feeling that someone was watching him. It was still black dark, but to one side of the sky he noticed it was a bit lighter.

"I guess that is where the sun is going to come up. Now I'll be able to keep my directions straight," he said as he rose to his feet.

The distinct feeling someone was watching him, again gripped him with fear. He forgot he was exhausted. Driven by fear as he went around the tree he had rested against, in the dark he broke into a brisk run and stepped

Map of Vermont

into space. "*AAAAAAAAAAAA*," he shrieked as he fell through the air, until something hard hit his head and everything went black.

*　*　*

When he woke he was looking up a long very steep wall of stones, rocks and a few small, stunted, deciduous trees. A couple of the trees directly above him were broken down. His head was throbbing! The sun was shining brightly on him. Mosquitoes had taken their fill, and were now replaced with flies. He looked at the broken trees for a few minutes. "I'm sorry I broke you off," he whispered, then staggered painfully to his feet. "Thanks for saving my life. I'm lucky I didn't break my neck in that fall. Boy does my back ever hurt... almost as much as my head."

John ran his hand through his hair and saw that his hand was covered with blood. Running his other hand over his face, it too came away bloody.

"My nose is bleeding, as well as the top of my head," he said aloud. He thought he could hear water rippling in the distance to the west. Walking stiffly and with difficulty through the bushes in that direction, he finally broke out of the shrubbery to see a lake lying before him. Going to the shore and looking out across the vast body of water, he pondered, Now what?

Looking at his clothes and the mess his hands were in, he decided to wade into the water, clothes and all, to splash around until he could wash some of the blood and dirt off.

"Oooooo! That's cold!" he said as he lowered himself into the water. Once he got used to the temperature he thought it felt good. When he felt refreshed and cleaner he left the water and stood, dripping on shore looking out across the lake, again.

I want to cross the lake, he thought. *But how?* He had been standing and praying for help for quite a while. His clothes had pretty well stopped dripping, when he heard a rustle in the bushes a bit to the north. He attempted to run back to the bushes, but found he was too stiff and sore to run or even walk fast. He would have ducked under cover, but there was nothing to hide under. He felt trapped!!

Standing on the shore and fearing the arrival of a bear emerging from the trees, he was startled, then frightened, when he saw two Indians appear carrying a canoe. When the Indians saw him, they dropped the canoe, then grabbed their bows and fixed an arrow into each one. They stepped forward a few steps in John's direction, arrows pointing to the ground ready for immediate use. John raised his hands shoulder high. The Indians stopped and spoke to each other. Then they approached him, one going to his left and the other to his right. They circled around him, carefully evaluating him.

What they saw was an almost six foot white man with the most of the back of his shirt torn open, revealing a back covered with bruises, scratches, scars and a couple of nasty cuts. His torn pants exposed bloody scrapes on both knees and legs. His nose, still bleeding a little was dripping blood onto his blonde curly beard. One blue eye was blackened and swelling, matching the ear on the other side of his head that was swelling and scraped and bruised. The cut on the top of his head was almost covered with his blonde curly hair, but a telltale mat of blood covered the spot.

If I was standing in their place and looking at me, I would be terrified, John was thinking as he watched the expressions on their faces. *I must look like something that fell out of the sky.* He learned nothing from their expressionless faces. One of them grunted, and they both turned and taking the arrows out of the bows, walked back to the canoe.

John heard Hooter baying in the far distance. Fear gripped his heart as he looked back up his trail. The Indians heard it too, and glancing in the direction of the sound picked up the canoe and came back to the shore near John. As they dropped the canoe in the water one of them turned, and to John's surprise, asked, "Where go?"

"Canada." John pointed to the far side of the lake as he spoke.

Both Indians looked at him long and hard, then climbed into the canoe and picked up their paddles. Hooter bayed again much closer than before. John looked back and saw the dog was on the bank that he – John had taken a great tumble from. Hooter was running back and forth along the top of the bank, looking for a way down. Desperation creasing John's face, he turned to see the Indians were well out in the lake and paddling rapidly. Putting his hands over his eyes, he fell to his knees,

"Dear Heavenly Father, please deliver me from capture by this dog and his owner. If it be Thy will, deliver me to Canada, and freedom from captivity."

John heard the water splash behind him, at the same time he saw the now limping Hooter coming through the bushes, baying all the way.

CHAPTER 3

RESCUE OR PRISONER?

Turning to see why the water was splashing, to John's astonishment the Indians had the canoe on the shore at his feet. One of them motioned for him to get in. Without considering the possible consequences, he climbed into the canoe, and the Indians started paddling again.

They were about forty feet out onto the lake when Hooter reached the water's edge. He ran back and forth considering jumping into the water.

While John sat helplessly watching the dog, the Indian at the back picked up his bow and fitting an arrow to it, let it fly at Hooter hitting him in the hind leg. With a yelp the dog sat down and bit at the arrow. John looked at the Indians. There was never a change of their expressions, but John felt a flood of relief.

"There Sheriff Polson, give up the chase and take care of your dog," he whispered.

* * *

The sun shone brightly all day. John being unaccustomed to so much sun realized his hands and face were burning. Dusk followed a glorious golden and pink sunset while they reached the other side of the lake. One of the Indians proceeded to make a fire while the other disappeared into the bush with the bow and arrows. A short time later he came back with a freshly killed grouse. They shared their meal with a very grateful John. There was no conversation during the whole time.

In the morning the roles were reversed. The hunter of the previous evening kindled a fire, which still had some red embers under the ashes, while his companion took the bow and arrows to the lake, and shortly came back with a large fish.

After eating, the camp-site was cleaned up until there was no evidence of them having been there. Picking up the canoe, they headed into the bush and mountains ahead, with John painfully struggling to stay close to their heels. John soon realized they were following an almost invisible trail, similar to the one he had followed shortly after he had left Bernard Brook.

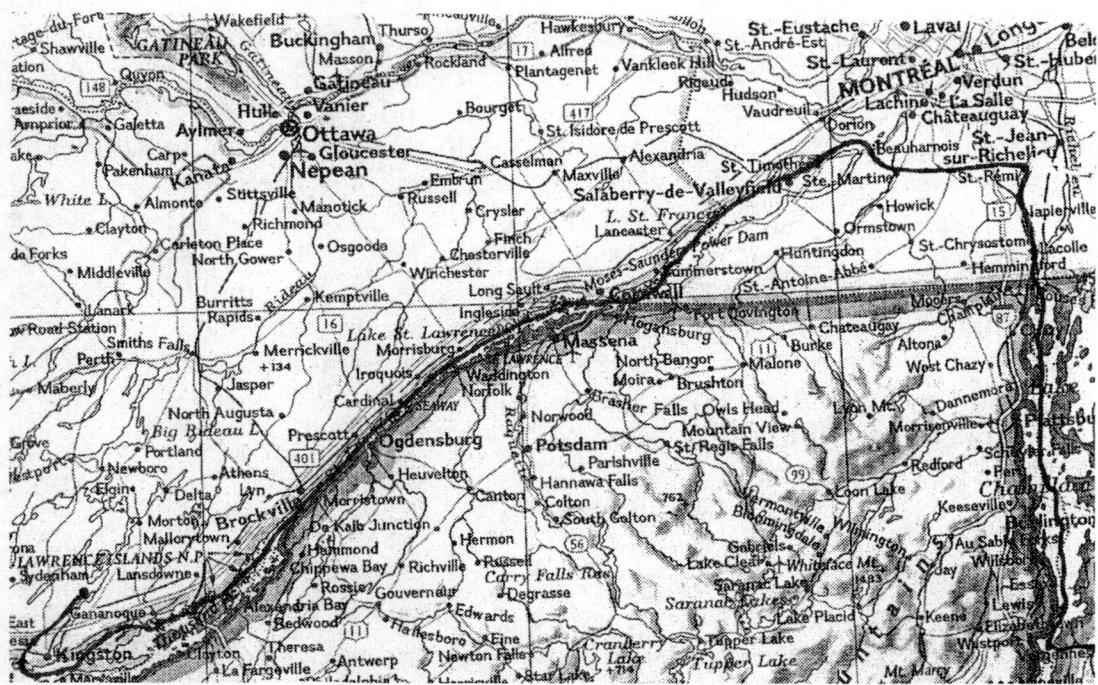

Map showing the terrain and lake along the west coast of Vermont and the approximate trail John Thomas may have used while traveling from Vermont to Canada.

For several days they wound around mountains, hills, rocks, and through dense bush. John lost count of the days. He felt like he had been away from Woodstock and Mr. Johnson for months, which gave him the feeling of being free from the apprenticeship.

They ate berries, nuts and plants they found as they traveled, as well as the occasional fresh meat. The Indians dressed John's wounds with the leaves of plants and pads of moss. They used mud to adhere the leaves and moss to his skin, and also on his face to protect him from the sun. He felt he was healing up fast, and was starting to feel relaxed and contented.

"Hosea, if only you had made it with me!" John lamented. "Oh, Hosea. What did you do wrong that prevented you from being with me?" he mourned. "Oh, my brother! My only brother! The last of my family!" Squeezing his eyes shut to fight back the tears that wanted to come, he opened them and gazed into the evening camp fire, lost in thought.

✳   ✳   ✳

Morning brought a clear golden sky with the rising of the sun, which John was able to use for a guide. He estimated they had been traveling north, but now the Indians turned into bush that had no pathway, and headed west. A day's travel brought them to the shore of another lake where they camped for the night. John was now helping with many of the camp chores and when they were on the trail he was carrying the paddles.

Daylight saw them putting the canoe in the water, and travel was taking them north. The sky was cloudy most of the time they spent on what seemed to be a very long lake.

The wind sprang up and began blowing rough waves that rocked the frail canoe. It was late afternoon when the first drops of rain came down. The Indians pulled to shore, and they all worked together to pull the canoe up on the bank and take their supplies into the woods where they found a large, heavily foliaged tree.

John helped set up camp for the night in the dry shelter of the tree. The dark clouds opened up, and for an hour rain poured down. No fire was made, but they ate some tasty vegetation. In the morning they found some bushes with nuts on them, then closer to shore they came across some smaller bushes loaded with berries. It was a very tasty and nourishing breakfast.

The sun shone unmercifully following the rain. They traveled all day to reach what seemed to be a point the Indians were seeking. They beached the canoe on the west side of the lake, and after resting for the night they headed west. Another long day's hiking through uneven boulder strewn scrub trees, and broken levels of cliffs, brought them to the shore of a very wide and fast moving river that was flowing to the north-east. On the other side of the river, John could see a town.

"Are we going to cross this wild river in that little canoe?" he asked himself, as he looked at the formidable current. His answer came when without hesitation the canoe was placed in the water. The Indians got in and beckoned to John to do the same. They rowed to the middle of the flow, then heading the canoe in a south-west direction, began rowing furiously to travel against the current. The wind was blowing strongly from the north-east, and helping them travel against the rough current.

John sat low in the canoe and tightly gripped the sides, as the rushing current almost possessed the delicate craft. They were buffeted about like a leaf, but the Indians kept to the middle of the river as much as they could, where the surface was the smoothest. They had to pass around some large boulders that splashed water over the occupants of the canoe and almost capsized them once. The wild current would have smashed the canoe against the huge rocks, but the Indians pushed against the rocks with their paddles to save it and keep going up stream.

At another time they were caught in an eddy that spun the canoe in three circles before the straining paddlers were able to pull it into the straight current again.

John was terrified! He could put his hand over the side of the canoe and touch the mad-rushing water, and know that if he should ever fall into it, he would not come out alive. He felt like he was staring death in the face.

"Please God," he prayed, "Deliver us safely to our destination."

Progress was much slower than had been experienced on the lakes. When the sun started curving over the horizon to the west, the Indians pulled into shore and beaching the canoe, prepared to spend the night. A fire was started and a large fish was brought in from the raging river. It was dark when they were ready to lie down to sleep.

* * *

The Indians slept until after the sun was up. They ate the leftover fish from the night before, cleaned up the camp-site and taking the canoe, went to the river's edge. Hanging on to the canoe, they beckoned John to get in, then they both sprang in, and picking up the paddles, were on their way again.

When the sun said it was mid-afternoon they passed another town that was on the west side of the river. An hour later they beached the canoe on the west bank and disembarked. John thought they were going to have an early evening. Instead, one of the Indians waved his arm to the trees and rocks to the west and said, "Canada... Go."

John knew he was free to leave when he wanted to. He wanted to thank his travel companions, but because of the language barrier, he bowed deeply to them.

He then, got down on his knees, and closing his eyes, he prayed, "Heavenly Father. Thank you from the bottom of my heart for bringing me safely to this country of freedom. I wish You could have seen it as right to have brought Hosea with me. He would have been so grateful to You. I miss him so much. Please take good care of him. I know You have been with me from the beginning of my time on earth, and I pray You will show me what You want me, Your servant to do next. Amen."

When John opened his eyes and rose to his feet, the Indians were nowhere in sight.

I guess they wanted to lose the extra weight I was putting in the canoe causing heavier ballast to be paddled against that furious current, he reasoned to himself.

He was on his own again...but in Canada!!

CHAPTER 4

REWARDS OF FREEDOM

It was near evening, and John didn't notice that he was tired, but he did feel the pangs of hunger, which was making him weak. He picked some vegetation and started eating. The first plant he put into his mouth was very bitter, and he spat it out, along with several gobs of saliva. He smelled the next plant carefully, and broke off a small piece to chew. Finding it was acceptable in flavor he put the whole thing in his mouth, then searched for a few more of the same variety.

When he had eaten enough to relieve the gnawing pangs of hunger, he began trying to break off some evergreen branches to make a bed. First he bent them down, which didn't break them. Next he tried twisting and wringing them, which cracked the branch lengthwise, but didn't remove it from the tree. He had nothing with which to cut or tear the tough wood.

After trying two or three branches he concluded he was not going to be able to make a bed. The Indians had sharp honed knives made from animal bones and flint stone that cut through the branches nicely. He – John – had nothing sharp to work with.

"I guess I'll just keep going. I'm not going to sleep on this hard ground. It feels like bare rock, and I have enough aches and pains without adding that kind of discomfort." He was talking out loud to himself as he proceeded to set the direction in which he planned on traveling.

He walked slowly so he wouldn't trip over fallen trees, or slip on the rock, which he now realized was bare and rolling. It was also rough with many boulders scattered along the route he took. He circled a small lake whose existence surprised him, as there didn't seem to be a stream emptying into it. He couldn't hear any water trickling to indicate there was a feeder stream, but in the dark he thought he could have missed it.

By daylight he estimated he had covered several miles, and being guided by the stars, he was going in a westerly direction. The firey red sky announced the rising of the sun, which verified the directional information for him, and he felt relieved that he had not been traveling in circles all night. He came to a grove of low growing trees that were loaded with mouth watering, plump black berries.

"Praise God for providing food for me." he whispered as he pulled a handful of the berries and put them in his mouth and bit into them. His face wrinkled up, as his mouth puckered from the bitter flavor of the fruit. He had just decided he was going to eat them anyway, when he heard a grunt that sounded like a pig, coming from the other side of the grove. Bending over to look under the branches of the trees, he saw a bear at the same time it spotted him.

John bolted on the run with all the speed he could muster, up an incline that formed the edge of the basin for the shrubs, then down hill. He seemed to be approaching a clearing, but he could also hear the bear coming behind him, rapidly gaining on him. He broke out of the thick bush into sparse trees and found he was following a path.

As he came out of the thinner brush he suddenly realized he was almost to the edge of a cliff. The bear was almost on top of him as he swerved sharply to the left. Making a guttural sound, the bear swiped at him, knocking him over the edge of the cliff. He grasped frantically for something, - anything to hang onto.

Oh no! not again! he thought as he desperately clung to some shrubs while he hung over the edge. He struggled and scrambled to get back on the level again, watching to see when the bear was going to appear to finish the job it had started. He felt relief when he finally got on the level and there was no bear in sight. His heart was pounding, and his breath was coming in short gasps.

Placing his hands on his knees to make breathing easier, he was standing thus when he heard a whining, squealing sound coming from where he and the bear had just left the bushes. Looking up to see what was causing this noise, he saw two cubs come galloping out of the bush and run to the edge of the cliff. Looking down they began running back and forth along the top of the cliff, until finally they both plunged over the edge and rolled and tumbled down to the bottom.

John looked over the cliff to see if they had survived, and saw the big bear who had chased him, sitting at the bottom of the cliff, shaking it's head and rubbing it's face with a front paw. Both cubs were standing on their hind legs, licking the face of what was obviously their mother. She slowly got to her feet and ambled north along the base of the cliff.

Shaking violently John sat down against a large tree and leaning up against it, closed his eyes. His heart was pounding so hard and loud he thought it was going to burst. While he was waiting for his heart to settle down, he directed his attention to his surroundings. The trees were beautiful some with gold leaves and some with red leaves. There were many dark green evergreen trees, and also trees that had not yet started to change their color from their green summer coat.

John realized his heart was getting too slow. Rising to his feet he began walking around. Going to the place where the bears had gone over the cliff, he looked down to where they had landed and figured it was about thirty feet. He then looked beyond their landing to what was across the way, and realized he was looking at a meadow.

A hay meadow!! A meadow with several haystacks in it!! Haystacks meant he was close to where people lived. Even though he could not see any sign of buildings, he knew he was close to civilization!!

"*Oh Blessed Jesus! Oh praise God!*" he said aloud, "*I might make it through this alive, yet!* If I can find a way down off this cliff and into that meadow I can go to that close stack and get some sleep before hunting for people."

Looking over the edge of the cliff, he saw that it tapered down to nothing as it went to the south and then turned west. He started walking south and a half hour later was at the haystack. The sun was shining down warmly on him as he pulled hay out of the stack to make a cover over himself, and to make a flat area to lie on.

"I feel weak," he spoke to the heavens, "I need something to eat to regain some strength. Please Father, show me some food, after I have rested for a while."

He crawled into the stack, then pulling the hay up he covered his feet so the sun wouldn't make them too hot, then he covered his body including his head, as he didn't want to get sun burnt again. With the sun warming him, he soon fell into a blessed deep sleep of extreme, exhausted relaxation.

CHAPTER 5

GOD BLESS CANADA!

Something bit deeply into John's upper leg, pinning him to the ground. Instantly he was awake from a deep sleep, terror filling his heart.

"The bear!" he screamed in horror, as he struggled to his feet. Propelled by sheer terror he started to run for safety, but blocking his way past the stack was a team of huge horses that were hooked to a rack, effectively fencing him in. Turning around, he came face to face with a large grizzly bearded man, dressed in black hat, overalls and jacket, standing with feet braced, eyes bugged out, mouth wide open, and a pitch fork held menacingly in his hands, blocking any escape in that direction.

John turned and bolted between the horses and the stack. Running toward the cliff, his breath coming in gasps, his feet were getting heavy. He had not gone far when the ground seemed to come up and hit him in the face, and everything went black.

✳   ✳   ✳

When he opened his eyes, he was staring at a ceiling, and was covered to his chin with blankets.

"Hello," a soft gentle voice spoke to him. "There thee be."

Looking in the direction of the voice, John saw a figure advancing toward him. Still filled with terror, he jumped up screaming, "A-a-a-a-a-a-a-h-h-h-h-h!" Turning to run, he fell flat on the floor, the covers piling up on top of him.

The voice kept talking, "Don't be afraid, I'm not going to hurt thee. God brought thee here to us for the help thee so obviously needs."

At the mention of God, John felt a calming effect coming over him. He looked over to the voice and saw a woman standing by the foot of the bed, alarm written all over her face. She had a blue apron pulled over her dark dress, and a blue dust cap made from the same material as the apron, tied on her head.

"What be thy name son?" she asked, "My name is Ann and my husband who brought thee in from the field is John. We are the Hodgsons."

John started getting to his feet, keeping his eyes glued on the woman.

"I d-didn't know I was on a b-bed," he said apologetically, "M-my n-name's J-John...John T-Thomas."

Looking down at himself, he suddenly realized he had on none of his own clothes. Gasping with shame, he dived behind the bed again, pulling the blankets on the floor over his body.

"Don't worry about thy appearance John," Ann said. "Thy clothes were in such a pitiful mess John and I took them off thee. We put the night gown on thee that I have just finished making for my husband. We will repair or replace thy clothes."

Hesitatingly John stood up, again looking down at himself, he commented, "Th-th-this looks l-l-like a long sh-sh-shirt."

Ann was pleased that he was making conversation with her. He was starting to overcome his traumatic fear.

"Well, that is actually the pattern I use." she busied herself with picking something up from the floor to see if he could tolerate her moving around, without becoming panic stricken again.

John suddenly felt very weak and tired. He was relaxing and needed to lie down. Ann helped him get the blankets back on the bed and covered him up again.

"I have something for thee to eat, also a drink of water for thee. Just stay there and rest," she said as she headed out of the room.

When she returned, she was followed by the bearded monster who was John's last memory before blacking out. John cringed under the covers and pulled them up higher until they covered his face with only his blue eyes showing above them.

"John, this is my husband, John Lampton Hodgson," she said as she brought the food and drink to the bed. "People refer to him as J.L. Don't be afraid of him. He is very kind and gentle. He brought thee in from the field, and helped get thee into bed."

Relaxing again, John pulled the covers down below his face. Starting to get rational thoughts, he sensed these were people he could trust. "God bless Canada!" he mumbled.

"What was that thee said?" J. L. queried.

Concern showed up in John's eyes and facial expression when he heard the deep voice. He involuntarily pulled the covers up again. "God bless Canada." John repeated weakly and unconvincingly. His courage had stumbled, and he floundered a bit, then he started recovering again.

J.L. and Ann helped John sit up and banked pillows behind him to make him comfortable. J.L. gave him a drink of water, then Ann held a dish of custard pudding up close to his face and proceeded to feed him.

"The puddin's good," he said. "Thank you."

"Now young man," J.L. spoke with authority. "Thee will stay here until thee are on thy feet again, and have put on enough weight to look better than a scarecrow."

Am I dreaming? Is this true? John wondered in amazement.

"In the meantime John, while thee are recuperating thee can decide what thee wants to do when thee has regained thy strength."

"Mr. Hodgson, sir," John spoke with a more positive attitude than they had seen of him. "I know what I want to do. I want to farm. I just don't know how I am going to get started at it, that's all. I have no money to buy a place. I was thinking I would maybe be able to get some kind of a payin' job to earn money. I also need to learn how to operate a farm, as I have no experience at it."

"Farming eh? Well thee came to the right place," J.L. spoke with rising excitement. We keep several horses to do the farming with. We also keep a few cows to provide milk, cream and butter to sell at the store in Kingston, and also in Battersea, as well as supply our table. We also sell eggs from our hens, so you see we are very busy."

"Also, our sheep keep us supplied with wool for weaving, as well as meat," Ann interjected. "It would be God's blessing to have someone to help us."

"There is also close to three hundred acres we are cropping," J.L. continued, "As well as about five acres that needs to be cleared of the trees so we can start cropping it as well. I plan on clearing about an acre each year. Almost everything we grow is used for feed for the stock, and household needs. Any surplus we are granted from God to produce is sold either to the stores, or individuals, or at the Kingston Market."

The more J.L. and Ann talked, the more excited they became, until John was starting to feel their excitement welling up in his chest. John was beginning to see that life was holding a good promise for him. He was overwhelmed with gratefulness to God for bringing him to this place.

"**God Bless Canada!!**" he said loudly, this time from the bottom of his heart. This time he knew it was a *REAL Blessing from GOD!*

CHAPTER 6

A PRAYER ANSWERED

During the following week, Ann and J.L. gave John more water and soup or pudding. His strength was returning and when J.L. asked him if he would like to join them at the table for breakfast, he was overjoyed. He dressed in the clothes Ann provided, but when he stood up to pull up the pants he would have fallen to the floor if J.L. had not been right there and grabbed him.

"Steady there boy," J.L. said soothingly. "Go slow. There is no hurry." John was astonished at how weak his legs were, and was very thankful that J.L. helped him to the table.

"Thank you, sir." he spoke softly, as J.L. seated him at the side of the table. Everyone took hold of hands, including John's. J.L. began speaking "Heavenly Father, bless this abundant food. Put it to Thy use in our bodies, and us to Thy service. Praise Thee Father for giving us all such good health and may Thee find it in Thy will to return John Thomas to good health so that he may work in Thy service. Amen."

Following this, the children were introduced to John. "This is John Ralph born May 1817, so he is now three years old, and this is our baby Elizabeth Ann born just last year in December," Ann said proudly, as she dished porridge into the bowls. Starting with J.L. she then served John, then the children and herself last. J.L. helped John get his porridge ready to eat, then he helped his son, John Ralph, while Ann cared for the baby.

John ate with a trembling hand, a small portion of porridge and half a slice of bread. By then he was feeling so exhausted he was having trouble holding up his head.

"Would thee wish to go back to bed?" J.L. asked.

"Yes, please," John replied, whereupon J.L. rose and took him back to the room and put him in bed. He fell asleep almost immediately.

* * *

John regained enough strength during the next week that he started going outside. For the first few days he helped Ann work in the garden, and as he got stronger, he ventured to the barn at chore time. Soon he was learning to milk the cows all over again and was also helping with the other chores.

＊　＊　＊

Winter of 1820 turned into spring and summer of 1821. John helped with the chores on a regular basis. He was feeling more like he did before he left Mr. Johnson's.

One summer evening as they were sitting on the porch, J.L. began discussing his plans for the morrow. "The new crop is looking very good, and now that the summer fallow is finished, it is time to clear that acre of bush. I want to get it plowed so that it can be sowed for cropping next year. Would thee care to join me in the work?"

"Yes. I would be very happy to help do that work," John replied enthusiastically. "That should help me get work after I learn how it is done. I want to get a job to earn some money so I can buy a farm some day. It will take me quite a while, but maybe God will show me a way."

"Thou hast much faith in God," J.L. observed. "It is good."

"God has been with me all my life, Mr. Hodgson. I know He will guide me if I trust in Him." John responded.

"Good, John," J.L. smiled, "we will get started at the clearing tomorrow. We have to cut the trees and haul them into the yard. That will take about a week. Then we will start pulling the stumps."

＊　＊　＊

It was about six days later when J.L. brushed his beard and said, "In the morning we will get everything gathered up to start pulling stumps. We will need two shovels from the buggy shed, and also the chisel bar. We will need the two axes we have been using, and I will take the oxen to pull the skid to load things on. We will also use them to pull the stumps."

In the morning when everything had all been gathered and put on the skid, J.L. left the oxen eating at some grass near the house. Then he said, "Come John, dinner will be ready." J.L. and John headed for the hot dinner they knew would be waiting. J.L. continued talking as they walked. "We will need a jug of water to take with us."

John was glad to hear it was time for dinner. He felt like he was always hungry, even though he had been with the Hodgson's for almost a year. He was gaining strength rapidly, and felt he was ready to take on heavier tasks.

John's appetite had also improved, and he felt like he should not eat his fill, as he thought it made him look greedy.

"Eat up, son. Eat up." J.L. and Ann both admonished him. "Thee has a lot of weight gaining to do yet. Don't be shy about eating." and J.L. would put another serving of food on John's plate.

"Thank you, sir," John would say meekly. "I am so blessed to have come to live with you folks."

✳ ✳ ✳

"Would thee be interested in coming to the Meeting House with us, on the Sabbath?" J.L. asked as they were walking out to the lot to be cleared.

"Do you mean to go to church?" John asked dubiously.

"Well yes," J.L. responded. "We meet on the Sabbath, and worship God with a free spirit, each in our own way, but all together."

"Yes, I would like to go to church," John replied. "It has been a long time since I have been to church."

"Good. Thee will come with us day after tomorrow," J.L. said as he picked up a shovel and started digging around the roots of the first stump.

CHAPTER 7

THE LEARNING EXPERIENCE

Digging out the sucker roots of a stump was started by first digging with the shovels and chisel bar, until the root went down a foot into the ground. Then using an axe they chopped it off. When all the sucker roots had been cut off, they started working under the stump to get at the tap root.

The oxen were hooked to the sucker roots on the opposite side, and asked to pull until the root was leaning, and the oxen couldn't move it any more. While the oxen held the stump thus, J.L. took an axe and getting down in the hole, began chopping the tap root. More dirt had to be moved out of the hole, and the oxen were asked to pull harder, getting more tilt on the stump.

The complaisant, obedient oxen leaned into the yoke, arching their backs and raising their tails until they were pointing toward the stump, indicating their exertion. John then took an axe into the hole and chopped, while J.L. kept the oxen pulling. Suddenly the stump broke loose and fell over onto its head. John finished chopping it free from the ground, and jumping out of the hole, pushed his cap back and wiped his sweating forehead with his shirt sleeve.

"There, we got that one beat," he commented as he sat down on the side of the hole to catch his wind.

"That took a bit more than an hour," J.L. said as he took a drink from the jug. "It goes faster when two are working at it."

"That's a lot of work," John said as he took a turn at the water jug.

J.L. headed for the next stump in one direction and John went to one in the opposite direction. When they had three stumps pulled they loaded them onto the skid, and taking their equipment, headed for the buildings.

It was chore time by the time they had the stumps unloaded. John stayed at the wood pile and chopped firewood off of the stumps, while J.L. went to the pasture and brought in the milk cows.

* * *

By the end of the following week they were bringing in from four to six stumps a day, and chopping the sucker roots off for firewood, leaving the stump and the tap root. J.L. said he wanted the big pieces to boil the sap in the spring when they tapped some maple trees.

*   *   *

The next morning after the last of the stumps were all pulled and brought into the yard, J.L. hooked the oxen to the walking plow and they went out to the freshly cleared piece of land. J.L. started plowing the area, going down one side and back on the other side. Stopping the oxen, he turned to John,

"The idea is to plow the high places into the low places until we have it fairly level. Thou take this outfit and keep working at it the way I have been. I am going to go in and get the team and harrows and will work on the plowed areas to level the ground out smoother. It will likely take us a couple of days to finish it up so that it will be workable next spring."

"Well, alright, if you think I can do that," John said dubiously. "I won't be able to handle the oxen very well, as I have never done such a thing before."

"If thou dost not like the job thou hast done the first time over, thou canst easily go over it again. Don't worry about what kind of job thou art making. This is a first class way to learn how to handle the oxen and the walking plow," J.L. said as he left for the barn.

John and the oxen made some pretty crooked furrows, and missed patches of sod, but by the time J.L. returned, John was starting to get them and the plow under better control, and was making straighter furrows.

"Now that is looking pretty good John," J.L. spoke admiringly when he returned with the team. "We should have this job finished by tomorrow afternoon."

*   *   *

The next big farm chore to be done was to bring the hay in and stack it by the barn. It was getting late in the fall and preparations for a snowy winter had to be made. J.L. used the team of horses on the rack for this job. It made a chill run down John's spine when he recalled the first time he saw them. He thanked God for the end result of that meeting, and cheerfully went to help with the hay.

"Be very careful when starting to dig into a stack," J.L. advised. "Thee wouldn't want to stick a fork into a hibernating bear. That's what I thought I had done when I stuck my fork into thy leg. I am so sorry I hurt thee."

"Don't apologize. I was covered with hay. How were you to know there was something under it? It is me who must apologize," John said apologetically. "Have you ever stuck a bear?"

"No, but I have talked to men who have," J.L. answered. "The most of them got pretty badly mauled. In fact one man was killed, and the ones who found him suspected he had stuck a bear."

"A bear chased me from the bush to the edge of the cliff," John confided. "I saw the cliff just in time to turn. The bear couldn't make the turn, and went over the cliff, but she hit me as she went past and knocked me down. I fell over the edge of the cliff, too, but was able to grab some bushes and hang on until I was able to get back on top of the cliff. Then two cubs came out of the woods, and finally climbed and tumbled down to their mother. It was after they left that I came and crawled into your stack." John was starting to sweat at the memory of that escapade. However he felt relieved to have told J.L. what had led up to his being found. He was not going to tell him why he was in the bush, as he didn't want anyone to know he was lawfully a wanted man. If he was found he could still be taken back to Woodstock, Vermont, and pay the dreadful penalty.

"Oh, I see," J.L. said with surprise. "I'm glad thee told me that."

*   *   *

The last of the hay was thrown up on the load, and as they were heading for the buildings, there was a cold north wind blowing.

"That feels like winter is soon coming," J.L. observed. "It is good to have the hay all in so early. God has been so good to send thee to me. The work has gone by much faster. It is so pleasant to have someone to work with. Now we will be able to start the threshing of the grain from the sheaves."

"How is that done?" John queried.

"The building beside those stacks of sheaves is the threshing barn. I will show thee the method," J.L. responded.

*   *   *

When they went in the building to start threshing the next day, John found on one side was a raised circular floor that was lower in the center. The rest of the barn area was a flat wooden floor, with many barrels and a pile of bags stored on it.

The sheaves were laid side by side around the outside edge of the circular area, with the grain heads pointing down to the center. The bands were cut to make the straw lay loosely. The men took what J.L. called flails, which were long handles with a paddle on the end that swiveled around. The men walked around the threshing floor, beating the sheaves with the flails. Sometimes they would get up on the floor to get a better whack at the heads of the straw.

The grain fell out of the heads, and slid down the floor to the center. The beating continued until they were sure all the grain was out of the heads. Taking the forks, they carried the straw outside and started building a stack of straw to be used for bedding the livestock during the winter.

While J.L. was flailing the sheaves, he sent John to carry a fork full of the freshly threshed straw to the chickens, and another one to the pigs. John stood and watched the chickens as they stretched and flapped their wings then happily talking and scratching in the fresh straw would lie down and roll on their sides, where they would begin dusting themselves. The pigs were the most fun to watch as they rooted through the pile of straw, then would buck-jump on top of it, with their mouth full of it, then would play-fight in the middle of the fresh straw.

When John went back to the threshing floor he was smiling. J.L. asked him what was funny, so John told him what the chickens and pigs had been doing.

"They like the smell of the fresh straw as much as we do," J.L. replied with a smile. "Now we will bag up the grain we have threshed, and set those bags over on that flat floor to keep." J.L. was taking pride in showing John how he managed his farm. John was fascinated with all the work they accomplished and admired J.L. for the ingenious methods he had employed or created.

* * *

When one stack of wheat was threshed, the threshing floor was cleaned up, and J.L. rolled out a large circular flat stone. John helped him lift it onto the threshing floor and take it to the center. It was placed over a shaft that protruded up through the center of the floor. They turned the stone until notches cut into the hole in the center fitted over a protruding key on the shaft. Next another like stone minus the notch in the center hole, was brought over and put on top of the first one. A long pole was fastened to this stone, and came out past the threshing floor.

Following this, J.L. spread a large robe on the ground outside, and set a bag of wheat on the up-wind side of the robe. Using a shovel he took a scoop of grain and tossed it into the air so it sprayed out in a fan shape. The wind blew through the spray of wheat, and deposited the wheat on the robe. The chaff and hulls were light so they blew farther away, most of it getting off of the robe. The wheat had to be clean to meet with J.L.'s approval before it was shoveled up and put back into the bag. The chaff was thrown up on the straw pile.

When a bag of grain was cleaned, an ox was brought into the barn and hitched to the pole. The bag of wheat was set on the stone, and J.L. started the ox walking around the outside edge of the floor, while he slowly poured grain into the center of the stone. The grain went down until it was between the two stones and ground. The crushed grain worked out between the two stones until it came out on the threshing floor as cracked wheat. This was shoveled up and put into a barrel.

John was sent out to clean more wheat, until he would be needed to help at the mill. As they were waiting for the last few grains of wheat to go through the mill, J.L. began going over the plans to meet the needs of people. "This will be enough cracked wheat for a while." J.L. informed John when they had a whole bag processed. "The next few bags will be put back through the mill two or three times until it is finely ground for flour. It keeps clean in the barrels, and the rodents can't get into it. Each barrel holds about a hundred pounds."

"The flour will have to be weighed as it is put into the barrels," J.L. informed John. "That is what that platform with the neck and scale does. We set the barrel on the platform and set the weight at one hundred pounds. Then when the out end comes up we know there is a measured load in the barrel."

"That is really an excellent idea J.L.," John admiringly praised his mentor. "What do you do with all the flour and cracked grain?"

"Most of it goes to Kingston to the store, and the hotel and a few private customers who like their flour and cracked wheat fresh from the farm. I also take some to Battersea to the store and hotel. We take flour and cracked wheat to the market in Kingston where there are more people and customers, too.'

"The cracked wheat will also be put in barrels for the same reasons," he continued. "But we will crack more wheat later. One barrel of the cracked wheat will be taken to the house today. The rest of the barrels of cracked wheat and flour can be stored out here where it is dry and cold."

So the pattern was set for the winter's work program. J.L. would hook the team to the wagon or sleigh, depending on road conditions, and load on as many barrels of cracked wheat and flour as he thought would be needed, then taking Ann and the two children, plus the cheese and eggs, and sometimes meat, would go into Battersea or Kingston. When the goods were delivered to all except the store, they would go there and unload all that was left. Ann would go into the store and do the shopping she needed for their home, then would go and look at the bolts of dry goods, sometimes bringing home a piece of material to make a dress or an apron or a shirt for J.L. and John.

They always asked John to go to town with them, but he always declined saying, "I have no need for anything. You folks have provided for my comforts. I am satisfied. I just hope I am doing enough work to pay for everything you are doing for me," he would say.

"Thee most certainly are more than earning thy keep John," J.L. kept informing him.

CHAPTER 8

SPRING! GLORIOUS SPRING!!

Winter brought lots of snow, which gave the men many hours of shoveling out pathways, and doorways. The beginning of March 1822 brought one huge storm. By the time the men had the pathways shoveled out, the weather changed and brought out the sun and it's warming rays. The men pulled on rubber boots to get around the yard, and put on lighter coats. The animals and poultry were delighted to get out in the warmth. Everyone was cheerfully looking forward to the coming season of growth and reproduction.

"Today we will go out and start tapping some maple trees," J.L. said at breakfast on Tuesday morning. "We will take a load of tree stumps on the skid with us, and unload them by the fire pit, then take the taps and pails on the skid to the trees. Those supplies are in the shack we built near the fire pit."

John was impressed with the speed with which J.L. bored holes in the trunks with a brace and bit. He then had John insert the tap. The pail was hung on the tap and they proceeded to the next tree. By chore time they had tapped two dozen trees. J.L. checked the shack to see what the squirrels had been into during the winter. Going back to the buildings he was quiet for a while. Then he said, "John, I have been thinking about thy desire to farm. Would thee like to take up a piece of land of thine own?"

"That has been my utmost desire." John was sounding interested. "What have you got in mind?"

"Well, thee applies at the Land Commissioner's office, and they will assign thee a piece of land. Thou must go and talk to the Commissioner to find out what thou has to do to aquire some land."

"That sounds great!" John said enthusiastically. "Can I go to town with you the next time you go in?"

"Of course thee can," J.L. replied. "We would be most glad to have thee come along. Tomorrow is Wednesday, the day we take supplies into Kingston. We can go to the Land Agent's office following the deliveries."

❋ ❋ ❋

After the supplies were delivered around town, they drove to the store where they dropped off the last of them. Ann and the children stayed at the store while the two men went to the Land Department office to talk to the District Land Agent.

"Hello Mr. Hodgson. What can I do for you, today?" a short stocky man with glasses on the end of his nose greeted them.

"Mr. McTavish this is John Thomas. He has been working for me for more than a year," J.L. introduced them. "We were wondering if thee would have a piece of land available for starting up farming this year?"

"Not out your way," Mr. McTavish responded. "There is some north of Battersea out by Dog Lake. It is good land, but has a lot of trees and bush on it."

"What are the terms of getting it?" John asked.

"A grant of fifty acres of land is free, but you will not be able to add any more land in the future. To get any other land, there is a fee of one dollar or two dollars per acre, depending on the quality and location of the piece of land. The piece by Dog Lake is priced at one dollar an acre. There are roughly two hundred acres in it."

"Would thee be so kind as to describe the reasons this piece of land had been priced in the lower quality range?" J.L. inquired.

"As I said there are many trees and bushes on it, also some very large rocks that cannot be moved. They are part of the land formation and go very deep into the ground," Mr. McTavish explained. "The soil there is very rich, but it will take a lot of work to get it cleared for plowing."

"We understand," J.L. replied. "We would like to go and look at it before completing the deal and signing the papers."

"I'll write the directions and information on a piece of paper. You can go and look at it whenever you like." Mr. McTavish picked up a piece of paper and began writing.

❋ ❋ ❋

As J.L. and John were driving back to the store, John gave a big sigh, "I sure will have to work a long time before I can come up with enough money to buy land, never mind the machinery to work it with." John's disappointment was clearly showing.

"Thee will need help. Don't lose heart. On the Sabbath we will speak to

That would be a good location for the barn and corral and that area out to the west that goes to that huge rock outcropping will be the pasture. I will build an eight by ten cabin south of what will become the path to the lake. I will build a decent house up in this area and the cabin will become the chicken house.

the Friends. It has been the policy of the Friends to assist Christian 'new-comers' to get started up in the farming business." J.L. spoke with a positive attitude. "Tomorrow we will have to go and collect the sap and get the fire started, but we should be able to go and look at the property on Friday."

"That sounds good," John replied with a dubious note in his voice.

✳ ✳ ✳

Friday John and J.L. had the chores finished before sunup. They ate a hurried breakfast, then hooked the driving team to the buggy and left. It was a ten mile drive to the lot location, and the sun was slanting in from the east when they arrived, indicating it was mid morning. The team was unhitched and tied where they could eat the hay the men had brought for them.

"There sure are a lot of trees," John commented as they started walking around the property. "I should have no trouble finding good ones to build a shack and a barn. This area down here would be a great place to have a garden and an orchard. It is low and the soil is rich. Look at this," he said as he held up a handful for J.L. to see. He then crumbled it and let it fall through his fingers.

They were near the east side of the property and turning to go west, they went to the top of the rise where John stopped. Looking to the east and indicating with his hand he said, "That would be a good location for the barn and a corral and that area out to the east that goes to that huge rock out-cropping will be the pasture. It is not far for the stock to walk to the lake for their drink. I will build an eight by ten cabin south of what will become the path to the lake. After I get my clearing and plowing done, that cabin will become a chicken house, and I will build a decent house in this area. For now I will leave it in the wild. There are not so many trees in this area, and they are backed by that huge rock outcropping that extends to the west. It should turn out looking pretty good. Let's go out north along the lake shore."

They went past a grove of saskatoon bushes and a patch of raspberries shrubs, then some hazel nut bushes, to a woodland of evergreen trees, birch and maple trees, ash and aspen.

"I will clear a hundred acres here, leaving groves of the trees that will produce food for me." John looked at J.L. and the expression on J.L.'s face caused John to hastily add, "Oh it will take me a few years to get all this done, but I like the place and would like very much to claim it."

"Thee had me worried there for a while." J.L. rubbed his hand across his chin. I thought thee was going to do all these things tomorrow," he chuckled as they turned around and headed back to the team and buggy. The horses were glad to be heading back home, and needed no urging.

"Thee can use one of my axes and shovels for a while. We will buy things as thee needs them," J.L. generously offered as they were driving home.

"Thank you J.L. You are so kind and generous to me. I don't know how I will ever repay you." John spoke from his heart.

"John, thee are like a most precious son to me. I have enjoyed having thee around this winter more than thee realizes. Our life is going to be so empty when thee leaves."

Speaking with difficulty, John replied, "I don't think you are going to lose me very far. I will be asking you about how to do things often, and will be seeing you in town, you know. You have been like a father to me, sir, something I have needed and wanted more than you will ever know."

"It has been wonderful how God has directed both of our lives. We have much to be thankful for," J.L. replied.

* * *

After the meeting on the Sabbath when the men had all gathered for their weekly visitation following the service exercises, J.L. looked around the group, then putting his hand on John's arm, began speaking, "My son here, has located a piece of land he would like to take up for farming. As most of thee know he has no money, nor a means of getting any. He is a devoted Christian in God's eyes, from many years back in his life. Would our brethren feel God's hand on thy hearts to set this man up in accomplished farming?"

A momentary silence followed, then a barrage of questions to John.

"Thou hast selected a piece of land. Of what size is it?"

"About two hundred acres."

"What is the price put upon it?"

"One dollar an acre," John replied.

"Is it good enough quality soil to support thee and thy family of the future?"

"Yes. It is very rich soil. It has a great number of trees of all kinds on it, and is situated on the shore of Dog Lake," John responded. J.L. shook his head in agreement. "It has several huge rock outcroppings that chops the layout up considerably, but I am sure there is a hundred and fifty acres that can be cleared and plowed."

"Will thee be able to do all the work necessary to get this piece of land under production?"

"If I can get the money to buy the land, and the necessary equipment to work with, - yes," John said with a positive attitude. "I can turn trees into many different forms of income to support the progress needed."

The men conferred for several minutes then one husky chestnut bearded man spoke, "We will let thee know our decisions next Sabbath, John."

"Thank you Mac," J.L. acknowledged.

"Thank you, sir," John said, then turned away to walk over to J.L.'s buggy. J.L. stayed with the group of men as they continued their visitations, until the group started breaking up to go home.

John had J.L.'s team hooked ready to leave when J.L. came over. Ann and the children were already in the buggy waiting on him.

✱   ✱   ✱

The week seemed to drag by even though John found plenty of work to do. He went out to where J.L. wanted the next lot of trees cut for clearing the land. By the end of the week he had all the trees cut that J.L. wanted cut for this year. J.L. had brought the oxen out and by Saturday noon they had the trees all pulled into the yard and more than half of the stumps pulled out.

Sunday, the Sabbath, they all dressed in their best clothes and drove to Kingston to the Meeting House. Following the praise exercises, the men gathered outside the House. John stayed back by the House so he would not interfere with their conversation. Soon J.L. called him over to the group. The chestnut bearded man that J.L. called Mac Innesfree, spoke for the group.

"John, I live close to the piece of land thou hast been looking at, and I will vouch for its good quality, and it's abundant tree growth. It will take a lot of work to get it producing for thee. We have decided to make J.L. the holder of the money we have decided to contribute. We have agreed to contribute enough money for thee to buy the land, and also some of the equipment thee will need. Thee are not obliged to pay the money back, but thee are expected to stay in the community for at least five years. Does that sound fair to thee?"

John's mouth was open. He closed it, then swallowed, and spoke, "It most certainly is fair, sir. I didn't expect so much help. I am so grateful to you people, but most of all to my Lord and Father for bringing me to this community. You can count on me to be here for many years. I will help any of you in whatever way you want me to. Please feel free to call on me whenever the occasion should arise."

The men started filing past J.L. giving him donations of money, then past John where they shook his hand warmly, and welcomed him to their midst.

CHAPTER 9

DEALIN' & WHEELIN'

The following Wednesday when J.L. and Ann took their produce to Kingston, John went with them and he and J.L. went to the Land Department Office. Mr. McTavish was behind his desk.

"Good day, Mr. McTavish," John greeted him. "Has that piece of land out by Dog Lake been sold yet?"

"Not as yet," he replied, "What was your name again? It has slipped my mind."

"John Thomas."

"Oh yes." Recognition brought a smile to his face. "Are you still interested in it?"

"Yes," J.L. and John confirmed in unison. "We want to sign the papers," John continued.

"And pay for it." J.L. concluded.

"You will be required to take the "Oath of Allegiance, and subscribe to the Declaration of it," Mr. McTavish said, "just in case the rule is re-instated."

"That's fine. I can do that," John willingly agreed.

John felt like he was dreaming when they came out of the office with the paper.

* * *

John went with J.L., Ann and the children when they took the supplies to Battersea on Tuesday. While they made their deliveries, John walked to the livery stable and started a conversation with the owner.

"Good morning, sir. My name is John Thomas."

"Good mornin'. Are you the man who has been helpin' John Hodgson all winter?" the tall gaunt man queried adjusting his cap on a head of thick, dark brown hair.

"I have been doing that, yes. He is a very pleasant man to work for," John replied. "Do you keep many horses around here that are yours?"

"Well, I have a couple of young colts. I would keep more if I could get my pasture fenced. There is always somebody wantin' a horse or two," he responded as he stuffed his hands in his pockets, and straightened his back. "Were you wantin' some?"

"I am certainly going to be needing some. I have just acquired a piece of land to farm and will be needing some sort of transportation. Could I ask you what your name is?" John asked as he removed his cap and brushed his hair back.

"Oh, my name's Bill Shakleton." He held out his hand to shake John's. "I have a pair of two year old Clydesdales here you can have a look at. I have had them since January." he said as he led John to the stall they were in. He backed out a pair of tall, gangly, long legged bays, with white feather on their legs, except one had a black front leg and feather. This one was a filly. They both had a wide white blaze on their faces, and the one with four white legs was a stud colt with a white patch on the left side of his body. Bill took the two outside into daylight so John could get a better look at them.

"Those two look like it will take all their strength to lift and carry their big feet. I could hardly ask them to pull a wagon load of anything," John commented.

"Oh, don't underestimate the pullin' power of these two. They can pull. I'll even throw in a set of good harness with them." Bill was in to the business of selling, now.

"How much are you asking for these two youngsters and the harness?" John put the crucial question to Bill.

"The whole package?" Bill looked at the ground and thought for a minute. "I will have to have sixty five dollars to break even on that deal."

John looked at him with his mouth open. "I think not," he said and turned to leave.

"Make me an offer," Bill called after him. John stopped and thoughtfully turned to face him.

"The best I can do is to offer you four loads of fence rails to fence your pasture with, but I also need a wagon."

Bill brought the team into the barn. "I've got a wagon out front. Let's go and look at it," he said. He was fervently hoping he wouldn't lose this deal, as it was his first deal of the week, and he had a superstition about the unfortunate luck of deals during the following week if he should lose the first one. The team were tied in the stall and Bill led the way out the other end of the barn and around the side to where a couple of wagons were sitting, as well as three buggies of different styles, and a couple of carts.

"Now this is a wagon that will serve you well, and pretty well matches that pair of horses for size." He had his hand on a three deck wagon with a tank grain box. John looked it over carefully, paying a great deal of attention to the under gear. He then went to the other wagon and looked it over just as critically. This wagon had a two deck plain wagon box, and a spring seat which was something new in the construction industry. Going back to Bill he asked, "How much do you want for the two deck wagon, the team and the harness?"

"Ten loads of rails," Bill said after some consideration. John thought for a minute, then started walking away. "I'll settle for eight loads, but no less," Bill stated loudly.

"Done." John turned back and shook hands with Bill on the deal. "I will be back to pick them up shortly."

"When do I expect to get the rails?" Bill asked.

"They will all be delivered before the summer is over. You can start making you plans to get your fence built."

*   *   *

John found J.L., Ann and the children at the store ready to unload the supplies. Ann said she didn't need anything today, so after J.L. and John had taken the barrel of flour into the store, they were ready to go home. As the two men came out of the store, John said, "I have made a deal on a team of horses and a wagon. Is it alright to bring them out to your place?"

"Of course, John. What did thee get? Where are they?" J.L. was curious. John told him all he knew about them. J.L. scratched his head.

"I think I had better come with thee," he said, "Just in case thee has bitten off something bigger than a bear. Clydesdales can be pretty thick headed, and since these two are two years old and not likely broken, they could give thee more trouble than thee can handle, even though they look thin and pathetically weak. That doesn't mean they think that way."

Going to his wagon, J.L. said, "Ann, you bring this team and follow us. John has bought a team and wagon, and we have to pick up a few supplies at the hardware store, then go over to the livery stable to get them. Just stay behind us."

At the hardware store J.L. bought a pair of leather gloves for both him and John. He also bought four hame straps and six strong halter rings, and last – two pieces of small rope thirty feet in length.

"Alright. I think we have all we will need," he said as they left the store and went over to the livery barn. Bill Shakelton helped pull the wagon out onto the street that headed toward home. J.L. and Bill harnessed the team putting one of the new rings on each of the belly-bands, and backed them out of the stall. J.L. looked at the fit of the collars, then instructed Bill to supply a pair of collars that would fit, as he didn't want them to get sweenied shoulders. John held the filly and Bill held the colt, while J.L. put the collars on the colts, then a hame strap and ring on the pastern of each front foot of each horse. He then took one of the long ropes to the colt, and ran it through the quarter-tug ring on the inside of the team. He pulled it down and ran it through the ring on the strap of the inside foot, then up to the ring placed on the belly-band, then down through the ring on the other foot and up the outside of the horse to tie it to the quarter-tug ring on the outside.

"This is called the running W," he explained to John. "When they get going too fast and you can't stop them, I can pull their front feet up to the belly-band and dump them on their knees and nose. They don't get hurt, but they sure learn to pay attention to the pull of the lines, and your voice commands." He had the running W just about completed on the filly by the time he had finished explaining it to John.

J.L. carried the long ends of both ropes while John and Bill led the team out to the rear end of the wagon. There they stopped and Bill and J.L. took the colt up to his place by the tongue. J.L. looped the rope loosely around the line stake, then went back to help John bring the filly with her rope up the other side of the wagon to her place by the tongue. The team was coupled together with the lines and the neck-yoke was put on them, followed by the tongue being placed in it.

"Get in the wagon, John and sit on the seat with thy feet braced against the front," J.L. instructed. "Wrap the lines around thy hands while I get them hooked up."

Bill stayed at the head of both horses, until they were hooked to the wagon, and J.L. was in it, standing behind John, with the ropes each wound around a hand.

At first the horses didn't move, but finally after a lot of chirping and clucking and line slapping, they started to move ahead. When they saw and heard the wagon following them they both bolted. By the time they neared the end of the first block, the horses were at a full gallop and trying to gain more speed. John was leaning back to an almost laying down position, pulling on the lines until they both had their noses bent back to their collars, but they didn't pay any attention to the pull of the lines. As they neared the intersection of the streets, J.L. pulled with all his might on both ropes, hopping back to the back end of the wagon, dropping both horses to their knees on the dirt street. The wagon came to a sudden stop.

Both men were talking soothingly to them. "Whoa boy. Steady girl. Easy now, easy. That's a good girl. There you are boy. Take it easy." J.L. got out

```

of the wagon and got the filly to stand up on her feet, while he loosened her rope and got it adjusted to its right tension again. Then he went around to the colt and did the same for him. He hurried back to the wagon and got a hold of the ropes again, to be ready when they should start. John let them stand and think until they showed signs of going to move, then he instructed them to do so.

They started slowly at first, then the colt seeing the wagon was still following them, started trotting, and the filly followed suit. Both men were talking continuously to them, and although they were starting to listen, the fear of the wagon overpowered their emotions and they broke into a mad gallop again. Half way down the second block, they were brought to their knees again on the earth street, and the procedure was repeated.

The next time they started, they didn't go past a trot, but were still not responding much to the pull of the lines. J.L. tripped them again at the end of the street so they would be able to make the turn onto their road to home without upsetting the wagon.

Once on the road, John let them trot as fast as they wanted to go, as long as they didn't start galloping. John and J.L. were discussing procedures to continue the training to make them safe for John to handle alone. The horses slowed down as they became winded. When they showed signs of responding to the lines, J.L. climbed onto the seat with John.

"Thee should drive them around the yard without a vehicle until they learn to steer and stop when thee says 'whoa', then thee can finish their training from the wagon seat," he said.

"Boy! I am sure glad you helped me. The wagon and I would have been piled up in a scrap heap somewhere if you hadn't. Thank you so much, J.L.," John gratefully acknowledged.

"Thee are most welcome, John. Look they are starting to walk. That is good." J.L. looked at the horses. "They must have run for about three miles. They sure are a tough pair." He looked back to see where Ann and the other team, wagon and their family were. "Ann must be nearly a mile back. She will likely catch up to us now that these two have slowed down."

They rode in silence for a while, then J.L. remarked, "I think these two are going to make a handsome pair of matched Clydesdales when they mature and fill out."

"I didn't have any choice. They were the only ones available, and I was able to make a deal with their owner," John admitted. "I hope they turn out alright. I want to get the colt gelded as soon as possible. Do you do that?"

"Yes. I have done a few," J.L. confessed. "I could do that when I am finished with the maple syrup in the morning. That will likely be close to noon.
```

Thee can drive them around the yard for practice until I come in."

"That sounds good," John said. He sat thoughtfully for a while, then shifting his feet to the floor of the wagon from the front, he said, "I have been trying to come up with names for them, and I think I will call them Bell and Bob. Those seem to be suitable names I think."

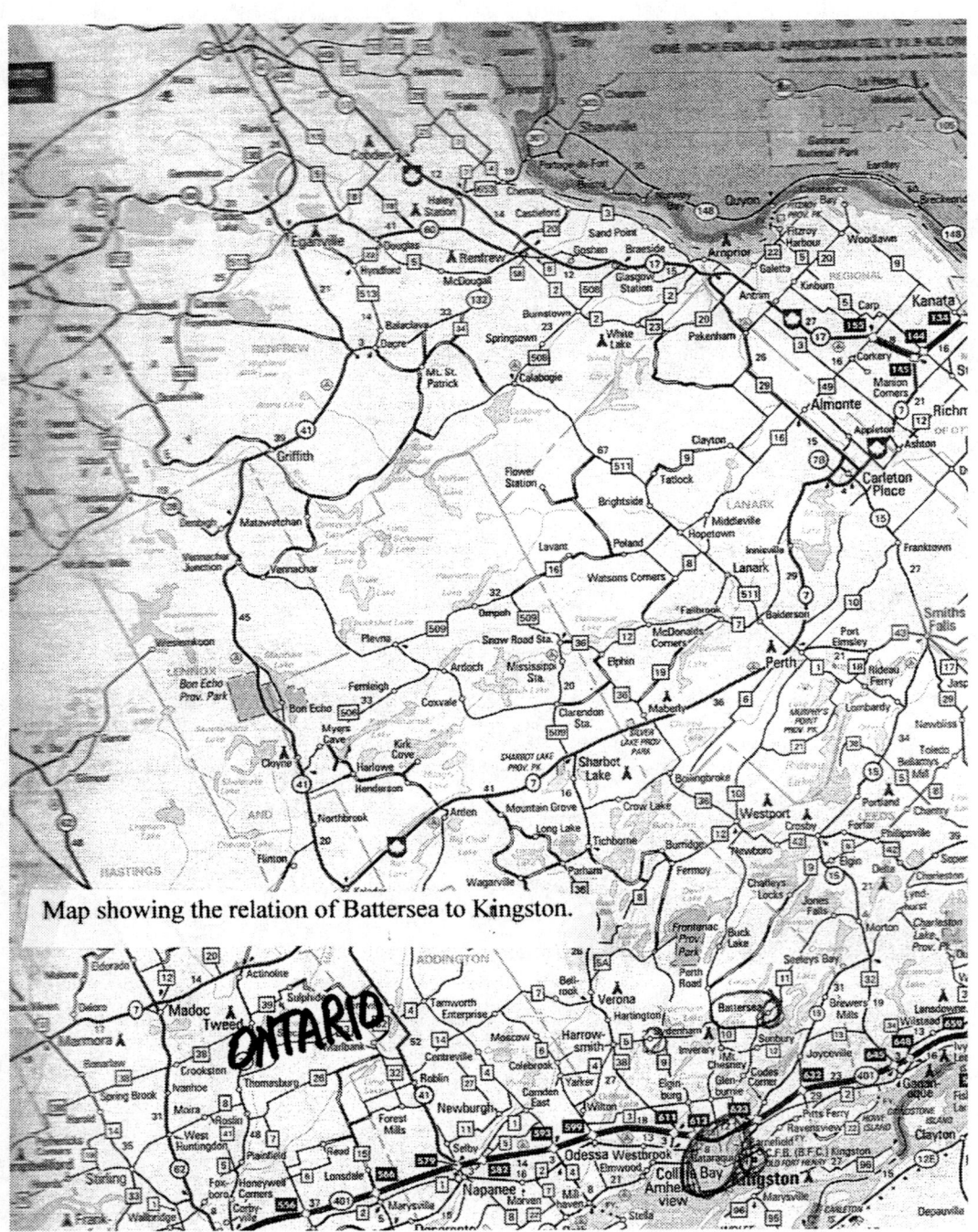

Map showing the relation of Battersea to Kingston.

CHAPTER 10

BEGINNING FARM LIFE

John spent Wednesday at the Hodgson's, going into Kingston with them to help deliver the supplies and take in the Kingston Market. He saw several things at the market that he thought would be good to have on his farm. *When I get things operating the way I want them, I am going to come back and look for useful things*, he thought.

* * *

Thursday morning after the barn chores and breakfast, he harnessed Bob and Bell. With J.L.'s help he hooked them to the wagon, and after driving them around the yard a couple of times, pulled up by the threshing barn. As he pulled them to a stop, he said to J.L. "They are easier to handle now. By the time I reach my place they should be pretty obedient. They were responding to the training quite well yesterday evening, especially after Bob was gelded. That has made a huge difference in the way they both handle. I think he was the instigator of all the trouble we have had with them."

"Thou art right," J.L. remarked. "That is often the way things go with horses - and all animals that get castrated. It turns them into civilized critters. Now we said we would give thee a barrel of cracked wheat, a barrel of flour, and two bags of oats."

When these things were loaded J.L. said, "Pull up by the house. I think Ann has some things for thee."

"Now what would she have for me?" John asked.

"She said something about some loaves of bread and a couple of hide robes," J.L. replied.

At the house four loaves of bread and two jars of last year's maple syrup were loaded into the wagon, as well as a horse hide robe and an elk hide robe. Ann also gave John a patchwork quilt and a feather pillow.

"There," she said, "that should keep thee comfortable until thee can build a house."

"I am so grateful I don't know how to thank you." John had a lump in his throat as he spoke. "How can I ever, ever repay you."

"Thee has already repaid us many times over, son," J.L. replied. "It has been God's blessing for us to have helped thee this far, and we are not done yet. If thee come back on Saturday and stay the night, thee can go to the meeting with us on the Sabbath. We would be delighted to have thee."

"That would be great." John picked up the lines and starting the team, he said, "I'll be seeing you on Saturday, then."

*   *   *

The team walked the four miles to Battersea. John drove them to the livery stable and was unhooking them when Bill Shakleton came out to help him.

"Say, have I got something to show you!" he exclaimed excitedly. As they were stabling the team Bill looked at John with a smile. "So you've been livin' with the Quakers all winter," he said. "Are you one of them?"

John looked at Bill with such a strange expression Bill started to cringe behind the shoulder of Bell.

"What do you mean – Quakers?" John asked as he came out of the stall.

"Their religion," Bill said as he came out of the stall to face John. "I heard they sing and dance at their church," he explained as he led John to the back of the stable.

"I have been to their Meeting House several times," John stiffly responded. "Yes, they sing and move about in freedom of expression. I wouldn't call it dancing. J.L. has some great inventions for his farm that he did himself, to make his farming and life easier. I don't think there is a kinder, more generous household of people to be found. I don't think you should criticize something until you know what you are talking about." he turned and was striding heatedly toward the front door.

"Wait, wait," Bill regretfully wailed, at the same time hurrying after John. "I didn't mean anything bad. You're right. I had no business asking. Don't go until you can see what I want to show you." Catching up to John he took his arm. John looked at him through narrowed, disgusted eyes, then turned and followed him to the back end of the barn, where Bill showed him a little starving foal.

"This little thing was born late in the fall and when it was about two months old, its mother died," he said. "The owner was debating between killing it or selling it. He couldn't do either so he brought it to me the next day after you bought the team. You can have it, no charge if you will take it today," then Bill added, "It leads, so you can tie it on the side of your team and take it with you."

"Bring it outside so I can get a better look at it," John instructed, doubting that he wanted to take on the extra work and expense of feeding it.

Out in the daylight John saw the foal had no feather at all on it's very fine slender legs. It was a dark brown or black color, and a filly. She had a very fine shapely head with a star and dainty stripe to her lip, but her eyes were sunken into her head, and John figured she couldn't see very well. His heart went out to the pitiful little creature. Her mane and tail had a lot of white hair in them. Both hind feet were white halfway to the hocks, and one front foot was white to above the ankle. John brushed her body coat backwards, remembering what his father and Fred had told the boys about checking for grey hair. John couldn't see any, so decided she was going to be close to the color she was now. *She could grow into a driving horse if she lives*, he thought.

"I'll think about it while I go for a few things I need," he told Bill. "I won't be gone long."

Entering the store, he was met by a man a little shorter than John, and slighter, who had black hair and beard.

"Hello," he greeted John warmly. "My name is Andy Smith. What can I do for you?"

"Hello," John shook Andy's hand. "My name is John Thomas. I have just signed an agreement for a piece of land out near Dog Lake. I need some things to get started with, and can either pay you with wood, or money after I sell some wood. Can you advance me some supplies?"

Andy was giving John a quizzical intense look. John looked at Andy and started to feel uncomfortable under the probing eyes of the man.

"I'll repay you every cent if you will stake me," John spoke defensively. "Honest I will. You can ask J.L. Hodgson. I have been at his place for about a year and a half. He will vouch for me."

"That's alright John," Andy finally spoke, "I'll stake you to anything you want. We will talk about settling up after you have had a chance to turn a dollar."

*   *   *

When he came back to the stable with a couple of parcels, he took another look at the filly. "I guess I'll take her. I just hope she lives until I reach my place."

They got the team out and Bill helped get them to stand one on each side of the tongue, then he put the tongue into the neck yoke, and helped hook the traces. Bill then went into the barn and brought out the filly and tied her on the side of Bell. The filly had only a rope around her neck. – no halter. John started the team and the filly started with them, without tightening the rope.

John drove the team over to the store where the storekeeper and his assistant brought out a barrel of molasses and put it in the back of the wagon. The team was started with the filly staying close to Bell's side. She stayed there like that all the way to the homestead.

When John got down off the wagon, he took the rope off of the filly to let her go loose. She stayed by Bell who she regarded as her baby sitter. John figured part of her reason for staying close to Bell was because she couldn't see very well, and used Bell like a guide. The filly had made the trip alright, but was exhausted and soon laid down.

John tied Bell on one side of the wagon and Bob on the other side so they could reach the ground and eat the hay from J.L.'s, which John had put under the wagon for them. Taking the axe he proceeded to clear a path to the lake, wide enough to drive the team and wagon through.

Going north from there, he went into the bush and started chopping down trees that were suitable to make corral rails and posts. He had about two hours of daylight, during which time he cut and limbed very tall, slender trees. At dusk he estimated he had enough rails to make a single rail and posts for the area he had selected for the barn corral.

Going back to the horses, he untied the team and led them down to the lake for a drink. The filly had gotten onto her feet and was eating grass when John showed up. She followed close by Bell and also got a drink. After they were finished drinking he took them back and tied the team to the wagon. He brought out three wooden buckets from the wagon and put oats in each one according to the size of the horse they were for. Opening the molasses barrel, he took a stout stick, and using it like a spoon dipped out some molasses for each bucket of grain. Saving that stick for a dipper, he got another one to mix the molasses into the grain.

Tying one bucket to each side of the wagon for Bell and Bob he set the third bucket on the ground for the filly. While they were eating, he rummaged through the parcels until he found one of Ann's loaves and a bottle of Maple syrup. Cutting a couple of chunks off of the loaf with his new jackknife, he smeared some Maple syrup on it and enjoyed his supper.

Making his bed in the box of the wagon with the two hides and the quilt and pillow, he heaved a big sigh of relief at the prospect of sleeping. Before turning in for the night, he gathered up the buckets, putting them in the wagon, then turned Bell loose.

*   *   *

Friday morning John was up before the sun, and fed the horses. Harnessing Bob he led him down to the lake for a drink, with the other two following. From there he took Bob to where he had the trees cut and limbed. Fastening a single-tree and piece of logging chain J.L. had given him, around the base of two trees, he led Bob and pulled them out of the bush, and up to where he was going to build the corral. After three trips like this he took the line out of Bell's harness and run it through Bob's hame so he could walk beside the logs and drive him. That worked much better.

The logs were all in by noon, so John took the harness off of Bob and turned him loose with Bell and the filly. The warmth of the sun was starting the grass to sprout, giving the horses a little nutritious greens to go with the hay and dry grass they had been eating. The horses wandered back east to the base of the cliff that ran along the border of John's property. They appeared to be pawing the ground and eating. John wondered what they had found that was so interesting. He decided he would check later.

He picked up the chisel bar and dug a hole for the corner post. Cutting the small end off of a log he stuck it in the hole, then with the bar whacked it in as far as he could. By nightfall he had all the rails fastened up making a single rail around his planned corral, plus two poles on for the second rail.

Saturday morning the sun was shining warmly, encouraging new growth on the trees and the grass. John checked to see what the horses had found so interesting at the back end of the pasture. The horses were there again, digging and eating the ground.

"What are you doing that for?" he asked them. Not getting an answer he went back to the fencing chore. First he estimated how many more poles he would need to complete the second ring, then fed the horses their grain. After eating he went to the bush and cut and limbed that number of poles.

The day was getting warm and the sweat was running down his face and back after cutting the trees. Catching Bell he harnessed her to pull in the rails. She was easy to catch, but needed some grain for a reward. John was willing to give her a bit extra for the hard work that was ahead of her of pulling the logs in. He was pleased with her.

*   *   *

When John had the rails on the fence, he fed the horses their evening ration of grain. It was mid afternoon and he figured he had enough time to go the ten miles to Hodgson's by dark, maybe before dark if things went well. Harnessing the team he proceeded to hook them to the wagon. John was feeling pleased with them and was smiling proudly when he drove them to the tongue to hook them to the wagon.

With Bell being the one to step over the tongue they both stopped and wouldn't go any further until John used the end of the lines and smacked them both on the rear. They jumped and went forward over the tongue, not stopping until they were well past the wagon.

"Come on you pair of dumb-dumbs. You have been doing pretty good. Don't stop now," he chastised them.

Circling them around to the wagon again, it was Bob who was obliged to step over the tongue. He ignored the clapping of the lines and waited until John again used the end of the lines on him. He then went forward hastily and stepped on the tongue with his hind foot. The tongue cracked!!

"*You big-footed clumsy ox!*" John berated him loudly, feeling the hair on the back of his neck starting to stand up. "*You did that on purpose.*" John tied them to the new corral fence, while he found a suitable pole and tied it on the tongue to brace it.

The third attempt, John drove them in front of the tongue so Bob only had to step over the end that was on the ground. Bob managed to step on the end of the tongue and push it into the ground. However, he arrived in front of the tongue where John wanted him to be. John then tried to back them up to their place. Neither one of them would move one foot backward.

"***You bull headed pair of good-for-nothing jug heads. You're not going to beat me out, you know!***" he roared at them. In exasperation he drove them ahead, and using the end of the lines on their butts, laced them until they were paying attention to him. When they were threatening to pull the lines out of his hands, he jerked on them until they stopped. He even jerked on them until they finally took a step backwards. He never ceased yelling and roaring at them until they stepped backward.

Driving them around again to have Bob step over the tongue, "***Git up there Bob. Git if you don't want some more training!***" John roared. Bob collected himself and lifted his feet high enough to miss the tongue while he stepped over. John pulled on the lines saying "***Back up!***" They both took a step backward, which gave John a pleased feeling. He tied the lines to the line-stake on the front of the wagon tight enough the horses had their necks arched and their noses curled in to their collars. John went to the front of the team to put the tongue up into the neck-yoke.

With the tongue in its place, he took both horses by the bits, and asked them to back up another step to hold the tongue. As they took that step backward, they both swung their rumps out away from the wagon tongue.

Going around the side of Bob, he held his line taught, and slapped him on the side of the rump with his hand, until he was in the right place. John quickly hooked the traces, then went around to the side of Bell and repeated the actions which loosened the lines. When he had them both hooked, he tightened the lines on the stake until they were prevented from going forward. Going around to the front of them again, he petted them on the necks saying,

"Good boy, good girl. You finally got it through your thick heads. I am so glad. I hope we don't have that kind of trouble again."

The filly went along with him to Hodgson's because he felt she would fret too much if she were left at home alone. As he was riding down the trail, he started talking to his animals again, "You need some company, don't you little girl? Steady Bob, we got plenty of time. Little girl, you also need a name. Something like Maggie? No, that doesn't fit you. How about Jessie? There must be a more suitable name than that." At that moment the filly, who had stopped to eat grass, broke into a gallop to catch up, then trotted smoothly up to the side of Bell.

"You certainly are a graceful little thing, even in your sorry thin state. There's a name for you!" he exclaimed, " Grace. I'll call you Grace."

*   *   *

When they reached Hodgson's, J.L. came out of the barn to greet him. "Hello John. What on earth did thee bring here?" he asked, as he walked around to get a look at Grace. John related the story to him.

At that moment Ann came out of the house, carrying Elizabeth Ann, and holding John Ralph by the hand.

""Come and see what John has got for himself," J.L. called to her. Noticing the spliced wagon tongue, he continued with a grin sneaking across his face. "Did thee have a bit of trouble getting thy team to step over the tongue?" he asked as he scratched the top of his head. "Get thy horses into the barn or corral where ever thou wishes, and help me get that tongue off the wagon and over to the shop. We will have it fixed before we go to bed tonight," J.L. instructed.

"How very fortunate I am to have such great friends." John said as he jumped down to start unhitching the team.

*   *   *

As they were repairing the tongue, John remembered the horses eating dirt by the big rock.

"Say J.L. my horses are going to that cliff at the east end of my place, and pawing and eating dirt. Why are they doing that?"

"They must have found some thing they are craving," J.L. informed him. "It won't hurt them. It's likely good for them."

CHAPTER 11

RAISING A BARN

"J.L. would you be able to come to my place and help me get my barn started so that it will be square, and put together right?" John asked as the two men were putting John's team away Saturday evening two weeks later.

"When does thee think thee would be ready for that?" J.L. queried.

"Well, I will need about another week to get enough logs cut to do the job. Then I don't know how to do the roof," John replied thoughtfully.

"I know one of our Friends – name of Mike McMurty - has a saw mill." J.L. scratched his head then replaced his cap. "I will speak to him tomorrow about sawing the logs flat on two sides, and see when he would be able to do that for thee. It makes the logs much easier to work with."

"That sounds good," John responded.

✳   ✳   ✳

After the service the men were standing in groups outside the meeting house, talking before they should leave for their homes. J.L. called John to come over to where he was talking to a thickset, chestnut haired man.

"Mike McMurty, I'd like thee to meet John Thomas," J.L. introduced them.

"Greetings to thee," Mike greeted John. "I have seen thee many times here and in town. How is thy home building progressing?"

"Some days it is going well, and some days it seems to be slow. I think I will have enough logs to build the barn by the end of next week though, if I can keep my nose to the grindstone."

Both men laughed. John looked at them quizzically for a moment. J.L. then started discussing the building of the barn, and the joke was forgotten.

"John thinks he can have enough logs cut in a week, to build his barn. I suggested we see if thee could cut them flat on two sides." J.L. looked hopefully at Mike.

"That I could. That I could," Mike said. "I am starting the sawmill up this next week now that the crops are planted. I have a pile of logs to cut into lumber, which will likely take about ten days. After that I could cut logs for thee. Just don't stop cutting trees when thee thinks thee has enough. Thee will be surprised how many more it will take than what thee thinks are enough."

"Well, thanks for the advice," John replied. "I will certainly keep that in mind when I am cutting."

* * *

During the next week John cut what he thought would be enough trees for the barn. He pulled them into the yard where he cut them off at twenty foot lengths, setting the smaller ends aside for corral rails. He finished early Saturday afternoon.

Not wanting to start cutting more trees at this time, he decided to go into Battersea to see if he could get another wagon gear. He was still keeping his supplies in the wagon box, and didn't want to unload them for fear that predators, - bears in particular - would come and destroy them when he was away from the yard. *If I had a wagon gear now, I could have loaded the corral railings and taken them to Bill Shakleton on my way to the Hodgson's. This situation has to be eliminated,* he thought as he set out to catch the team.

* * *

Bill Shakleton met him at the door of the livery barn. "I must congratulate you on the progress you have made with the Clydesdales, John. They are behaving very well," he complimented him, "Look at that little starving filly. She is filling out and her eyes are brightening up."

"I think she can see pretty well now," John responded. "She is doing a lot of running around showing how she feels. As for the other two, I have had a major amount of help from J.L. Hodgson getting them to where they are today. He sure knows the tricks to get unbroken colts started thinking without doing them any harm. It sure has been God's gift to me that I should have encountered J.L. when I did."

"How is your bush clearing progressing?" Bill enquired. "When do you think you will be bringing some of those poles in for me?"

"I would have brought a load in today if I had a wagon gear," John related.

"I don't want to unload my supplies out of the wagon until I have a building to put them in. So I came to town to see if I can find another wagon gear."

"The only thing I have is that wagon you looked at before," Bill said, "Try Harry Potts the blacksmith. He builds wagons, so he may have a gear already to sell."

"Thank you," John said as he turned the team around to go to the blacksmith shop.

Bell and Bob both snorted at the strange fire-tinged odors emanating from the open shop doors. Grace stuck her head in the doorway and gave a big snort.

A medium height, heavy shouldered man came out to see where the disturbance was coming from. He was rubbing his hands on his leather apron, as he looked at Grace then at John and his outfit.

"I'm John Thomas, recently moved to this district. I have a farm six miles to the north, and have come to see if you can help me."

"What can I do for you?" the blacksmith said.

"Well I need another wagon gear for moving logs and poles from my place to town, and also to the sawmill." John reset his cap as he spoke.

"I have one wagon gear that I am in the process of building a box for," the man replied. "I guess I can sell it to you without the box. Come around here and have a look at it."

John turned the team and followed him around to the back of the shop. The horses settled down after they got away from the rancid smoke, so John tied the lines around the line-stake to be able to get out of the wagon to look at the gear.

"Would you be interested in taking poles to pay for it?" John asked after he had looked the wagon over thoroughly.

"I guess I could do that," the blacksmith replied after a few minutes consideration. "I guess since you are starting farming you haven't started making any money yet. Yeah, we burn wood at our house, and I also use some here at the shop. By the way, my name is Harry Potts," he reached out to shake John's hand as he introduced himself.

"You're right about the money," John spoke as he shook Harry's hand. "I have lots of wood on my place, but it is all standing waiting on me to cut it down. Could you wait until fall for it?"

"Yeah I could wait that long for it. I will want four loads of wood for the gear."

"For a fifth load of wood, could I get a set of double trees, and a good loggin' chain?" John asked. "I would like to tie this new gear on behind my wagon now, and I need the chain to do that."

Harry opened the door at the back of the shop, and picked up a logging chain. Handing it to John he went inside and came out with a set of double trees and swung them up into the wagon box. John jumped up and grabbed the lines to prevent the team from leaving when the doubletrees rattled and banged into the wagon. Harry finished fastening the wagon gear onto the back of John's wagon. Thanking Harry again John climbed onto the wagon seat and left for Hodgson's place.

* * *

By Wednesday night John had another big pile of logs cut to the twenty foot length, and another load of rails laid aside, all in the yard. Thursday morning he was loading logs onto the new wagon gear, when four men and two teams of horses pulled into the yard. The men were Friends from J.L.'s church meetings who lived in the Battersea area.

After greetings, Mac Innesfree explained, "We thought we would give thee a hand for a day. Tell us what we can do."

"I could use some help to get this load of logs on the wagon. If you want to do some field work, you can pull stumps. I am needing to get some plowing done, and some oats sowed, and the stumps have to be pulled out before I can do anything," John said. "I am so grateful for your offer to help, I don't know what to say to thank you enough."

"That's alright boy," Mac was taking charge, "Thee three go out to the field and start pulling stumps. I will help load these logs, and will be out later to help thee."

The trip to the sawmill was two miles one way. When John got back he started a fire and set a large pot of beans on it to cook, then he started loading another lot of logs. Mac came in from the field and helped put the load on and secure it.

"I'll keep an eye on these beans," he offered as John was leaving with his second load. When John returned again, Mac was stirring the beans. "I put some molasses in them to improve the flavor." Mac was smiling as he told John. They loaded another lot of logs onto the wagon for John to deliver in the morning.

"Mike says he should be able to start sawing my logs tomorrow," John said as he unhitched his horses for the night. "He says he will be able saw them faster than I can bring them to him, so I should get as many over there as possible."

"I don't live far from here," Mac commented as he turned to go to the field to get the men to come in for a bean supper before they started for home. "I will come back in the morning and help thee again tomorrow," he spoke over his shoulder as he walked.

* * *

Friday morning as John was about ready to turn at Mike McMurty's road, he saw a team and wagon gear coming toward him. He stopped and waited until they drew along side. It was Mac Innesfree as he expected.

"Good morning," John called to him.

"God's grace to thee this fine morning," Mac greeted. "I'll come with thee and give thee a hand to unload those logs."

* * *

Mike McMurty came over, "I'll be starting cutting thy logs about noon," he informed John. "Does thee want the ends of the logs sawn flat?"

"I think I would like that." John rubbed his forehead. "What do you think Mac?"

"That would make the building look much nicer," Mac replied.

"Thee will also need at least a load of logs to be sawn in two foot lengths," Mike informed them. "They are used to build doorways and window holes and the like. They are also used to splice the ends of two logs to make more length."

"Say that's a good idea. I never thought of that!" John exclaimed. "I will keep that in mind when I am building my house."

* * *

John and Mac took two more loads of logs to Mike's sawmill, and when they took the last one, they also loaded up two loads of finished logs, and the slabs that were cut off the sides. They unloaded them near where the barn was to be built, and then loaded up two more loads of logs. Mac took his load to the mill on his way home.

Saturday morning Mac drove into the yard as John was hitching his team to the load of logs. Mac pulled up to the dwindling pile of logs. John tied his lines so the team couldn't move forward, then went over to help load Mac's wagon.

Grace was locked in the corral, as she had been the day before, and was fussing a bit.

"Good morning Mac," John greeted him. "Did you skip out on your chores this morning?"

"God's morning to thee John," Mac responded, "My two oldest boys are doing the chores today. They have become quite capable of taking care of things."

*   *   *

John and Mac made two trips to Mike's sawmill, and on the return they loaded logs onto Mac's wagon and a load of corral poles on John's wagon. John helped unload the logs off of Mac's wagon, then drove on to town. Grace was happy to be able to come with the team.

John drove down the street to the livery barn. Tying up the lines he went in to find Bill Shakleton, who was doing up his night chores before going home for supper.

"Hello John," Bill greeted him. "What can I do for you today?"

"I got a load of poles out there for you," John responded. "Where would you like them put?"

"Oh...I'll show you." Bill set his fork down and went out to inspect the load. "They look fine, John. Follow me."

They went around the barn to the pasture that was to the north. "This is my pasture that I want to fence. We will unload the poles here."

It was after dark when John reached J.L.'s place and turned his team out to the pasture.

*   *   *

Monday morning dawned bright and clear. The sun rose warm and golden above the hills and trees to shine down on a long string of horse drawn vehicles converging on the road to John's farm. The birds were singing merrily as John was measuring out the feed for his horses. He whistled and they came in from the back end of the pasture at a trot.

He was putting the harness on them when the string of vehicles started driving into the yard. Four of the wagons had their boxes lifted off, and they pulled up by the pile of logs to load up. One of them was Mac. When they all got loaded the pile was cleaned up.

When these five wagoneers got back from the sawmill with five loads of finished logs and slabs, J.L. had arrived and had the foundation of the barn started. He had a group of men sawing and chipping the notches in the ends of the logs, and the rest were bringing the logs to the foundation and placing them to J.L.'s satisfaction.

Right behind the loads of finished logs, came a half dozen horse and buggies driven by women, many of them having children on board. The women drove to the east side of the yard, and began unloading baskets and boxes, and spreading blankets on the ground. By the time the wagoneers had their loads off, the women called,

"Dinner's ready. Come and get it."

"There is something I would like to say," John said as everyone gathered around, "I am overwhelmed with the kind friends and neighbors I have and who I am becoming acquainted with during my barn raising. I thank my Lord and Saviour for bringing me to this wonderful country and placing me among so many great people. I thank God our Father for the wonderful food that has been supplied this day, and the ladies who have prepared it, and brought it to us. I pray that I may serve You Father during my life, and may my life be spent here. Amen."

As John finished there was silence until J.L. said, "Well, come and get it before it gets too cold."

John was the last to pick up food, and repeatedly thanked the ladies as he moved down the table.

"You're most welcome Mr. Thomas. We are so glad to have you settle in our neighborhood. We hope you will bring a wife, too."

John felt embarrassed by the direct implication, as he replied, "Someday ma'am, but not until I have this place under production, and a house built."

"I don't know where you will get a woman your age. All the women around here are already married, and the unmarried ones are still children," another woman commented, as they started gathering up their things and getting ready to head for home, and their night chores.

The barn was already up to shoulder height, and John liked what he saw. He and the other men with wagons left as soon as they could, to go back for more logs and slabs. One load of two foot logs had been brought in the first trip in the morning, and another one would be coming in the afternoon as they had to be carried in a wagon box.

John and Mac got the other three loaded and on the road, then they waited for the final cutting and trimming to be done. They arrived back at the farm in time to see the roof being put up. Slabs were laid flat side down against the top rail of the walls and the ridge pole that was in place. They were nailed down, then another layer of slabs were placed round side down cradled by the trough between the slabs of the first layer, making a smooth top roof that would run the water off.

Harry Potts had made hinges and was busy hanging the doors. There were two large doors on the south end, and a smaller dutch door on the west side for easy entering during times when the large doors were to be kept shut.

The whole job was finished by evening. John thanked each man, shaking his hand warmly as he was preparing to leave. Mac and J.L. got all of John's barrels and bags inside the barn through the side door, then shaking John's hand, Mac spoke for the both of them, "John we are so glad to be able to help thee. We will be seeing thee on the Sabbath at the meeting."

"By all means," John replied.

When everyone had left, he went into the barn to see what it was like. He found two double stalls had been built complete with mangers, The partitions were made from the logs up to waist high, and the head partitions were made from slabs. The mangers were made from double ply slabs the same as the roof, with a pole across the top for the horses to be tied to.

"Wow!" he said in amazement. "Wow. Those people are sure good."

John had one more load of logs and slabs to bring home, and he also had to see what Mike would be wanting for his work. He would do that tomorrow.

CHAPTER 12
FACING THE PAST

In the next two weeks John got some land worked and oats sowed, then cut more trees for another two weeks. Harnessing the team he hauled the trees into the yard, where he cut them off at the twenty foot length. He piled them in a cross-thatch pattern until they were shoulder high, to leave them to dry until next year.

When all the trees were in the yard he used the team to pull stumps. On rainy days he worked inside the barn making a single stall for Grace, then partitioning off an area for his household goods and his straw bed. The field grew a nice crop of oats, which he cut with a cradle scythe, while they were in the shot blade to avoid freezing, which would have made them inedible. He tied the oats into sheaves by twisting the heads of two whisps of the oats together, then around a bundle, then crossing the ends and twisting them under their own band. He then stood them in stooks. This was quite time consuming and winter had arrived by the time he had finished.

John was able to get the oats hauled in and stacked by the barn before the snow started coming. During the winter he cut trees and hauled them into the yard, until the snow got too deep to negotiate. With no one around to talk to, he had lots of time to plan...and think.

"I need to do something to get some money to talk with," he said aloud. "First I need to buy a gun and ammunition so I can get some meat to eat. I also need a lighter rig for traveling to town in the winter. Maybe I can sell some firewood around Battersea. If I need to sell more than they need, I will take it to the Kingston market. I could sell poles as well as firewood there."

* * *

He went into Battersea knocking on doors until he had negotiated the sale of four loads of firewood. Then he went to the store.

"Good day sir. I am selling fire wood or corral rails to raise some money. Would I be able to put an ad up in your store to see if someone might be interested in buying some? I need to buy a gun and ammunition among other things. My name is John Thomas as you likely remember from the time I got the molasses and other things. Was the wood I brought you satisfactory?"

"Yes it was fine, John. I remember you. I got a couple of men with a circular saw driven by a gas motor, to cut it up for me. Sure you can put an ad up in the store, John," he readily agreed. "By the way, since you are going to be living in this area, I would like to properly introduce myself. I am Andy Smith - originally from Woodstock,...Vermont." Andy held out his hand to shake John's.

John's mouth was hanging open and he could not get any words to come out. He looked at the man and tried to make a connection to the Andy Smith he had known so many years ago. John looked around the store, and to his relief it was empty. His mouth was dry as he took Andy's hand.

"Is your father Fred Smith?" John falteringly asked. The blood had all drained from his face and he was feeling faint. He sat down on a flour barrel.

"Yes," came the response.

"Have you come here to collect the bounty that hangs over my head?" John asked quietly.

"Not on your life. You are my brother and I would never do a thing like that to my brother. After your family was gone father didn't have the heart for the business any more, and after a year he sold the lumber business and turned to raising and training horses and selling them. Mother and father are still living in the valley we all loved so much. Ricky is helping him."

"How long have you been here?" John could feel the blood slowly returning to his face.

"Nearly three years. Have you told anybody where you came from?" Andy asked. John shook his head in the negative. Andy could see he had put John into great shock, so not waiting for an answer he continued talking. "I got married just a little over a year ago. I found a lovely girl here in this town. She will never know that I knew you before you came here."

"Thank you, Andy. If it should get out, I could still be taken back to Woodstock and pay the penalty." John stood up. "I must get going. I will likely be bringing a load of firewood to town tomorrow."

"What do you mean by bounty hanging over your head?" Andy asked as he set a new rifle and ammunition for it on the counter.

"I guess you would have left Woodstock before we did. Mr. Johnson was impossible to please. Hosea threatened to do something desperate, so to try to keep him out of trouble, we devised a plan to run away. We still had a year and a half of apprenticeship time to put in, plus three years of obligatory employment with pay. It felt like we would be there forever, particularly to Hosea. We were to get together to travel, but he didn't show up and I had to leave without him. I ended up at J.L. Hodgson's place and spent the last two winters there. Now I am trying to get started on my own."

"Oh." Andy's face sobered, "It sounds like you have been to hell and back and you don't want to talk about it. I understand," he said. "I could use a couple more loads when you have the time to bring them in." Andy looked thoughtfully at John as he left the store.

"You forgot your gun, John. You will need it to survive, you know."

John hesitated, then turned around and picked up the rifle and ammunition. "How much for these things, Andy?" he asked.

"Let me see." Andy squinted his eyes and tilted his head sideways, "That will cost you two loads of firewood when you can get them here, plus a meal for me and my wife and family out at your place when you get a house built."

"Good. I will get the wood in here as soon as I can. I hope we can have more than one meal out at my place before too long."

On the way home John didn't know whether to feel dreadful or happy that he had met Andy.

"I can trust Andy," he told himself. "I should feel happy."

CHAPTER 13
BUILDING ASSETS

Winter turned into the spring of 1823, with John busy hauling poles and firewood into Battersea, making spigots for tapping the Maple trees, and many other jobs that he could do when the snow was too deep to go to the woods to cut trees. He had accumulated a bit of money, and was looking for ways to make more.

When the thaw started he went to the maple trees and tapped a dozen with the spigots he had made during the winter. Once the trees were tapped, he started setting up a fire pit to boil the sap. He went to the Kingston market with J.L. and found a barrel suitable to convert into a boiler. It would need legs and would need an opening cut in one side to make the top. *I can cut the hole*, he thought. *I could even make the legs if I bolt some pipes together right.*

Tuesday, John went to see Harry Potts, the blacksmith in Battersea and asked him if he would create a set of harrows. John explained how he wanted them made in four sections.

"Alright. It will take me a week to get them made for you that way, but it looks like a good plan. They should work good for you." Harry seemed to be quite interested in producing the planned harrows.

* * *

As John was on his way to Hodgson's on Saturday, he called in to see how progress was coming with the harrows. Harry was working on another project, as he turned toward John with an air of satisfaction. "Hello John, I got them all made for you. They went faster than I thought they would," he spoke enthusiastically as he showed John the finished products. "You can settle up for them later in the summer. I think about twenty five dollars should do it alright. Bring your wagon around by this door and we can load them for you."

When the harrows were loaded, John shook Harry's hand. "Thank you Harry. I really appreciate what you have done for me, including the hinges on my barn doors. I will be paying you in full this summer. Thank you." As he was climbing up on the wagon, Harry spoke,

"Your horses sure have grown and filled out during the winter. They are starting to look like a very handsome team, and well matched, too."

"Thank you Harry. I guess all the laying around doing nothing during the winter paid off that way. They could each use another four or five hundred pounds, but that will likely come with time, and feed," John replied as he picked up the lines and started the team.

✳ ✳ ✳

Monday morning Bell and Bob were harnessed while they ate their breakfast. John ate his, then set the harrows on the ground and attached a set of double-trees with a chain. He brought the team out and hooked them up, then headed for the field to harrow the piece that was cropped last year. By noon he was half done. The harrows were doing a nice job of disturbing and smoothing the soil surface, and he was pleased with the outlook of things to come.

Arriving in the yard to give the team a noon rest and feed, he was surprised to see a team and democrat with some horses tied on behind, turning into his place. I can't see who it is, and I don't recognize the team, he speculated as he pulled his team to a stop. He tied the lines up on the hames, and put Bell and Bob in their stall, then went outside to greet his visitor.

"Good day, sir. My name is John Thomas. I haven't seen you around these parts before. Were you looking for someone?"

"Only someone who would be interested in buying horses. My name is Walt Isaacs," the man replied. "I came from the other side of Kingston a couple of weeks ago. I usually spend the summer and fall on the road buying and selling horses. Have you got any for sale?"

"No sir, I only have three and one of them is a driving horse. I am in need of more work horses, but am not yet ready to buy any." John was giving the horses a casual glance as he spoke. "Would you like to put your team in the barn, and the others in the corral and come and have dinner with me?"

"Why that is right neighborly of you. I certainly would appreciate taking you up on your offer." As Walt spoke the horses behind the democrat began squealing and biting at each other, then two of them turned to start kicking at each other. Walt and John grabbed their heads to stop them. They untied them and the other two who were at the back, and put them in the corral. "Those two have never seen each other until a couple of hours ago," Walt explained. "They'll be alright when they get something to eat."

John and Walt unhooked the driving team and put them in the barn, feeding them some oat sheaves, and also carrying some oat sheaves to the horses in the corral. While the men were eating some venison sandwiches, Walt started a sales pitch, "Those four horses I was leading are all experienced work horses. The bays will make a nice team. They came from two different places, but I bought the second one at quite a price because he looked like he would mate the other. They will make a fine pair of geldings for someone. The black mare is a hard worker. She is keen and will do a great days work. I'll be honest with you." (This latter remark got John's guard up.) Walt continued, "They are all ten years old. They have smooth mouths. The grey mare is blind in one eye and I plan on taking her to some wolf hunters that I know of. They can use culls like her for bait when they are hunting."

The men picked up their sandwiches and went out to the corral to hang over the fence for a better look at the horses. John was paying closer attention to them now.

"How much are you wanting for them?" he asked as he scrutinized the grey. She had one eye knocked out, and was overly pot-bellied and a little low in the back. She had a great set of feet and legs. Her head was beautiful and followed by a lovely slender neck. John climbed over the fence and caught her to look at her teeth. From what J.L. had taught him, he estimated she was about fifteen or more years old.

"Are you interested in the grey?" Walt asked. "I would sell her for ten dollars, same price the hunters would give me. How about that black? There's a horse that will give you a good days work every day. She has energy to burn. Her and the grey are sisters. The black is two years younger than the grey."

John began looking at the black. Suddenly he was taking a bigger interest in her. He didn't mention to Walt that he had seen signs of foal movement in her. He caught her and checked her teeth.

"Are you sure the black is the younger of the two? Her teeth say she is about twenty years old." John looked at Walt to see what his expression was.

"Well, maybe they are a little older than ten, - maybe twelve, but no more." Walt was beginning to squirm a bit at the unexpected knowledge of this young newcomer to the country.

"They both are at least twenty, Walt. Neither one of them are good for anything other than wolf bait. I admit the quality of the black in some areas is better than the grey, like in the back. They both have good feet and legs, but there is only a year or so left in their life, if a person is lucky, and they are both so out of condition they couldn't do a days work. It would take a month to get them in workable condition."

"Well, what about the bays. They will do a days work." Walt was directing

John's attention away from the two mares.

"Not interested," John retorted.

"Tell you what I'll do. I appreciate you stabling and feeding all my horses, plus my dinner. I'll sell the two mares for twenty five dollars. You should be able to get twenty five dollars worth of work out of them."

"Why is the black's disposition so different from the grey, if they are full sisters?" John asked.

"They are not full sisters. They are from the same mare but different sires. Both sires are Percherons, a relatively new breed from France. They are more agile than the Clydsdales, Shires, Belgiums and Freisans, and they can do as much work as them. They don't usually require as much grain and hay either," Walt informed John.

"Well, I got to get back to my field. I guess I will take the black and the grey. I will help you get your team out." Turning to go to the barn, John was now in a hurry. He was hoping to finish harrowing the field before sunset, and a lot of the afternoon was now gone. When Walt took the team out of the barn to the democrat, John went to his bed and got the money out of the straw mattress. Next he went out the south door and took the two mares over to the gate and turned them out in the pasture. Catching one of the geldings he took him over to the fence and tied him with one of the ropes. He took the two mares ropes into the barn, then went out and helped Walt catch the other gelding. Leading one of them to the back of the democrat, he tied him where he had been tied when he arrived. Pulling the money out of his pocket and counting it out into Walt's hand, he bade him farewell.

As Walt was leaving the yard, John went into the barn and got Bell and Bob out to go to the field.

* * *

He was glad to see the field finished before sundown. Taking the harrows over to the side of the field he unhooked the two outside traces of the team, took the double trees off of the harrow bar, stood the harrows up in a stook fashion and laid the harrow bar across the top of them. Going to the barn he let the team pull the double-trees in. Unharnessing the team, he turned Grace loose and took the three of them down to the lake for a drink.

When they returned he let Bell and Bob out in the pasture, and watched for a while as they became acquainted with the new horses. The black decided to attack Bob, but he just stood his ground and roared at her. She decided that was more noise than she wanted to contend with, so left him and went to the grey mare.

The sun was setting into some dark clouds that were scurrying across the sky. At length John noticed a breeze springing up, and looking up into the sky saw that a storm appeared to be coming. Hurriedly he caught the grey mare, but the black one wouldn't let him catch her, so he took the grey mare down for a drink. The black one was ready to be caught when he got back. He was tempted to let her wait until morning for her drink, but when she stood and waited on him to catch her, his heart softened and he took her with the grey to calm her nerves, and made another trip to the water hole. The oncoming storm was flashing lightning, and the thunder was grumbling louder, now.

When he got back to the barn, he put the new horses in the other double stall. After he had eaten his supper, he let Bell and Bob and Grace in and stabled them for the night. The storm had arrived with brilliant bolts of lightning and deafening cracks of thunder, along with vicious winds that were coming in off the lake. The trees between the lake and the buildings, though bowing deeply to the wind, diverted most of it, but enough got through to lift the roof off of one side of the barn and throw it into the pasture in broken splinters and kindling wood.

The horses all jumped nervously, and the black mare pawed the floor frantically. Torrents of rain were hammering down, drenching the horses and soaking John and all of his possessions. It also flattened most of the vegetation and created temporary ponds of water everywhere.

* * *

When sunrise came John went out to see what damage had been done to his crops. Since the plants were flattened and hammered into the ground, he was not sure he would be getting a crop. There was nothing he could do but to wait a couple of days to see if the plants would make a come-back.

Going back to the yard he decided to take a load of logs to Mike McMurty and get them all sawn into one inch lumber, with which to repair the roof of the barn as quickly as possible.

When Mike heard what had happened he sawed the logs right away, and John was able to bring them back with him.

* * *

The next morning he was up on a ladder starting to get some boards fitted in, when Mike drove into the yard. "Could thee use some help, John?" he called.

"I sure could. When I am up here that end gets out of place, and if I fasten it first, this end moves out of line. Put your horse in the barn under the roof that is left, and give him a sheaf of oats."

By supper time the two men had one layer of boards on the whole length of the roof.

"That should give thee a considerable amount of protection," Mike observed as they stood back from the barn and looked at their handiwork. "I'll come back in the morning to help thee finish the job."

True to his word, Mike drove into the yard as John was about ready to tackle lying on the second layer of boards to cover the cracks. This side went faster and they had the job completed by mid-afternoon. Mike then helped John clean up the broken and splintered boards from around the pasture. They were finished as the sun was starting to slant toward the tree tops. Mike looked at his watch. "It's six thirty. Time to go home," he said.

As Mike was driving out of the yard, John having thanked him profusely, now thanked our Heavenly Father for providing such wonderful neighbors.

*   *   *

Saturday, John decided to take the new team to Hodgson's to find out what they were like. He wanted J.L. to help him with any problems that he may discover in the test drive. For that reason he didn't make any deliveries to Battersea. He left Bell and Bob and Grace in the pasture, and opened the gate to the lake so they could get a drink when they wanted.

The team gave no trouble getting hooked to the wagon, but the black jumped violently and tried to get things going when she saw John climb up over the side of the wagon. John jumped and grabbed the lines before the grey got motivated to go. The black had her head in the air and agitated to go faster, prancing a bit and pulling on the lines as they got on the trail. John found it was not as relaxing to drive them as it was to drive Bob and Bell.

He let them trot when they were on smoother ground, and the black wanted to go faster and kept going faster until she finally broke into a gallop. John immediately pulled them back into a walk, and maintained that until they reached Hodgson's place.

"What has thee got this time?" J.L. was walking around the team, giving them a thorough going over. "Where did thee get these two?"

"Well, they just walked into my yard behind a democrat. They are a little long in the tooth, but they are both with foal, and they came at a price I could afford." John went on to relate the rest of the story, finishing with "I don't trust the black mare. I think she would run away if I relaxed my hold on her. It is tiring for me to drive her a distance."

"How about giving her the same treatment we gave Bob and Bell?" J.L. asked.

"I had that in mind, but thought I would ask what you thought of the idea," John admitted. "Would there be any danger of her losing the foal if we did it now?"

J.L. thoughtfully considered the situation. "I don't think so. It wouldn't be as stressful on her as running away would be. It should change her mind-set so that a run-away can be avoided. I'll get the straps and rope so we can do it now. That will give her all night to think about things."

As J.L. climbed into the wagon, the black mare jumped and would have left had John not pulled her back. J.L. took the rope from John.

"Go out to my summer-fallow field. It's not plowed yet so we won't do it any damage. Once we get to the field, drive them with the tension of lines that thee would like, and we will see what this old girl has in mind. I think it would be a good idea to make a bridle for her that has sides that prevent her from seeing what is going on behind. She has too many vices to be trusted. The more you can take away from her, the better."

When they got to the field, John slackened off the lines, and the more line the mare got, the faster she went. When she had reached a gallop, J.L. said, "Now say whoa as thee would under normal circumstances."

When John said whoa, J.L. pulled the ropes and dumped the mare on her nose. The other mare didn't stop until John pulled hard on the lines, and the wagon was nearly on top of the black.

When J.L. had the mare back on her feet and the rope adjusted again, he jumped into the wagon. The mare jumped and would have taken off if the grey had worked with her. John commanded, "Whoa," whereupon she waited for a further command, tossing her nose impatiently.

"That's good," J.L. said approvingly. "She is starting to listen."

J.L. gathered up the ropes and set himself for the next trip. When he was ready John started the team again, repeating the system. It took the mare a little longer to reach the gallop, but when John gave the command to whoa, the mare's ears came up just as J.L. pulled the rope and dumped her again. This time John jerked the grey mare and made her stop before the wagon was on top of the black.

"Now the next time we will dump her when she reaches a fast trot, before she breaks into a gallop. Thee say 'whoa' and I will pull the rope."

Everything went as planned. When John said 'whoa' the black mare went down, and the grey mare stopped before she got jerked.

"One more time." J.L. said, "only this time I won't pull the rope unless she doesn't stop." The black mare was carrying her ears differently. Instead of having them almost pinned and paying attention only to what she wanted to do, she now had them turned back toward the wagon paying more attention to John.

When John started the team he had to make them trot. When he said 'whoa', both horses came to a stop faster than the wagon did. John let them stand and think about their lesson for ten minutes while they regained their wind, then they drove them around the field at a walk with lines on contact, to cool the mares down before driving to the yard.

"I think that did it John," J.L. said. "She doesn't seem to be so rammy now." As they were unhitching J.L. looked at their teeth. "They both seem to be crowding twenty years. They have likely worked all their lives, and when they got old their owner bred them to make them more saleable. Thee are fortunate they are both with foal. Their owner likely didn't think they would get with foal at their ripe old age. I am surprised the salesman didn't tell thee they were bred."

"I think he would have if he knew. It seems like a strange case. Anyway I am happy they are both with foal." John was pulling the harness off of them as he spoke. He turned them out in J.L.'s pasture.

✳   ✳   ✳

Sunday afternoon John harnessed them both and headed for home. They made the whole trip at a walk. John was very pleased. Looking at them from the wagon seat, thoughts run through his mind. *From up here I can see you are both better than I thought when I saw you from ground level. You are both nice through the withers, and both have a great spring of ribs that is not all caused from the foals. You're looking better the longer I look at you.* Now he had time to think about names for them, instead of having to concentrate on keeping them under control.

"When we were going to J.L.'s," he thought aloud, "I was thinking of calling you Mud and Lazy. I think you have earned better names than that. Let me see," he scratched his head thoughtfully, "I will call you Maud instead of Mud. That ought to be a decent name for a black mare. I hope your foal will be a black. For you Lazy, - you're not lazy, you're just sensible and relaxed. That is why you make a good mate for Maud. You're like an anchor that holds her down and keeps her more controllable. Let's see," he stroked his beard thoughtfully, "how about Mandy. When I hear Mandy I think of a warm hearted woman bustling about the kitchen and hugging the children. I think that picture suits you pretty well."

CHAPTER 14

A HOUSE! A HOME!!

That year of 1823, John cut and piled enough logs to build a good sized house, then decided to wait until next year to build it to let the logs get well dried.

He sowed about ten acres of wheat and the rest in oats for stock feed, estimating it to be about ten acres, also. He figured he had about ten acres of stumps to be pulled this summer, after first pulling the last of the felled trees off of the ground from his winter and spring cut. Progress was being made, and John felt happy, until he would go in for his meals. *It would be so nice to have a house with a woman in it, who would have a warm meal ready when I come in,* he thought. *Oh well, maybe someday I will.*

Maud and Mandy both foaled in late June, both mares having fillies.

That is surely God's blessing on me. Thank You Father. I know You are still with me.

Maud's filly was a brown, and Mandy's filly was a black. J.L. told him that Maud's would become a black horse and Mandy's would become a grey. John decided to call Mandy's filly Daisy, and Maud's filly Darky. *Those names don't seem to be suitable now, but they will be when they grow up. They look like a handsome pair of foals.*

* * *

At the Meeting the following Sunday, John heard of three stallions that were in the country. Monday he went to look at them to see which one he would like to mate the two mares back to.

The first one was a fine, big Clydesdale, black with four white feet and legs. He had a wide face blaze that encompassed the end of his muzzle and one eye. He also had a white patch on the left side of his body that went under his belly to the other side and also went back to his left hind leg and down the stifle and gaskin to the hock, and then encompassed the whole leg to the ground. He also had two glass eyes. His conformation was superb. John liked the horse even though he had more white than John liked. *I don't like the glass eyes. I will hope that feature is not too strong. I will keep this one in mind for Bell when she is matured enough.* This year Bell was only three years old.

* * *

The next stallion he looked at was a Belgium, brought from the home-land last year. He had won many Championships in his homeland. John was impressed with the huge size of him. He also liked the conformation of the animal, and the color. He was a sorrel with a flaxen mane and tail. His owner said he weighed a ton. *I'll keep him in mind, but he is not right for any of the horses I have just now,* he thought.

* * *

The last place he called was the home of a Percheron stallion who had been brought to Canada from France two years before. His first crop of foals were in the process of being born. He was a solid black with a small star on his forehead. He was a huge horse in a different way than the Belgium. He appeared to be more agile and moved freely and with ease, even though he would weigh almost as much as the Belgium. John liked him a lot. He even liked the manners and disposition the horse displayed. Although it was a thirty five mile drive, he decided this was the horse he would bring his mares for rebreeding.

* * *

The busy summer went by quickly. John took his driest piles of logs to Mike McMurty's and got them sawn ready to start his house.

He used Bell and Bob to pull the stumps from the ten acres he had cut trees from during the past winter, and also to plow and harrow it smooth enough to be ready for seeding next year.

Grace would be three in the fall, and had grown to more than fifteen hands. John started getting her used to having the harness on and being driven around the yard, teaching her to steer and stop on command. She also had to learn to back up. She seemed to be happy to have someone pay-ing attention to her, and willingly learned to do all that was asked of her.

* * *

John bought a binder in the fall of the year, to cut and tie his crop with. It required three horses to pull it, so Maud and Mandy worked half day about, while Bob and Bell worked full time. The crop was cut and tied in ten days. John stooked the wheat to keep it dry until Mac Innesfree could come to thresh it with his new machine. The oat sheaves were stacked by the barn to be fed without threshing.

John had Mike saw one load of logs into one inch thick lumber. From this he built many things, among which was a rack that he mounted on the newest wagon gear for hauling sheaves and hay, etc. He also made a third deck for his wagon box. He made a bed for himself, so he wouldn't have to sleep on straw any more. He piled a thick layer of hay on the bottom and covered it with the skins of the animals he had shot for food, making a nice comfortable mattress. He used the hide robes Ann Hodgson had given him for his covers. It was comfortable. He also built a stone-boat with a tongue, and used that to clean the barn among it's many uses.

During the fall and winter he got another ten acres of trees cut and about half of the trees pulled into the yard, and sorted and trimmed for building logs, corral rails and firewood, before the snows stopped him.

* * *

Spring of 1824 John processed enough maple syrup that he was able to take some to Andy to pay bills, and also some to sell for cash.

That summer after the crops were all in John was at J.L.'s to go to the Service with him and Ann.

"Do you think you could come and supervise the building of my house?" he asked J.L. "I think I am ready to have it constructed. I have been piling logs for it, and have them all sawn flat on two sides, so that should save time and labor during the building."

"So, thee thinks it is time to get ready for a wife, dost thee?" J.L. responded. "When did thee have in mind that thee wanted to do this?"

"Whenever the time suits you." John had a twinkle in his eyes that J.L. didn't miss. "Are you feeling able to do it for me?" John asked, knowing that question would put J.L. on the defensive, and get the conversation off of the topic of a wife for John.

"By all means, I can do it." J.L.'s eyes snapped. "If thee has everything in readiness, we can start next week. Just make sure thee has everything ready so thou dost not slow me down."

John was smiling by the time J.L. finished his speech. Nodding his head in agreement, John responded, "Next week it is then."

* * *

He let the word out at the store, and at the Meetings that he was ready to build the house. The men got their heads together and set a day to come. J.L. came to size up the situation on Monday.

"My goodness John thee has enough trimmed logs here to build thyself a fancy house. Does thee still plan on building a small one to later be turned into a chicken house? Or does thee wish to build a grand three bedroom and a bathroom house now?" J.L. asked.

"I hadn't really thought about building a big fancy house now. Do you really think there are enough logs ready to do the big one?" John was quite surprised.

"Aye. That I do. That I do." J.L. responded.

"Well, I had planned on putting the permanent house back there on that flat piece of ground, where it will be above everything in the yard. Let's go there and stake out a plan for it. If you think there are enough logs ready, we might as well build it and get it done right." John was getting excited. He hadn't thought this house would be built for several years.

The men walked to where John indicated he wanted the house, and began measuring and driving stakes in the ground to mark corners, door, windows, partitions inside, and when they were finished they measured the outside of the house. By putting in extensions across the ends, and using full double lengths on the sides, the house would measure forty feet long and thirty feet wide. It would contain three bedrooms and a bathroom in one end, using slightly more than half of the dwelling.

The other end would be the kitchen with room for a large table and chairs, with a cook stove at the end of the house, complete with it's own chimney. The entrance to the house would be at the center of the east side of the kitchen.

A fireplace would be put in the center of the dwelling between the kitchen area, and the bedrooms area. It would be placed to the west side of the area to heat the whole house. The space in front of it could be used for sitting in while reading the Bible, which John wanted his family to do as he remembered doing when he was a boy. The area could also be used to seat company when they came to visit.

"This will be the grandest house in the neighborhood," J.L. commented.

"You must be planning on getting a wife. It should make a woman happy."

"I am planning on getting a wife someday, but not for a few years yet," John confided, "I still have a lot of work to get done before that happens."

*   *   *

Tuesday John hooked Bell and Bob to the wagon gear and loaded as many finished logs onto it as he could. He took them up to the house sight and left them just outside one of the marked walls. Then hooking to the wagon box he filled it heaping high with the blocks for windows and doors and took them up and unloaded them where they would be handy to get during construction. Lifting the wagon box off the gear, he loaded the gear as high as he could get it with the two inch planks that he had Mike cut for him.

When he put the horses in the barn for the night, Maud and Mandy didn't come when they were called. John went out to see what was the reason, and in the dusk, saw Maud had just dropped a foal which was struggling to get onto it's feet. Mandy wouldn't leave her and kept circling nervously around the pair, snorting and tossing her nose in the air toward the bushes.

John stood by and watched Maud clean the foal. Both mares were nervously agitated, and kept looking toward the shrubbery at the back. John kept very quiet and still until he saw a wolf poke it's head through the curtain of leaves, look around, sniff the air, then pull back and disappear. He immediately jumped out in the direction of the bushes, yelling and waving his arms.

The foal was on it's feet and had suckled by the time John got back from the bushes. It stayed close to Maud as John got them moving slowly to the barn, with Mandy right with them. John noticed Mandy had a long string of wax on her teats, so when he got them to the barn, he put Maud in their stall, and put Mandy in the box stall he had made.

Morning brought him wide awake before the sun was up. *Got to see what Maud's foal looks like, and see what Mandy is doing*, he told himself. He sat up in his bed to see Mandy had foaled during the night. Her foal was already dried and fed. John fed the horses their grain and some hay. After eating his breakfast he took the two mares with their foals to the water hole, then turned them out in the corral. *It looks like both foals are going to be black when they mature. Maud has a colt, and Mandy's is a filly. That is nice. They both look healthy. Ned and Nell, that's what I will name them.*

*   *   *

Wednesday there was a larger group of men arrive to help with the construction, than had come for the barn raising. Also the men who had been going to the sawmill before had none of that to do, so there were more hands assisting with the building. J.L. and John were kept busy supervising the work, helping to carry the heavy logs to where they were needed, and checking to make sure everything was going according to plan.

By night the walls were up ready to start building the roof. All the men had brought big bundles of food to be used for the volunteers. John had put a fire in the maple syrup pit a few days before, and had wrapped several large venison roasts in wet burlap then plastered them with clay, and had them cooked for the crowd. There was more than enough for two days feeding. Many of the men stayed over night to work the next day. Several went home, some of them intending to come back the next day.

* * *

Harry Potts came in the afternoon of the second day, to put hinges and latches on any doors that would be put in. Andy Smith also came out in the same afternoon with the windows John had ordered. He had ordered two, and now decided he wanted one in each bedroom and the bathroom. Andy said he would see what he could come up with, and would bring them out the next day

J.L. got some men working on putting in a two inch thick plank floor with planks ranging in width from fourteen inches down to ten inches. J.L. was particular that there should be no cracks anywhere on the floor.

Another crew was set at putting up a one inch thick ceiling for the whole house, with a trap door type entry to the attic, in the kitchen. These boards were also from ten to fourteen inches wide, making the work go quite fast. A third crew put the roof on, using the same type of slabs that had been used on the barn.

By the end of day three the house was finished except for the fireplace and two chimneys. John and J.L. planned on doing that alone. Andy had even been able to find enough nice windows to complete the house to John's delight. As he and J.L. were installing the rest of the windows, Mac Innesfree came to help them finish the installing, since his assigned part of the project was completed.

When the work was finished, the men all gathered in the yard and stood talking about the finished product and their part in it. Everyone felt pleased with their handwork, and congratulated J.L. for his expertise, and John for producing the materials and the ideas for the rooms.

"Everyone will be invited to the house warming when the house is completed." John spoke appreciatively, "I thank all of you from the bottom of my heart for your help in this project. Please feel free to get my help for things you want to do on your own places. I will be most glad to return the favor you have given me this week. I know it has not been easy for you to spend so much time here, and leave things at home undone. Thank you so much."

"You're most welcome John." came a chorus from the men, then they turned to leave.

*   *   *

There was not much time left to build the fireplace, as the crops would be ready to cut in about a week. John took the team and wagon and went down by the lake to look for stones suitable to build the fireplace. He made three trips to the house with all the weight he thought was safe for the wagon to carry. Each load also made Bell and Bob straighten out and lean hard in the collar.

On Saturday he told J.L. he thought he had enough stones for the job.

"I'll stop in Battersea and pick up some things that will be needed," J.L. said, "like cement for the mortar, and a damper, plus thee will need a flue to insert the stove pipe through. I should be out to thy place by mid morning Monday."

It was after dark Monday, when they finished the fireplace, and J.L. was leaving for home. As they were hitching J.L.'s team, John heaved a big sigh, then said, "I think we can have the house warming on Monday a week from today. How does that sound J.L?"

"Sounds good, John. We will see thee on Saturday and discuss it further," He clapped the horses with the lines as he spoke, and they rattled out of the yard.

John turned to go to bed in the barn, then stopped and looked at the house. "A house," he said aloud, "*My house...My home! Oh praise You, my Heavenly Father.* Three years ago I never thought it would ever happen, and here it is."

He was overwhelmed with what he saw, and bowed his head to thank God for having such wonderful neighbors, but most of all *Thank You Father for guiding me in all of my efforts and endeavors. You have Blessed me so wonderfully. Thank You blessed Jesus. Amen.*

*   *   *

Tuesday John started building the chimney for the cook stove, going by what he had learned from J.L. while they were building the fireplace chimney. He brought up a load of smaller stones than were used in the fireplace, then went to Battersea to get some supplies to complete the job. Working in all his spare time Tuesday afternoon and all day Wednesday he had the job almost finished by evening, and got it completed by noon on Thursday.

* * *

To prepare for the house warming, John got a fire going in the maple syrup processing pit, after removing the boiling barrel. That evening - Thursday - he took his gun out and shot a large buck deer. He eviscerated it and hung it high in a tree to cool.

Friday dawned bright and clear, promising great weather for the day. John went to the fire-pit and stoked the fire. He returned to it several times during the day to stoke it and develop a deep bed of coals.

Saturday morning, he skinned the deer carcass and cut it into large roasts wrapping them in jute grain sacks that he had cut up, and tying them with wire, making a piece of the wire into a handle. Plastering the roasts with clay mud was a messy job, but he got it finished by mid-afternoon, and using the team and stone-boat took the roasts up to the fire pit and buried them under a large pile of red coals. Satisfied with his work so far, he piled more tree roots on top before driving the team and stone-boat back to the barn.

Saturday evening he started his first fire in the fireplace. When it was going to his satisfaction, he went outside and brought in the saw-horses the men had made during the construction. He set four of them up in the house, then brought in two planks that were about fifteen feet long, and set them across the saw-horses to make a table that went almost all the way across the kitchen-living room.

* * *

John drove to J.L.'s early Sunday morning to go to the Meeting with them. He arrived just as they were about ready to leave their yard. Hurriedly he put his horses in the barn, and joined the Hodgson's on the ride to the Meeting.

* * *

About two o'clock Monday, the vehicles started coming into John's yard. Every man who had worked on the house, came and those with wives and families brought them all. When they started getting out of their buggies, democrats and wagons, they brought bundles that John directed for them to take inside and put on the make-shift table.

"I'm going to get my team and go up to get the meat from the fire-pit," he said to Mac Innesfree. "Could you look after the incoming people until I get back?"

"Sure thing." Mac agreed.

John had the team harnessed, so it wasn't long before he was gone. When he got back Andy was in the yard with a borrowed democrat, to carry a large table and four chairs. John waved to him then took the meat up to the house, where many hands helped carry the bundles in and deposit them in the fireplace. John took the harness off his team as soon as the stone-boat was put away, then the team was turned out to pasture. He went over to Andy who was still sitting on the democrat seat. His wife and child had gone into the house with the other women.

"What have you got here, Andy?" John asked as he approached the democrat. "A table and chairs? They look well used, but they look as solid as a dollar. Where are you planning on setting them up?"

"Wherever you want them John. They are for you." John was looking closely at them as Andy was talking. "When I was leaving home mother and father knew I wanted to start up store-keeping, so they told me to take the table and chairs out of the house that your family occupied. I have since purchased a set for my wife, and I thought you would like to have these."

John grabbed the side of the democrat, as his knees buckled and he was going down. He sat for a few minutes, the tears running down his face. Andy got down and put his arm around John's shoulders.

"Are you alright, John?" he asked, "Did I do something wrong?"

"No Andy," John mumbled as he struggled to his feet. "This is the table and chairs that our fathers made for their wives that they both loved so much. This table is such a treasure to me. Thank you Andy. Thank you. How can I ever repay you for such a treasure?" John wiped his eyes on his sleeve.

"You already have John. Just turning up in my area is one of the greatest gifts I could have ever received. Just don't tell Maria that she comes second in my life. I love her dearly, too, you know. Promise me John."

"I promise Andy." John said as he started to laugh. "Bring the table and chairs to the house and we will unload them in the kitchen."

Many willing hands took the set into the house, and put them just inside the door. John went in and when he looked around he was amazed at all the things that had accumulated there.

"Hello John. I am Hazel Innesfree, Mac's wife." a plump jovial faced woman held out her hand as she spoke. John liked her immediately, particularly her reddish brown hair.

"Hello ma'am," John found she had a strong hand as he shook it. "I am so glad you have taken over the organization of the kitchen."

"Sam Shewfelt opened up one of thy crocks of roasted venison and sliced it for us, so I think everything is in readiness for eating now if that is what thee wants to do." Hazel continued.

John noticed that one of the women was scrubbing his precious table with a stiff brush, and another lady took the brush when the first lady was done with it, and began scrubbing the chairs.

"It is such a beautiful day Harriet, that I think we will take them outside." Hazel said to one of the women, as she went out the door. She gave a shrill whistle and a bellowing holler, so that everyone turned to see what was up. She beckoned for everyone to come toward the house.

"Come on. Come on. Gather round here. Reverend Samuels is going to say a prayer." she said as everyone was gathering around.

The ladies were bringing the table and chairs out and were followed by Reverend Samuels, who was from the Methodist Church in Battersea. He had a booming voice, so everyone would be able to hear him. John was astonished at the huge crowd that had gathered.

"Friends," Reverend Samuels started, "We are gathered here today in the sight of God to give thanks for all the wonderful things Thee has provided for these men to build this house, and also the barn, and for you women to provide such a wonderful banquet as is laid out in the kitchen. It is by God's good grace that we are gathered this day to welcome John Thomas to our community. Bless this food Father, and put it to Thy use in our bodies, all in the name of Jesus Christ. Amen."

Hazel took over again, "John, go into thy house, pick up a plate and help thyself. When thee has what thee wants, come out here and sit at this table. Everyone else follow John."

When they had all had their fill, the women took the dirty dishes to the kitchen, then started bringing out home-made quilts, feather pillows, the dishes as they were cleaned, loaves of bread, cutlery, bowls and many other things used to run a good house. Every woman brought something, although some of them said what they had brought had been cleaned up for the meal they just had. Everything was put in front of John, on the table until it was full, then the overflow was put on the ground around it.

John stood up and took a deep breath. A hush fell over the people as they strained to hear what he was going to say. Finally he started, "Friends," he said, then stopped and swallowed. "I didn't know I had so many friends." Everyone laughed. "If you wanted to see a grown man cry, you have succeeded." Everyone laughed again as John wiped his eyes. "I am so glad the Good Father has led me to this community, and I pray that I and my future wife will live the rest of our lives here. Thank you all so much for all the gifts you have presented me with. They will certainly make life easier. I am not sure I deserve all these things, but rest assured I appreciate every one of them."

Everyone applauded loudly, then started a line of people shaking John's hand and welcoming him in person as well as introducing themselves when they thought he might not know who they were. They then went to their rigs and left for their homes. Andy and Maria, and J.L. and Ann helped take the things into the house, then J.L. said, "Come with me John." and they went to the barn and got John's bed and brought it to the house and set it in the first bedroom. The hay and straw mattress was now replaced with a feather tick and a couple of quilts. Then the pillow was put on and two more quilts were put on for covers.

"There," J.L. and Andy said in unison, "now we must be on the road."

John went out and helped them hook their horses, then helped the women get into their rigs, and with bursting heart he watched them drive away. When he went into the house, he found an oil lamp burning warmly, another gift from someone. The food that was left was piled on the makeshift table. He would have to find a place to keep it tomorrow. Right now he had to take care of his animals, and then he was going to bed.

✳   ✳   ✳

While he was watering and feeding the horses, he couldn't keep his mind on them. *The transformation of the house to a home with just the women bustling about making the meal, made everything seem so warm. The men looking after the children, he thought, just like Father and Fred used to look after us kids. Just like Mother and Betty used to make the meals and turn those houses into warm homes. And now on top of everything else, I have a thick feather mattress to sleep on. I don't think I will be able to sleep with so many things to think about.*

CHAPTER 15

PROGRESSION!

During the winter of 1824/1825 there was not as much snow fall as the previous years. John was able to cut trees all winter, and haul them into the yard. He cut them off at the twenty foot length, and sorted them into piles of the big ones being set aside for constructing buildings. Some that were not quite as big were moved up his yard entrance to where he planned on building a large shed to house his vehicles and implements. Then there was a pile of poles for corral rails, and the crooked and uneven ones were piled for firewood.

With the arrival of spring 1825, John began getting anxious to start constructing the shed. He talked with Mike McMurty at the Meeting and made arrangements to get his logs sawn ready for building. Mike was able to do this for him before it was time to start on the land.

He found that harrowing the fields took a long time. He now had forty acres under cultivation and would add another ten acres this summer. While he was walking behind the harrows, he had lots of time to think and plan. *If I had twice as wide a set of harrows, I could hook on four horses and get this job finished in half the time. I can afford to get another set of harrows made now.*

He talked to Harry Potts the next time he went to Battersea and had the wide set of harrows ready to harrow the seed in after he got it broadcast. Using Maud and Mandy half day about with Darky and Daisy and with Bob and Bell working full time, he was able to get the forty acres harrowed in three days. His three oldest mares in the hitch were all pregnant to foal in July, and he wanted to be easy on them, especially the two older mares.

He had used Bob to train Darky and Daisy during the winter when they were rising two year olds. He made life as easy as he could for the brood mares, but he needed their help to handle the work.

During the early part of July, Maud had another black colt that John named Coal; Mandy had a grey filly he named Daphne, and Bell had a black filly, well trimmed with white, that John named Shadow because she was marked like her mother, but with four white feet. John was keeping the three mares with foals in the corral for the night until he was sure the foals were strong enough to evade the wolves.

A week after Mandy foaled, as John went to do his chores, he found Maud standing over Mandy who was lying down. Maud was nuzzling Mandy's foal. *That's strange*, John thought as he walked over for a closer inspection. He found Mandy was dead.

He put Maud and the two foals in the barn, then harnessed Bob and Bell. He tied Bell's foal – Shadow, in the barn next to Maud, then took the team out and pulled Mandy out to the very east end of the pasture. When he got back to the barn he found Maud was letting Mandy's foal suck, much to his relief.

✳ ✳ ✳

During the summer, John got his vehicle shed more than half built while the mares were nursing their foals in the pasture. He had the north end built up high enough he was able to put the bob-sleigh under shelter, He also backed the rack on the newest wagon gear into it.

He decided he had better leave building the shed and pull stumps. He used Bob alone for a while, then started teaming him with Darky and Daisy, alternating them half day about to teach them how to pull. It was slower going because John had to do more cutting of the roots, but they got about half of the stumps cleaned out before it was time to cut the crop.

Darkie and Daisy were hooked with Bob to the binder to cut the crop. It was great training for them. By the time the crop was all cut they were responding to commands and signals as well as Bob, plus their fear of noise was gone by the end of the first day.

✳ ✳ ✳

John fed Maud extra grain all summer, but she continued losing weight from feeding the two foals. When they were a month old they started eating oats with her, which helped keep the both foals in good condition, but Maud remained thin. John was glad he had decided to not rebreed her. However, he did take Bell over to the Clyde stallion again.

The beginning of October 1825 John weaned Coal and Daphne and Shadow, and kept them tied in the barn for a month. They learned to lead well when he took them down to the lake for water twice a day. He also tied them on the sides of Darky and Daisy on Saturdays when he would go to Hodgson's, alternating the three of them so that each one would make two trips, then stay home for one trip. It was a very educating exercise for them.

The trip to J.L.'s was good for the two-year-olds too, as the wagon was empty. John was not taking loads of poles to Battersea now, since those bills were all paid up. He had several orders for fire wood for the winter, but would deliver them after the harvest was completed.

* * *

During the summer John dug a root cellar north west of the house. He built a roof and entrance over it himself. *There, now I will have a place to store meat and any vegetables I might grow, or have given to me as happened last year,* he thought to himself. *Next I will build a chicken house.*

"Ha ha," he chuckled, "That was going to be the second building I was going to build. How things can change."

* * *

John took a team and rack over to drive on the threshing gang for Mac Innesfree, to pay for Mac threshing John's wheat. He took Bob and Darkie one day and the next day – Bob and Daisy and alternated them until all the threshing was finished.

After the harvest was finished, John went back to building the machine shed and got it finished before winter set in.

* * *

Late in the fall John was doing up the night chores. He went to the barn door and whistled on the horses to come. They all came except Maud. He went out looking for her, but since it was after dusk, he was unable to see her.

The next morning he went out again. This time he found her lying near Mandy. She was also dead. John had stretched Mandy's hide, so now he spent the rest of the morning removing Maud's hide and stretching it.

"You two old girls have certainly done well for me. I'm glad to see you are both resting together in your afterlife," he remarked. He picked up the hide and headed for the barn. "Six foals in the three years I have had you. You certainly deserve your retirement. Rest in peace girls."

CHAPTER 16

THE SEARCH BEGINS

Spring of 1826 John began looking around his farm, evaluating how much he had accomplished so far, much with the help of his friends and neighbors, calculating what he needed to do before bringing a woman home.

"I think I have things ready enough now for a woman," he said to the sun as it was rising over the rock behind the barn and pasture.

"I have fifty acres producing and will get another ten acres worked up this summer. I would be able to have more time for clearing land if there were someone here to do the chores. If I get the right woman I could get a few cows and we could start selling cheese or milk. We could keep a few sows and sell pork meat in the fall or maybe more often. We could increase the farm income considerably from what I am getting from the grain and wood."

"It would be so nice to come in to a warm meal and someone to talk to every day. Heavenly Father, where can I find a suitable woman?" he asked as he closed his eyes. "Church. Of course, church would be a good place to start looking. There is no one at the Friends Meetings that I think of as suitable. They are mostly too young or are already married. I will have Andy and Maria out for supper some night. They might have some ideas of places I might look."

John began preparing his land for the coming seeding. He had a fine crop of maple syrup, and was able to sell all that he didn't want to keep for himself. Having increased the number of trees he was tapping was paying off.

*   *   *

After the seeding was harrowed in, and the spring work finished, Bell dropped a black Clyde colt who had a glass eye, as well as an abundance of white on his left side and under-belly, to go along with his four white legs and bald white face and chin.

"Well, you finally arrived. I have been expecting you," John told him when he saw him. "I will call you Ben and hope I can find a nice home for you."

* * *

John took a load of rails to town for Bill Shakleton, who wanted to put a third rail on his pasture fence.

"Hello John," Bill greeted him as he came across the road to the pasture to help John unload. "What are you driving today? I don't think I have seen these two before."

"Greetings Bill," John replied. "No, this is the first time I have brought them to town. These are the first two foals I raised. I was very fortunate to get a pair of fillies. They are now three year olds, and are doing very well."

"Do you still have the Clydesdale team?" Bill asked.

"Yep," John said as he dropped a rail on the pile. "Although the mare has had her second foal, I don't drive them as a team as much, because she is raising her foal."

After the rails were unloaded, John put Daisy and Darky in the stable, and walked over to the store. From behind the counter bagging up some flour Andy looked up as John entered. "Hello John," he cheerfully greeted him. "You're looking like you're on a mission today. What are you up to?"

"Well," John raised his cap and scratched his head. "I just brought a load of rails in for Bill Shakleton, using my three year old fillies. I thought I would give them an hour's rest before I head back home. They're in the livery stable," he finished as Andy was looking out the window for the team.

"I'm glad you thought of coming in here to kill time," Andy said with a grin. "We don't see much of you."

"Well, I keep pretty busy," John shuffled his feet. "Actually one of the reasons I came to town was to ask if you and Maria would like to come out to my place Friday for supper and a visit."

"**Maria**," Andy called to the back of the store. Maria appeared carrying a baby of a few months of age. "John wants to know if we would be interested in going out to his place Friday evening. What do you think? Is the baby ready for outdoor travel, yet?"

"I think she is." Maria looked tenderly at the bundle in her arms. "I think it would be nice to get away from the store for a few hours. Thank you for asking us John."

"What have you got there Maria?" John asked as he went over to look at the baby.

"This is Elizabeth." Maria said as she passed the baby to John. "She is two months old, now." He took the baby awkwardly, and turned her around so he could look into her face.

"Isn't she a miracle?" John whispered as he looked into her tiny face. "And her hands. They are so perfect, so tiny. Truly a miracle." He started crooning a tune to her, much to the amazement of Andy and Maria. They hadn't seen this side of John before. He always seemed to be so quiet...so shy... so much in a hurry.

A toddler came out of the living quarters, and Maria scooped him up into her arms. "John, I would like you to meet little Fredrick." Maria said proudly, "He is going to be two years old tomorrow. Would you come and join us for supper to celebrate his birthday?"

"I'd be most happy to," John replied.

Half an hour later John decided he should get on home, and passed the baby back to Maria. He was feeling happier than he had felt for a long time, as he rumbled on his way home in the wagon.

*   *   *

When he had his chores finished, John gathered up some pieces of wood that was left over from the construction jobs, and took them to the house. With his jacknife and the saw he worked on the wood pieces for a few hours before going to bed. In the morning he got his chores done, hastily, then went back to his wood project again. By three o'clock he had a miniature wagon and removable box completed.

Going to the barn, he whistled on the horses and while they were running in from the pasture, he put some oat sheaves around the corral for them.

"Come Grace," he said as he took her into the barn. "Now the rest of you can look after yourselves. I will open the gate to the lake so you can get a drink. I will also close the barn doors so you can't go in there and spend your time. Then Grace and I are going to town for the evening."

Taking a grain sack to put the miniature wagon in he jumped on Grace's back. After she had smelled it they left the yard, and soon were loping down the road, the precious cargo being held to one side at arm's length to keep it safe from breakage.

*   *   *

Andy and Maria both met him at the door when he knocked. "Come in. Come in." they both chorused.

"What have you got in the bag? I hope that's not your dinner," Andy teased.

"No," John replied. "I trust Maria will have something to eat that will be more edible than this. I brought a little something for the birthday boy."

"Freddy, look what Uncle John has for you." Andy took Freddy by the hand to the middle of the living room. "Come on Uncle John, show us what you have there." Andy looked at his wife's startled expression, and winked at her. John sat down on the floor and withdrew the wagon from the sack. Freddy sat down beside him and reached for the toy.

John leaned over and thrust his feet out behind himself, so that he was lying on his stomach, and Freddy did the same. The fun began with John being the first to pull the wagon by the tongue, up to Freddy.

"There Freddy," he said, "now you do it. Here hold it by the tongue." Andy squatted down to sit on the floor to watch the two of them play with the wagon. There was a knock at the door, which John didn't notice. Andy got up and went with Maria to the door to greet their other guest.

"Come in Mary," Maria warmly invited. "We are about ready to sit down."

"Thank you. Here is a little something for Freddy," she smiled warmly.

"You give your gift to Freddy, Mary," Andy grinned. "He's in here." Andy was still grinning when he took Mary to where John and Freddy were playing on the floor.

"Mary Brown I would like you to meet my dear friend John Thomas, and my son Freddy. John is the biggest one." The grin had not left Andy's face, and now Maria who was standing by Andy's side, was smiling pleasantly.

Embarrassed, John rose to his feet and held out his hand to shake Mary's hand. "Hello ma'am," he sheepishly greeted her, "I was just showin' little Freddy how to play with that thing," he indicated with his hand. John thought Mary's hand was awfully limp, and moist. The thought flashed through his head, *Kinda like a dead fish. Stop it John. She may be a very nice girl.*

Mary gave Freddy her gift and helped him open it, to find a light blue shirt.

"That will be great for him to wear to church." Andy spoke for Freddy, "Thank you Mary. We really appreciate it." He took the shirt to show Maria who was dishing food into bowls. "I'll put it in his bedroom," he told his wife.

"Thank you Mary. Freddy will look so well dressed in that shirt. It looks like it will be just the right size, too. Thank you Mary," Maria exclaimed.

Setting a bowl of potatoes on the table she went to the stove for a plate of meat, then called, "Come to supper. It's getting cold."

John picked up the birthday boy. "Come with Uncle John, Freddy. We don't want supper to be cold."

Freddy clung to the wagon and when John tried to take it away, he kicked and screamed. John turned him around to bring them face to face.

"Freddy," he spoke sternly, "We don't want our new toy to get all dirty with supper. We will leave it here until we are finished eating, then we can come and play with it again." As he was talking, John took the wagon out of Freddy's hand and put it on the floor. Freddy looked at it, but said no more while John took him to his chair and fastened him in. Andy and Maria looked at each other in amazement.

Supper went very well. Mary was very dainty and polite the whole time, showing her excellent breeding.

"Mary works in the bank, John," Maria said. "She also comes to our church. That is actually how I got acquainted with her. I am so grateful to have a friend like her to talk to."

"I'm glad for you Maria," John replied. "Mary would you be interested in coming out to my farm on Friday evening? Andy and Maria are coming and you are perfectly welcome to come, if you so wish."

Mary fidgeted with her fork, and kind of tipped her head a little to the side. Looking at Maria, she replied, "Why thank you. I guess I can do that if you have room for me to ride with you." She looked at Maria the whole time, never once looking at John.

✳   ✳   ✳

Grace cantered her smooth comfortable gait for a couple of miles. John pulled her down to a walk to spend more time considering his thoughts about Mary.

"She has a pretty face and a nice figure. I just can't seem to picture her in the role of the farm wife I would like to have. I will have to think about it for a while."

✳   ✳   ✳

John's supper with Andy and Maria went fairly well. John had roasted venison with some potatoes he had grown in his developing garden. He had also gone to the woods and picked a bowl of greens. During the morning he had made some biscuits, and had bought some butter from the store when he went to the birthday party.

Mary ate sparingly and went with everyone when they went out to see the horses, but showed no sign of interest in anything. She seemed to be glad when it was time to go back to town.

* * *

During the summer John took Mary out to various things, - the church picnic. The carnival when it came to Kingston. Andy and Maria also went to the most of these things. John was enraptured with their children, and helped with the care of them on these outings.

Early in the summer John had told J.L. and Ann that he was going to start attending the church that Andy and Maria went to, so from that point on he went to the Methodist church in Battersea. Their services were almost the same as the ones he remembered going to when he was a youngster. The familiarity of the services made him feel more comfortable.

He saw Mary every Sunday and spoke to her, making plans with her to go places she chose. He thought things would work out better if she liked the entertainment.

Late in the fall they went to the hotel for supper. It was a scrumptious dining event. John felt as much out of place there as she did out at his farm.

When he met her at church the next Sunday, he took her hand and walking down the path to the sidewalk, he stopped and turned to look into her eyes, which she tried to avoid. He spoke softly, "Mary, you are a pretty girl and should have no trouble finding a mate more suited to you than I am. We are not comfortable with each other and that is not how it should be after the number of times we have seen each other. I think the right thing to do is to stop seeing each other, and search elsewhere. What do you think, Mary?"

Mary lowered her eyes and withdrew her hand, then after a brief moment she responded, "You are right John. I could not fit into your way of life. I thank you for being so honest with me," she turned and walked down the street.

"Good bye, Mary," he spoke to her retreating figure.

* * *

During the fall and winter John got the trees on another ten acres cut, but left them where they fell, planning on moving them in the spring. During the maple syrup time he pulled about half of them into the yard, and got them cut and sorted.

His chores were taking more time each year. During the winter months he got his two year olds started under harness. He hooked them with Bob when spring was coming, and drove them into town to see the sights. He also used them with Bob when he went collecting the syrup.

He took loads of firewood or poles to The Kingston market, but used Bell and Bob for those trips. His firewood was now cut in stove lengths by the men who had cut Andy's wood, so when he took a load of firewood to Battersea or Kingston he used the wagon box to transport it.

Wednesday when he had taken a load of rails to the Kingston market, he heard that a boat carrying a shipment of immigrating women from the British Isles, had arrived in Canada. They were taking the train from Montreal and travelling west. They would be stopping at Kingston next Wednesday. A few minutes after he had heard the news, a man came along and bought his load of rails, and also ordered two loads of firewood.

On his return trip to home, John stopped in at J.L.'s to pass on all the good news.

"Would I be able to spend Wednesday night here?" he asked.

"Of course thee can. So can thy selected wife, John," Ann added.

"If I have one, Ann. Looking does not mean I am getting one, you know. Look what happened with Mary," John reminded them.

"Whatever thee brings thee are most welcome to stay," Ann responded.

✳   ✳   ✳

John stayed only a short while at Hodgson's, then was on the road again. He called in to Mac Innesfree's and was talking to Mac in the yard, when Hazel came to the door of the house and invited him in for supper.

"We are just sitting down, John and I won't take no for an answer."

"Alright Hazel," John agreed, knowing there was no use arguing with her on this subject.

"We will be a few minutes, as we are going to put the team in the barn," Mac called to his wife.

"Would I be able to borrow a wagon and driver next Wednesday?" John asked as they were stabling the horses. "I have sale for two loads of fire wood and would like to take them both at the same time. Also there is a train coming into Kingston that day, with women from the British Isles. I thought I would look them over to see what the possibilities are. I have made plans to spend Wednesday night at J.L. Hodgson's so would need somebody to do the chores for me Wednesday night and Thursday morning."

"Why sure John," Mac responded with a big grin. "We would be most happy to help thee out. It is high time thee had a helpmate."

"I would like to leave about four o'clock or before in the morning to be able to make the three and a half hour ride by seven," John explained as they walked to the house, "I want to get the wagons loaded Tuesday. We will use my horses for both wagons."

"The boys and I will come over on Tuesday and get the loading done." Mac was entering the house as he was talking, so right away after the blessings were said, he had to explain to Hazel and the family what was up.

Hazel immediately became excited and started making plans.

"Hold on Hazel," John cautioned her. "Don't start making plans until I bring a good woman home. That might not even be this year, you know. Things don't always go the way we would like them to."

"Alright John," Hazel giggled. "I'll wait until thee're outside to finish making plans."

CHAPTER 17

IN SPRING A YOUNG MAN'S FANCY TURNS...

Sunday, word was passed around both among the women and the men, at both the Methodist Congregation, and the Friends of J.L.'s Meeting place, of John's intentions. Mac talked to several of his neighbors about loading the wood on Tuesday, which brought quite a few helping hands to complete the work.

Mac told John he would be taking the load to Kingston, as his boys were able to do his chores, and would also do John's. While they were hooking Darkey and Daisy to Mac's wagon, John outlined the requirements for his chores. Mac said he would meet John at the junction of his lane and the Battersea road. "Don't be late. I don't want to have to sit out there very long," he teased.

Wednesday morning John was up shortly after midnight, and got his chores done. He harnessed Bell and Bob, then went to the house and packed up a few things to eat on the road. Opening the gate to the lake, he threw out a few oat sheaves, then took Bell and Bob down for their drink. He closed the barn doors so the horses wouldn't be able to get into it while he would be away. Climbing up on the wagon, he drove to the intersection of Mac's road. It was still dark so he couldn't see anything and he couldn't hear anything. Lying back on the pile of wood he closed his eyes. When he heard the rattle of the trace chains, and the rumble of the wagon he opened his eyes and sat up.

"Did you have to wait long?" John called out to Mac, giving him a dig for the remark Mac had made the day before. "I was afraid you had gone on without me."

"If I was goin' huntin' for a wife, I might not have gone to bed either." Mac retaliated. "It was too early for these two. They didn't drink."

"Neither did mine," John admitted. "We will try watering them later when they are more ready to drink."

The two teams and wagons started down the road as the eastern sky began coloring up with the coming of the sun.

John decided a stop at J.L. Hodgsons would be a good place to water the horses. They all drank readily while John and Mac had a short visit with J.L. They were soon on the road again.

✳ ✳ ✳

They had just nicely pulled into their market stalls, when the man who was to get the wood, drove in with two teams and wagons. The two empty wagons were pulled up beside the full wagons, and two boys for each wagon began throwing the logs over into the empty wagons. While the wood was being transferred the man paid John. He even produced a broom to sweep the wagons with. "I want the crumbs, too." he told them. "They make good chips for starting the fires."

When the man was gone, John looked at Mac, "Do you want to go home now, or do you want to look around for a while?"

"I think I will take a walk through the Market to see what is here." Mac responded.

"Alright." John agreed. "I will stay with the horses until you get back. I would like to go to the hardware store to see if I can afford a new stove. I think that would be a nice addition to my home."

"I won't be long here. I would like to look around the hardware store too." Mac adjusted his cap as he left.

"Pick me up a bag of potatoes, and a bag of onions," John called after the retreating figure.

✳ ✳ ✳

When Mac came back he was not carrying anything.

"Was there no potatoes or onions?" John asked.

"Yeh. There are lots of them. I want to get five bags of potatoes as well as a bag of onions, so thought I had better drive the team down there," Mac said as he climbed up on the wagon.

"You're sure you didn't want to carry them all up to here?" John was teasing again. He pulled his team and wagon in behind Mac and followed him to the stall.

When they left the market place they drove to the hardware store where Mac pulled his team in behind John's wagon. They tied the lines to the stake at the front of the wagons and went in.

A jovial middle aged, black haired, black mustached man came toward them. "Good day gentlemen." he greeted them, "Can I do something for you?"

"My name is John Thomas from the other side of Battersea. I was wondering if you might have a kitchen stove to sell."

"My name is Mac Innesfree. I am a neighbor of John's. I don't have anything in particular in mind to buy, but would like to look around your store."

"Welcome to Kingston, gentlemen. My name is Ray Hunter. I have a very serviceable stove over here. It just came in two weeks ago. It has a warming oven, and a reservoir at the back end to keep the water heated. The oven is a good baking oven, and I am sure any woman would think she was in Heaven if she had one of these. This one is a Great Majestic. Actually I have two of them. The salesman was sure they would sell quickly, and suggested I get more than one."

"What is thy price for one of them?" Mac asked.

"A hundred and seventy five dollars. That price includes a sheet of galvanized tin to lay on the floor under the stove for protection from fire starting from red coals, ten feet of stove pipe, one section having a damper in it, two elbows, and a can of wax to polish it up at times. This stove has a brick lined fire box and brick lining around the oven to keep the heat more even for a longer time. It is much better when baking. This actually is an excellent deal," Mr. Hunter ended.

Mac looked at John. John looked at Mac.

"I'll take it." John started digging out his money.

"John," Mac looked at John pleadingly, "would it be alright with thee if I took one home for Hazel?"

"Of course, Mac. Why would you even think you should ask me?" John looked at him quizzically.

"I didn't want thee to think I was trying to upstage thee," Mac replied.

"I am so glad to have someone else have things as good as I have, there is no way of me being jealous. Look around and see if there is anything else you would like," John said as he put a hand on Mac's shoulder.

While John was paying for his stove, Mr. Hunter informed him that it was very heavy, and would take four men to move it out to the wagon.

"I'll back the wagon up to the door. That should help. First I have to move the bags of potatoes," John was still talking as he was going out the door.

He got the potatoes and onions all moved up to the front of the wagon, then picked up the lines and maneuvered Darkey and Daisy around until he had the wagon backed up to the door. He saw some men coming down the street, and when they came to the wagon, he asked them if they could help move the stove out into the wagon. Two of them volunteered and the other two older men stayed to watch.

John brought the men into the store and pointed out the stoves to be moved. Mac and John took the leading end of the first stove, and with the two volunteers help, got it into the wagon. Then followed the second stove, and then all the items Mr. Hunter had named. John gave each of the two men a dollar, and they gratefully left. Mac also put two coal oil storm lanterns in the wagon. Everything done, Mac drove the wagon away toward the hotel for a lunch to eat on the road home, and John drove his wagon toward the livery stable, eating had not yet entered his mind.

* * *

John had the team in the barn before the stableman showed up. "Give them some oats and good hay," John instructed him, "I'll pay for it all," he followed the man to the stall where the oats were kept and made sure the measures were full. He also went with him to the hay pile and personally picked out hay for the team.

"Say, you're a fussy horseman," the stableman exclaimed.

"I expect my horses to do a day's work for me. I feed them accordingly," John explained. "These horses pulled a three deck wagon load of wood seventeen miles this morning. They have earned their rations."

"I appreciate a man who looks after his stock. My name is Tom Afton," he held out a gnarled, calloused hand to John.

"I'm John Thomas," he said as he took Tom's hand with an equally calloused one.

"Sure is a lot of excitement 'round town 'bout that train load of wimmin comin' t' town. Did you hear about it?" Tom asked.

At that moment John heard a train whistle in the distance, so he started for the door.

"Yeah I heard about it," he tossed over his shoulder.

"Come here, John," Tom called, "Have a look at these b'fore yu' leave." he showed John a gangly two-year-old colt, and in the next stall was a dry cow and a calf, then in the next stall stood a red bull with some white markings. The animals were all so thin their hip-bones were sticking out, and you could have counted their ribs from across the street. Their hides were tight and their hair was dry and standing on end.

"What are you showing me these terrible looking animals for?" John asked. "Somebody should have fed them."

"Well John, the man who brought them here was heading west. He brought his stock to the market last week. The mature horses and the two milking cows sold, but these didn't. He brought them to me and told me to send him the money I could get for them after the stable fees were paid," Tom hesitated, giving John time to think about the animals, then added, "Would you be interested in them?"

"Tell me something interesting about them," John instructed.

"Well, the colt is bred for saddle work. He was brought up from Kentucky or someplace as a weanling, then this man bought him a year ago."

"Bring him outside so I can see him," John instructed.

John looked him over very carefully. He was a red sorrel with a flaxen mane and tail, except they were very dirty. He had a small star but no other white marks. In spite of his thin condition, he was about sixteen hands high, with a strongly built back and loins. He seemed to like to carry his head higher than the horses John was accustomed to. John turned and walked into the barn. Tom put the colt away.

John was looking at the bull, so Tom took him outside into better lighting. He was a deep red, almost black around his head. He had a nice straight topline, and a good spring of ribs. Although he was not big, he seemed to be of good quality.

"The bull is an import from Scotland. He is a Shorthorn mooly. His calves will not likely grow horns. He is from a milking strain of Shorthorns," Tom informed him.

John entered the stable to look at the cow. Tom put the bull back into his stall. "The cow is from a milking herd from Nova Scotia, as were the other two cows," Tom said as he untied her to lead her outside. The cow was a golden brown of very fine bone, with large beautiful eyes, and of small stature.

John grew impatient to go to the station when he heard the train whistle blow again, much closer to town.

"The calf is from one of the other two cows, and is sired by this bull," Tom continued talking without let-up. "They are actually all good stock. When the man's wife died he lost heart and neglected his livestock pretty badly. He finally decided to go west to get away from things."

John thought for a while as he was giving the animals consideration. They were all animals he could make use of after they got some flesh on their bones. He thought the colt might have a pretty good conformation. If he got the right woman, he could make good use of the cow. She looked like she was carrying a calf. The bull was a purebred, which spoke for the care that went into his breeding, he should be good. "What do you want for them? I don't have money to spend on such a risk as these animals are," John was being perfectly honest with Tom.

After some thought Tom suggested, "How about trading your team for these four animals? Two animals for four is a pretty good trade for you."

At that moment the train whistle blew a long announcement that it was

One tall lady had her hair done in a braid twisted up the back of her head and topped with a saucy little hat. She appeared to be shy and stood to one side and back near the station. John, suddenly feeling intimidated, stood back, watching.

about to enter the town limits. John turned to leave.

"No," John spoke firmly. "Those animals are too thin and may die even before I get them home. The best I will do is to trade my gelding for the three grown ones. You can keep the calf," he called over his shoulder.

"OK," Tom called after him, "I'll throw the calf in too. It needs company," Tom finished lamely. John turned around and went back to Tom. They shook hands on the deal, then John left.

"What have I got myself into this time? Will those skinny animals be able to walk even as far to home as J.L.'s? I guess we will just have to go slow to find out."

* * *

The train was puffing and steaming into town, as John crossed the tracks to join the crowd on the platform. There were only two girls on the platform that John could see, and they stayed close to each other. They were dressed in skimpy, rather revealing clothes, so John assumed they were from the hotel. The rest of the crowd on the platform were men of various means.

The weather had turned into a lovely warm spring day, and the men were standing around with their coats unbuttoned, some of them showing a watch-fob and chain. Some of those attending this exciting event were obviously farmers, who didn't have fancy clothes, and then there were a few who looked like they came from the bar in the hotel, and didn't care what they looked like. Knowing these women had come over the ocean and would not be able to go back was all they needed to know to try to capture a poor unsuspecting lady.

The train puffed and steamed into town, and as it ground into the station, John forgot all about the deal he had just made, and watched proceedings. The train squealed to a halt, emitting a huge cloud of steam over everyone on the platform. The regular baggage was unloaded onto station wagons, and also the delivery wagon that would take things around town to their destinations.

Passengers were coming out onto the platform, most of them women, who were dressed in neat colorful clothing, some had hats on neat coiffures. Others had a brightly colored scarf tossed around their neck. One tall lady had her hair done in a braid twisted up the back of her head, and topped with a saucy little hat. She appeared to be shy, and stood to one side and back near the station.

A few well dressed men emerged and headed off toward uptown. Several men were talking to prospective wives, but John suddenly feeling intimidated, stood back, watching.

The lady who was standing to one side, caught John's eye. She was broad shouldered for a woman, and tall and slender. She was also watching proceedings, looking over the men who appeared to be looking for a wife. Her eyes fell on John. She studied him until he felt uncomfortable and began to squirm. At that moment one shabbily dressed man approached her and spoke to her. She looked at him thoughtfully, then shaking her head in the negative, spoke to him. He left to talk to another woman.

John liked what he saw of her. She was dressed in a black two piece cotton pique' dress that had a white stand up collar, with matching ruffles all around the collar and down the front and around the bottom of the jacket. The skirt was full and to the ground with ruffles around the bottom. She had strong features, with a turned up nose. Her thick chestnut hair was braided and pinned to the back of her head. A few stray whisps had come loose at the front and sides, wrapping around her beautiful face. A pair of snapping emerald green eyes looking out from under the brim of a saucy little hat, riveted John in a steady, evaluating gaze. She was admirable to view. Even pretty, John thought. Was she too pretty to live on a farm? I think I will ask her.

The lady had gathered up her skirt with both hands and was starting up the steps of the train, when John said, "Good day, ma'am." She turned to look at him. "My name is John Thomas. I have two hundred acres of farming land. Sixty acres are now broke and with crop. I have about fifty more to turn into cropping land in the near future. I would sure like a woman like you, to keep my house and be my wife. Would you be willing to take a gamble on me?"

She descended a couple of the steps of the train. Steady pools of emerald green eyes looking him straight in his blue unwavering eyes all the while. Her soft red lips pursed in a permanent smile as she spoke,

"Ma' name is Jane Sleith, and I have cum from Norrrthern Ireland, where there is a severe drought. I'm a farrrmer's daughter and have come to Canada, hopefully to marry a gooood farmer and raise a healthy family, I have."

She has such beautiful green eyes, and such beautiful chestnut hair tucked under that little hat. How could I be so lucky? And a farmer's daughter, too. Praise God for bringing me this woman. John suddenly realized he was staring. Embarrassed he said, "Shall we take your things off the train?" he asked. "We can store them on one of the station wagons, and put it in the shed over there. Then we can go for something to eat," he held out his hand to receive hers.

Jane looked at John again, appearing to debate a decision. "Verrry well," she said at length, taking his hand while she decended the rest of the steps.

"I will go with you John, I will."

John shook her hand in agreement of the deal. He found she had a strong hand with a firm grip. He was pleasantly surprised. When her luggage was safely stored in the shed, John took Jane's hand and placed it around his arm, as they headed for the hotel.

* * *

The hotel dining room had several small tables, each with four chairs. John selected one near a window. The place was bustling with people, many of them women who had come on the train, and were with a prospective husband, John assumed. Many of them were sitting four to a table. John was trying to make conversation,

"This hotel is beautifully decorated," he indicated the woodwork and the big chandeliers, then brushed the cloth on the table.

"Yes," Jane replied. "I haven't seen such a nicely decorated place forrr public to dine in. Aye there are some in Irrreland, but I was never out to any of them."

The waiter came at that moment and took their orders. When he left, John started the conversation again. "I have been on my farm for five years. I didn't have any money to start up, but my Friends the Quakers gave me the resources to get started and kept me going for about two years, until I was able to support myself. I have finally got going good enough that I have been able to move on. I brought two loads of fire wood to the Kingston market today. I have been bringing either building logs, or fence rails to the market for a couple of years. Lately I have been able to sell fire wood here. It keeps things going for me."

"Who fells the trees for you?" Jane asked.

John looked at her, then realized what she had asked.

"Oh, I do," he stated. "I have been cutting trees and pulling stumps for a year before I got the farm."

The waiter brought their dinner of roast beef and gravy, with mashed potatoes. When he left, John placed both hands half way across the table, palms up. Jane looked at his calloused hands, then looked at John. Hesitatingly she placed her hands in John's. They both bowed their heads, while John spoke: "Thank you Father for bringing me this lovely lady. Bless our lives and bring us much happiness and fulfillment in our relationship. Bless this food we are receiving this day, and put it to Thy use in our bodies, and us to Thy service for Christ's sake. Amen."

Jane's face lit up and crinkles appeared around the corners of her emerald green eyes, revealing a warm sparkle that went with a little smile of approval. While they were eating they revealed things about themselves.

"I have some muurrrphys and garrrlic bulbs in my parrrcels. I hope they don't get frozen, as I brought them from Ireland for seed."

"I'll wrap them in a hide robe to protect them." John's heart was beating rapidly. *A farming woman! How lucky could I have got. God is surely guiding my life,* he thought.

"Tonight we are going to go seven miles to my friends place, - J.L. Hodgson's. They will be able to put us, and my livestock up until morning. I lived with them for a year and a half before starting the farming business. They are like father and mother to me." John suddenly remembered the deal he had made at the livery stable. "By the way when I stabled my team, I was offered a deal on a horse and some cattle that I felt will turn out good for us if I can get them home alive. They are pretty thin, so we will have to go very slow."

The conversation increased as they dined, until they were both relaxing with each other.

"Will you wait here at the hotel while I go and get your things loaded into the wagon?" he asked her.

"A wagon?" Jane looked at John with raised eyebrows. "Oh, tu be shore, John. I'll still be waitin' when you come back."

CHAPTER 18

MEETING THE GANG

John hurriedly left the hotel to go to the stable. It was about three o'clock. *I hope we can get to J.L.'s before dark*, he told himself as he entered the stable.

"Tom, would you help me get my team hooked up?" Tom and two other men came out of the office.

"You betcha," Tom responded.

"I will need a collar for that colt. Bob's collar would be 'way too big for him. Have you got one to sell?"

"I have some spares in the office. Bring him here and we will see which one fits him," Tom instructed.

John went to Bob to take the harness off of him. He patted his neck, saying, "Goodbye Bob. You have been a great servant for me. Be the same for your new owner. Goodbye old buddy," As John hung the harness on the colt he jumped a little nervously. "Steady bud. Easy now. Nobody's going to hurt you. Back up boy. Now come with me." John kept a steady, soothing conversation going to the colt while he took him to the office door. Tom had a collar ready to try on. John looked at it, then complained,

"This collar isn't fit to put on a horse, Tom. Get me a good collar. It can be a little big as long as you supply a sweat pad to line it with."

"How's this one?" Tom asked passing a collar to John.

"This one is better, but it will need a sweat pad. I don't want to sweeny him before I get him home," John waited until Tom produced a sweat pad, then he instructed Tom to bring Bell up beside the colt, while he got the collar on and the hames buckled in place. When Bell came up beside the colt, he paid her no attention. John tied his halter shank to Bell's quarter tug ring to help guide him, also to prevent him from bolting after they were hitched.

John paid Tom what he owed him for stabling his team, then asking the two men to come with him to the station to help load Jane's things, he started the team. The colt didn't seem to know what to do, but went along with Bell when the harness pulled on him. He didn't seem to be nervous of what was coming behind him, much to John's relief.

At the station, John tied the lines to the stake and stayed in the back of the wagon to help get things loaded. No problems arose, not even when John laid out the horse hide to wrap the box of potatoes and garlic in. They drove back to the hotel, where John helped Jane into the wagon.

Next John took the two men to the livery stable where he was going to pick up the cattle. John got Tom to put a pile of straw in the back end of the wagon box to make a bed for the calf to be tied there. The tail gate was put in place, and the bull and cow were brought out and one tied to each corner of the back end of the box. John paid the two men who had helped him load everything, then bidding them all farewell, started the team. The three men from the stable chased the cow and bull until everyone was walking down the street.

"Faith, John. These animals are as thin as many I saw in Ireland when I was leaving. Is this common in Canada?" Jane asked.

"I hope not," John answered. "I hope this is just an isolated case. Come on Bud, get your feet in the rut."

"Do you have names for all yorrre animals?" she asked.

"Yeah, that's a good way to identify them."

"What's the name of this big brrrute?"

"That's Bell. I just traded her mate for these pathetic critters." John sounded like he was regretting the deal. "She is going to have a foal in July."

"Don't feel bad John. They may turn out to be exceptional animals," Jane consoled him. "So this one is Bell and this one is Bud."

"Yeah, I guess that is his name," John spoke thoughtfully. "I hadn't really named him, but since you have pointed it out, I guess I have been calling him Bud ever since I started working with him. I like it. Thank you Jane."

"I didn't realize I did anything. You're welcome," she paused, then continued, "What is the name of the cattle?."

"I haven't named them yet. You can do that if you want."

"Really? You mean you will let me name yorrre critters?"

"Yes, ma'am. Just remember they are yours, too. So give them names we will like."

"I didn't think of them that way, John. Thank you so much."

John looked at her in wonderment. They had traveled three miles, so he pulled the team to a stop to let them all rest for fifteen minutes. He and Jane got down off the wagon and were stretching their legs.

"Jane?"

"Yes, John?"

John took her hand while he went down on one knee, then looking into her beautiful emerald green eyes he said, "Jane will you marry me?"

She looked at him a moment, then her eyes crinkling at the corners, she replied, "Yes John, I will marrry you," a smile spread across her face.

Still on his knees John kissed her hand, then reaching into his pocket, pulled out a ring and placed it on her finger. It was a little big, but she clenched her hand so tightly there was no way it could fall off. John rose to his feet, and taking both of her hands, he looked deep into her sparkling eyes.

"Jane, I have a good feeling about our future. I think God has been guiding us both," his heart was pounding until he thought she might hear it.

"I think so too, John. I am so happy to have found a man who is a Christian," she lowered her eyes and was studying the ring.

John put his arms around her to hold her close, his nostrils picking up the perfume from her hair and hat. A moment later he helped her onto the wagon. As they drove another two miles, conversation continued.

"It is going to take me a while to get used to your accent," John commented, "I hope you will forgive me."

"Oh, I'll forrrgive you John." Jane put her hand on John's arm and patted it. "I hope it's not intimidatin' you. I guess when yu grows up in Canada, you don't larn to speak proper English." she felt a little miffed, but was too happy to let it last.

John laughed. "I didn't—," he stopped his statement in mid stride.

"You didn't what?"

"Well, never mind. It doesn't matter anyway. I started farming five years ago. I have a house built, thanks to my friends and neighbors. I also have a barn built...Actually that is what I had built first. I have a machinery shed built, but as yet have to build a chicken house."

John was anxious to change the subject. He was not yet ready to tell anyone where he had come from, before arriving at the Hodgson's.

"Now with these extra animals I will have to build an addition onto the barn," he added thoughtfully.

They let the stock rest for another fifteen minutes before continuing on to J.L.'s place. It was about eight o'clock when they arrived, but the welcome mat was out. John got down off the wagon, then went to Jane's side and helped her down.

"I'd like you to meet my good friends John Lampton Hodgson and his wife Ann," he took Jane's elbow to escort her closer to the Hodgsons. "Here comes their family, John Ralph now ten years old, and Elizabeth who is growing like a weed, and is now eight years old," Everyone shook hands with Jane. John continued, "We are going to be spending the night here, Jane. Is there anything you would like from your things?"

"I would like the valise. I think that will be enough tonight." John climbed into the wagon and gave her the case.

Ann took charge of Jane, while the men put the animals away for the night. Ann picked up Jane's left hand and looked at the ring.

"Thee already have an engagement ring?" she queried.

"Yes," Jane replied, her eyes sparkling. "John asked me to marrry him when we stopped to rrrest the animals on the waaay here."

"Well, wasn't that thoughtful of him," Ann smiled and patted Jane's hand warmly. "It is a beautiful ring. He must have been planning this for a while. He does have a way of keeping things to himself."

✱ ✱ ✱

"Ho, what has thee got here?" J.L. asked as they were unhooking the team. "It looks like thee has been rummaging through the slums again," he exclaimed.

John Ralph was standing behind his father with his hands on his hips, and had a big grin on his face like his father did.

"Just you wait until they get fleshed up," John said defensively. "I think this colt has pretty good conformation, and that bull is a purebred Shorthorn mooly, as well as being from a milking strain. The cow originated from a dairy farm in Nova Scotia. The calf is a heifer from a cow that came from the same dairy farm, and is sired by this bull. I think all of them will eventually make money for me, if I can get them home alive," John stopped talking to look at the calf. "That calf hasn't had any milk for at least a week, so maybe for tonight we should give it some water, and start mixing a little milk in for it tomorrow," John informed J.L.

"Ralph thee fetch the calf into the barn, slowly and carefully. We don't want it to die from shock just now," J.L. instructed his son. Turning to John he commented, "It is too young to be eating grain, but in it's starving conditions it may nibble on some."

"Don't overfeed that colt on oats. I don't want him to develop colic in the middle of the night," John worried.

"Right John," J.L. agreed. "Thee learns fast."

While they were watering and feeding the animals for the night, J.L. was unusually quiet.

"I take it you don't think I did the right thing," John commented.

"Huh?" J.L. sounded like he had just been awakened. "Oh, I was just thinking,... maybe thee should leave the calf here so I can feed it milk for a while."

Ten year old Ralph brightened up, and looking at his father, asked, "Can I look after it father? Can I?"

"Yes, my boy. Thee can care for the calf," J.L. smiled as Ralph threw his arms around the calf's neck and hugged it.

"Oh, that would be great!" John exclaimed. "Are you sure you don't mind?"

"No. I was also thinking you won't be using the bull for a while, how would you like to leave him here?" J.L. suggested, "I think I would like to run him with my cows."

"You sure you want to mess your cows up with something I got out of the slums, J.L.?" John teased.

"After he gets some flesh on, he might look fit to associate with my herd," J.L. countered.

"If you think you would be happy with him, you sure are welcome to keep him," John put his hand over his mouth to hide the smile that wouldn't quit.

"I think I will keep him in the barn corral for a while and get some flesh on him before I turn him out,"

"Great. I hope I am not causing you too much trouble,"

"Not at all, John. I was thinking I was going to look for another bull. The one I have has too many heifers on the ground. I am not going to be able to use him next year," J.L. said.

When the men entered the house, the odors of a hot meal tickled their nostrils.

"Smells good," John complimented Ann.

"We had already eaten before you two arrived. The children must soon go to bed," Ann informed them.

"Awww," Elizabeth complained

"I get to feed the calf," Ralph gloated at Elizabeth.

"Now Ralph," J.L. reprimanded him. "If thee wishes to not go to bed before Elizabeth, thee had better change thy attitude."

"We will still be here in the morning Ralph," John informed him. "You should go to bed now. I wouldn't want to miss seeing you in the morning."

Ann started dishing up plates of food for John and Jane, then J.L. got a plate from the cupboard and gave it to her. "I'll have more of that if thee is so minded," he said to his wife.

"I want some too," both children chorused, so with a sigh, Ann dished up a plate of food for everyone, including herself. The pot was a dish of chicken and dumplings.

An hour later they all went to bed, Jane in Elizabeth's room with Elizabeth sleeping on the couch in the living room, and John with Ralph in Ralph's room.

*   *   *

The three men went to the barn in the morning to milk the five cows and feed everything up. When they came in for breakfast, J.L. said, "After breakfast, Ann, fix John with thy scrub pail and a big rag. He brought home a load of lice. We will bathe all four animals with a solution of sheep dip in water before he leaves,"

After breakfast Ann produced two buckets, and several rags. The two men and Ralph went out and had the animals all bathed by noon. While the men were doing their job, Ann and Jane prepared a stew for dinner, along with some biscuits. When the meal was finished, the men hooked John's team to the wagon, then tied the cow on behind. Jane and John were soon on the road to Battersea, with only the cow leading behind the wagon. Andy and Maria's store was John's next destination.

*   *   *

As they were riding along Jane told John a great deal about her life in Ireland. "We worrrked long hours in the Muurrrphy fields," she related, "hoein' weeds, 'n hillin' day after day. Then when the rrrains didn't come, the plants didn't grrrow very well and it all seemed to be for naught. I felt I was a burrrden to m' father," her eyes clouded and for a moment John thought she was going to cry. Raising her sad eyes to John she took a deep breath, then continued, "That's when I decided to come to America. I wanted to go farrrther south, but when the time came to get a ticket, the forrrst ship out was coming to Canada. So here I am, I am," she paused and reflected on her home for a few minutes. "Father had two horses to plow the fields," she continued, "and cultivate the rows of Murphy's. They were prrrretty thin when I left. They were not big like either one of these two. They would pull harrrd without slackin'. That's what mattered most,"

They rode in silence for a while, each thinking about the past they had left behind.

"We are going to the Battersea store," John broke the silence. "My friend Andy Smith and his wife own it. They have agreed to take in a woman I might bring home, at least until after the wedding."

"We are going to have a weddin'?" Jane queried.

"Of course, Jane. You promised to marry me, didn't you?" She nodded her head. He continued, "Well, there is a Methodist church in Battersea that Andy and Maria go to. I have been going there most of the time for the past eight months, and I like it. Do you want to change your mind about marrying me?"

"Oh no John," she said hastily. "It just seems so sudden."

"Today is Thursday. I thought you and I could go to the meeting with J.L. and Ann and their family this Sunday. You pick out the day we shall get married. You can also decide where it will take place. It matters not to me as long as it is a Christian service,"

"I'd not be pleased with anything other than a Christian service," Jane assured him, pursing her full lips into stern assurance. "T'would be nice to have someone to help me plan things a little."

"I think you will like Maria. I think she can give you the help you would like," John tried to make her feel a little more comfortable about their forth coming marriage.

"If you drop me off, when will I see you again?" Jane sounded concerned, her green eyes clouding up.

"I will see you tomorrow. I have some shopping to do, and may have to go to Kingston. You may come along with me if you wish,"

"I would like that," she replied, appearing to be more at ease.

They turned off the main road, and shortly were traveling down the streets of Battersea.

"Welcome to Battersea," John said, and put his arm around Jane's shoulders. "This is our home town."

"Oh, it is a nice little town, John," she sounded more cheerful, but John wondered if she was putting up a good front for his benefit. As they pulled up in front of the store, John stopped the horses and wrapped the lines around the stake. Bud was very tired, and John was sure he wouldn't move unless Bell did.

John was helping Jane down off the wagon when Andy and Mrs. Waggoner came out of the store. Mrs. Waggoner was carrying a bundle of supplies.

"Hello, Mr. Thomas," she quipped as she stared at Jane. "How are you today?"

"Fine Mrs. Waggoner, fine," he answered. "You're looking fine today," Turning to Andy he put his arm around Jane's shoulder. "Jane I want you to meet Andy Smith." Jane and Andy shook hands. Mrs. Waggoner was still standing there. John turned to her, "Mrs. Waggoner, I would like you to meet Jane Sleith."

"How do you do, my dear," Mrs. Waggoner never took her eyes off Jane.

Putting his hand around Jane's waist, John ushered her into the store, and left Mrs. Waggoner standing on the walk, by the wagon, still staring after them. Andy took them through the store to the living quarters in the rear. "Maria," Andy called.

"Just a minute Andy, I'm changing Freddy. I'll be out in a minute,"

"Can I take your coat and hat, Jane?" Andy asked.

"Thank you," Jane replied as she took them off.

Maria appeared carrying Elizabeth, and holding Freddy's hand.

"Unca John," Freddy squealed as he ran over to John.

"Freddy," John said picking him up. "Maria I want you to meet Jane Sleith. Jane these are my good friends Andy and Maria Smith, and this is Freddy," John added giving Freddy a squeeze.

"Hello everyone, and hello Freddy," Jane smiled while shaking hands with them all.

"Come with me Jane," Maria invited. "I will show you where your room will be while you are here. John, I will have supper ready in about an hour."

"I must get home to care for my animals." John turned to go out. "I'll be back tomorrow. In the meantime Jane can fill you in,"

Andy went with John out to the wagon. Mrs. Waggoner was gone, so they felt they could talk freely.

"Jane has promised to marry me," John's blue eyes were shining like blue diamonds on water. "I am letting her choose the church and the day. She is too tired to be able to think now, so tomorrow I hope she will be rested up some. Will you get that cow up on her feet and start her after the wagon. I want to get these two animals home as soon as I can so they can also get some rest."

"Will do John," Andy had not missed the sparkle in John's eyes. "Come on cow. Get up. Come on, up with you. We will see you tomorrow, John."

*   *   *

It was getting dark when John got home. He put the cow in the corral, then unhooked and unharnessed the team. He took them down for a drink, then brought a pail of water up for the cow. Locking Bud in the corral with the cow, he turned Bell out with the other horses, who had come running in when he drove into the yard. Throwing oat sheaves out for all of them he went to bed without lighting a lamp. Being totally exhausted he was soon asleep with a smile on his face.

CHAPTER 19

THE SHOPPING SPREE

John was surprised to see the sun was up well above the trees when he arose. Feeding everything more oat sheaves, he was able to check on them to see how they all were. Bud and the cow were looking a little more rested, and attacked the sheaves with vigor. He caught Ned and Nell, the three year old blacks, and stabled them with their own sheaves. Everyone else looked fine, so he went to the house to get some breakfast.

When he walked into the kitchen, he came to a full blown stop. His new stove was completely and properly installed. Examining it carefully, he decided to not light a fire in it until Jane was there to do it, which would be after they were married. He wanted to let her enjoy doing it for the first time.

After his breakfast he went to the barn and watered Bud and the cow, then threw two more oat sheaves to them. After Nell and Ned were watered, he harnessed them and hooked them to the wagon, then left for town.

* * *

Stopping at Mac Innesfree's was a must. He had to tell them the news, and thank them for installing the stove.

Hazel met him at the door. "Did thee not get a woman?" she asked. Disappointment clouding her usually jovial face.

"Hazel, I got the 'Bell of Ireland' but I left her in town until after we are married." He couldn't conceal his joy in telling her.

"Halleluia !!" she shouted, then puckering up her mouth, she emitted a loud shrieking whistle, followed by a bellowing roar. The men quickly emerged from the barn, and seeing John at the door, hastily came to the house.

"Thank you for setting up my stove." Getting down from the wagon, John warmly grasped Mac's hand.

"Thanks be to thee John, for talking Mac into getting a new stove for me." Hazel flung her arms around John's neck and gave him a squeeze.

"Be careful," Mac cautioned, "he's not used to having women hug him."

"Well, he's gonna to have to get used to it," Hazel said with a happy grin. "He brought hisself home a woman." She hugged him again with gusto and a pat on the back.

"Congratulations, John. I pray thee has found the right one." Mac shook John's hand. "I got Mike McMurty and Sam Shewfelt to come and help the boys and I unload and set up both stoves. They also helped move our old stove into the porch and set it up for Hazel to use on the hot summer days. Hazel has already baked a batch of bread with the new stove. It is the best bread she has ever made."

"Jacob, run into the house and get a loaf of bread for John," Hazel instructed. Jacob came out with the loaf wrapped in paper. John took it, and thanking them profusely, climbed up on the wagon.

"I have to get going," he said as he picked up the lines. "Jane and I are going shopping today. She is feeling like she is among strangers and was anxious that I should see her today. Thank you so very much for everything you have done for me," he called to them as he left their place.

✳   ✳   ✳

Jane was smiling when she came quietly into the store behind Maria.

"Hello Jane," John's heart started pounding. "How are you today? Are you rested up enough to go for a ride around town?"

"I'm so ashaaamed to tell you I have only been up long enough to have my brrreakfast, I have. That surely is a comforrrtable bed, it is." She took John's hand and brushed her lips across it.

"Mrs. Waggoner, has certainly done her duty." Andy was grinning again. "I have had more customers than usual this morning and they are all asking about John's lovely bride-to-be. I think Mrs. Waggoner was well impressed... and v-e-r-y happy to be the first to know, and first hand at that."

"Stay for supper John. We have so much to talk about," Maria requested.

"Alright Maria, I can do that." John readily accepted the invitation as he ushered Jane out the door.

They went on a slow drive around town looking at all the stores.

"Are you needing things out of your trunk and boxes, Jane?" John queried. "What of them would you like unloaded at the store?"

"Yes, I will need many things from some of them. There is the valise that could be brought in the store. What I need from the trunk, I can take out and leave the trunk in the wagon. It has mostly books for educatin' my wee ones when they are old enough."

"You mean you brought a trunk almost full of school books?" John asked in amazement.

"Well yes, I'll not be plannin' on goin' back to Irrreland when my wee ones are ready to start larnin' readin', writin' and 'rithmetic," she retorted. "So I brought them with me. I want my children to be at least as well educated as their mother."

"I never went to school," John admitted, "My mother taught me to read and write and do arithmetic."

"I never went to school, either John," Jane said. "M' mother taught us children all she knew. That's m'education, it is. I brought m' books that I larned from."

John spotted a clothiers store, and stopping the team in front of it, helped Jane down and into the store. They walked around the store, looking at men's suits, and ladies dresses, as well as coats and shoes, scarves and even jewelry.

"If you see anything you like," John whispered to Jane, "take it. I will pay for it. I am going over here to talk to the owner." Crossing to the other side of the store, he approached the owner.

"Good day, sir. Would you have a dress suit in my size?"

"I may have. Come over here and try on some jackets." John tried on six jackets, but they were all too tight across the shoulders. "My name is John Macey," he offered during the try-ons. "I'm sorry. Those are the biggest jackets I have in the store. Let me measure your waist and leg length to see if I have pants that might fit you."

After measuring John, he checked the sizes of the biggest pants he had, and came up with a pair of grey pants with narrow light grey and dark grey stripes.

"Try these on to see how they look," he instructed. "The fitting room is right there," he pointed to a door. John went into the room, and put the pants on. There was a mirror there for him to see himself in. He liked the way the pants fit, and he was impressed with the striping. Coming out of the fitting room, he passed the pants to Mr. Macey.

"I like them, and I like the way they fit, but I can't take them until I get a jacket. I want them to look like they belong together. If you could hold them until the end of next week, I will let you know as soon as possible, if I am taking them."

"I can do that. I will need to know your name, though," Mr Macey agreed.

"I'm sorry. My name is John Thomas. I live west of here six miles."

"Oh, you're the young man who has set this town on it's ear. You are going to be married soon, so I hear."

"I guess most of that is right. The last part is. That's why I need these clothes. I also want to get a pair of dress shoes, good socks, and underwear.

I need the whole uniform," John said with a little laugh.

Mr. Macey picked out everything John had mentioned in sizes he was sure would fit, then sent him into the fitting room. He went over to see how Jane was making out with her selections.

"Are you the lovely lady John Thomas is planning to marry?" he asked.

"That I am," she admitted meekly.

"Are you looking for a wedding dress?"

"No. I have that in m' trunk."

"Can I help you with anything else? Would you rather I got my wife to come and help you?"

"Yes, that would be most kind of you."

Mr. Macey went to a door at the back of the store. Opening it he stepped inside, and a few minutes later emerged following a woman. They came to where Jane was standing.

"This is my wife Hannah, and I am John Macey," he introduced himself and his wife to Jane.

"Hello. M' name is Jane Sleith, recently from Ireland. I was looking at some things in here and see a few that I would like to try on, if I may." John Macey left to wait for John. Jane and Hannah soon were heading to the back room with an armful of clothing and things.

When they came out a little later Jane was carrying a few things and Hannah was carrying the rest. Coming to the till where John and Mr. Macey were talking, Hannah totaled up the bill and John paid for it. Picking up their parcels, John and Jane left.

Continuing their tour around the town, John started talking again,

"I couldn't get a suit jacket big enough here. He has a pair of pants that fit and I like, but I wouldn't buy them until I see what I can get for a jacket. How did you make out?"

"I got some things. I was hopin' to get two house dresses, but I didn't like only one of those that were there. I got a pair of shoes, though that I liked," Jane shyly told John.

"I am planning on going to Kingston next Wednesday again." John kept talking, his mind on their purchases. "I don't think I will take anything to market, but we can look through the market to see what you would like to bring home. When we are finished at the market, we can go to the business stores to look for the things we can't get here." John looked at her steady green eyes. "You would like to go wouldn't you?" he asked as they pulled up in front of the livery stable.

"Yes, I guess I will have to get used to these very long rides," Jane replied.

"I'm sorry Jane. We can't step out of our door to go anywhere without taking at least an hour to get there," John said apologetically.

*   *   *

Leaving the stable they stopped to look at several buggies and carts lined up along the fence.

"Do you see a buggy that you like?" John asked her.

"They all seem to have something wrong with them, like a cracked shaft, or loose spokes, or broken down box. No I don't think you would want to take any of these home," Jane said, then started walking toward the store. John walked beside her, and taking her hand told her of his plans for the week end.

"I thought we could drive to Hodgson's tomorrow after noon, and go with them to their Sabbath Meeting. That will give you an idea of how they worship. I find it very interesting, but you need to form your own opinion."

"That sounds like a good plan to me John," Jane remarked. "I'm so grateful you think of me when yor' makin' yor' plans. I'll be happy to go with you."

*   *   *

When they reached the store, Jane took her bundle through to the back where her room was, while John stayed in the front to talk to Andy.

"We were looking at those buggies by the livery stable. They are a pretty sad lot of buggies. Would I be able to borrow your buggy and harness to go to Kingston next Wednesday?" John asked.

"I'll check with Maria to see if she will be using it that day." Andy looked toward the living quarters door. "You are most welcome to it if it is free. You can also use my horse, if you like."

"Thanks Andy," John said, "Thanks for the offer of your horse, but I think I will use Grace. I want Jane to get used to my stock as soon as possible. She is going to have to be working with them when I am out in the fields, so the more she knows about them the better."

"I see your point. You are welcome to whatever you want, my brother," Andy remarked with a smile.

*   *   *

Jane went with John when he went to get his team and wagon to go home. They stopped by the store, where John handed Andy the valise Jane wanted. Jane opened her trunk and took out a large bundle wrapped in paper. She

They were locked in a fond embrace and were deep in a kiss when the horses came to a stop.

got John to help her down out of the wagon, having entrusted the parcel to Andy, who couldn't resist winking at John as John jumped out of the wagon. When John took Jane into his arms for a farewell embrace, she turned her face up to his. He kissed her lightly on her soft red lips, then saying, "Good bye my lovely Jane. I will see you tomorrow about one o'clock." Jane turned to go into the store, her face flushing a warm pink. So was John's as he got into the wagon to go home.

When he got home, he unloaded all of Jane's things, and put them in the house.

* * *

Saturday morning, John hooked Daisy and Darky to the wagon and headed for town to pick up Jane to go to Hodgson's. It was a beautiful, bright, sunny day. Jane was in a delightful mood, chattering endlessly, and at times teasing John, at one point saying, "You're too fat to fit the coats in Battersea. I hope you won't have to go to New York to find one big enough to fit."

John grabbed her around the waist and laid her over his knees, and kissed her soft lips, while his whiskers smothered her face. Finally she cried "I'm sorry John, I'm sorry I called you fat." He let her sit up.

Suddenly she stopped talking, and sat quietly for a time. Fifteen minutes and a mile went by. John was beginning to think he had insulted her, but he kept quiet to see what was coming next.

"John?"

"Yes Jane."

"Tomorrow we go to the Quaker's church, right?"

"Yeah, that's the idea."

"Then the next Sunday we go to the Methodist church, right?"

"That's what I thought you would like to do."

"Then the Monday after that, I will decide which church we will get married in. Then we will get married the next day – Tuesday. Does that sound agreeable with you, at all, at all?" She turned her emerald green eyes toward John as a smile spread across her lovely soft mouth.

"Tuesday?" John exclaimed, "That sounds great. That's wonderful. We can tell J.L. and Ann and they can spread the word around." John took Jane in his arms and laying her across his knees kissed her tenderly, absorbing the softness of her mouth, then kissed her again with passion.

"Jane I love you more than you know."

"And I love you John." she whispered. They were locked in a fond embrace, and were deep in a kiss when the horses came to a stop. John looked to see why. They were in Hodgson's yard, and J.L. was standing in front of them with his arms raised to stop the team, a grin on his face that went from one ear to the other.

* * *

Jane and John told their plan to J.L. and Ann and the children. J.L. cleared his throat, then said,

"Thy plans sound all very well, except for our circuit official who does all the marrying at once, won't be in our meeting house until November. He comes around every eight to twelve months, and notifies us ahead of time of his expected arrival. I expect that will have a bearing on thy place of marriage."

"That it does, that it does," Jane said somberly. "We will have to use the Methodist church and minister. We feel we cannot wait for six months to become united."

"Then everything is all set," John remarked, "except speaking to the Methodist minister, which we will do next Sunday. I hope you folks will feel free to attend our wedding."

"Of course we will be there, John." J.L. nodded his head, "Thee being my son, I wouldn't miss thy wedding."

* * *

While John and Jane were on their way home to Battersea, they had many things to talk about. They discussed at great length their experience at the meeting this day. John ended it with, "I think a person would have to grow up with them to really become comfortable with it as a ministerial service after attending the kind of services you and I grew up with. They are happy, and understand that God is with them there in their meeting house, and at home where ever they are. That is what is most important."

Their conversation turned to plans for their wedding, and other things to be attended to.

"I have to get more trees cut to make an income to support us." John spoke thoughtfully. "I guess I will cut trees Monday and Tuesday, then Wednesday we are going to Kingston Market, then if all goes well I can spend the rest of the week cutting."

Jane took a long hard look at him. "Do you always work that much in the fields?" she asked.

"Well if I want to make a living, I do. The trees don't fall over by themselves, nor do the roots jump out of the ground by themselves." he answered. Then nudging her with his elbow he added, "That is why I am so fat."

"Is that going to be our style of life?

"Pretty much. We will go to church Sunday mornings, and visit friends or stay at home Sunday afternoons, whichever you want to do. Then Wednesdays, we will go to the Kingston market, and take in our weeks produce. The rest of the time I will have to spend in the fields, either cutting trees or pulling stumps, or I will be either putting in crop, or taking it off. It is a year round job," he ended with a sideways glance at her. "Do you think you can handle the routine?"

"I will larn. I will larn, John."

✳   ✳   ✳

Wednesday morning John jumped on Grace's back and arrived at Andy's store a little after ten in the morning. Andy called Maria out to look after the store, while he went out to help John harness and hook Grace to his buggy. Jane came out the back door, as they were finished.

"Look John," she smiled, and twirled around. "This is the dress I got the other day. How does it look?"

"It looks great Jane." John complemented her. Andy gave a shrill wolf whistle.

Jane couldn't conceal a smile and a light flush creeping up her face. "I need a jacket," she informed John, as she turned to enter the house again.

"You know John if I wasn't married, I think I would be looking for an Irish bell." Andy grinned. "You sure seem to have picked a good one."

"Thank you." John responded, "It is God's doing. She was the first one I saw that appealed to me. It was God who had her in the right place at the right time." He paused thoughtfully before asking, "Andy, will you stand up with me at the wedding?"

"I would be so proud and happy to do that. That would be like the icing on my cake. Of course I will John. Of course I will."

Jane came out with a jacket and a small case that Andy said Maria had loaned her. John put the case in the back of the buggy, then helped Jane onto the seat. He then thanked Andy for the buggy and harness, and climbing onto the seat they turned to go past the front of the store to wave to Maria and were on their way to Kingston.

Grace held her head high while traveling. She also lifted her feet with a lot of bending of the knees and hocks. They flew down the road fast enough the spokes of the buggy wheels were a blur.

"Gracious John, this is much different than riding with the other horses." Jane was hanging on to the arm rest of the buggy. "It will take us no time to get to Kingston at this speed."

"I don't think she will be able to keep this up all the way. It is eleven miles from Battersea to Kingston, and I think Grace will soon have to slow down to catch her wind."

Grace was breaking out in a sweat, when John pulled her down to an impatient walk. "This is the first time I have had her hooked to a buggy, but I am going to get a buggy so she can be used in the summer as well as the winter on the cutter. I have been driving her in the winters when I didn't need to take a load of wood." Looking at Jane, he added, "You will have to get used to driving her as she will be your means of transportation."

"Mmmeee! Drive hheerrr?? John, are you crrrazy? She is too wild for me. I couldn't ever drive such a wild horse."

"She is not wild, and she is not crazy. She is very gentle and loving. She is also fun loving, and her fun is to hit the road at top speed. She never slacks off on the six mile drive into Battersea, which she and I have done many times during the winters. When I say whoa she stops." Grace came to a sudden stop. "Just like that," John finished his statement as Jane grabbed his arm to stay in the seat.

"Now you take the lines Jane and drive her for a while." John showed Jane how to hold the lines.

"Now what, John. How do you get this gorrl going?"

"Lift the lines and chirp like this." John chirped and Grace started and was soon going at a fast clip down the road. "Let her have a slack line on contact to maintain the speed you want her to travel at. If you want her to slow down, just pull back on the lines. It is that simple, Jane. You can also talk to her, and tell her what you want her to do, like easy Grace, take it easy. She will slow down when you ask her to."

Grace was well lathered up when they reached Kingston. Walking through town she was sedate and patient. They drove through the whole town, locating the stores they wanted to call on. Their next call was the livery stable, where they stabled Grace.

Walking over to the Market place, Jane was still excited about driving Grace.

"I think she and I are going to get along just fine." she gave John's hand a squeeze.

"I'm sure glad of that." John replied.

"Look John, there are some buggies. They look to be in pretty good shape."

"They look like they are brand new, out of the factory." John commented as he walked around each one.

"They are sir," their agent said. "They are fresh in from Pennsylvania. The best buggies money can buy. One of these McLaughlan buggies will out last any other buggy you will find."

"John, look at this one," Jane called.

Going to where she was looking at a buggy, John asked.

"Are you sure you want a buggy like this one. Where will we put the children when they are old enough to sit by themselves?"

"Well," Jane had moved to another one. "How is this one? It has two seats."

"That is a dandy for a large family." The agent informed them. "The rear seat is removable, which turns it into a democrat, a very serviceable vehicle. It has already been sold to a man who has a large family. How many children do you have?" the inquisitive agent asked.

"None yet." John answered his question.

"Well, how about this carriage?" he asked. "This is a beauty, and has two seats besides the driver's seat, which also carries two. At the price, it is by far the best buy."

"What price do you have on it?" John asked.

"Only two hundred and fifty dollars."

"I can't afford it today. I agree the price is alright, but I have other things more important than a buggy right now. Let's go Jane."

They left the market and went to the hotel. John booked two rooms before they had their supper. Following a delectable meal of beef steaks, vegetables, potatoes and gravy, they retired for the night.

✳   ✳   ✳

When morning came John knocked on Jane's door. She opened the door, dressed and ready to go. They had breakfast, then proceeded to the clothier's store, both of them feeling rising excitement.

At the clothier's they were met by a man of short, slight stature. "Can I help you folks?" he asked.

"M'lady would like to look at some dresses, and I would like to look at a dress suit coat, or maybe a suit." John put his hand over Jane's, which was around his arm.

"Good, sir. My name is Harold Millburn. My wife Ethel will wait on m'lady. Ethel, can you come to look after this lady?" he spoke to a woman in the next isle. When Ethel arrived, John indicated Jane, saying,

"This is Jane Sleith, recently of Ireland. I am John Thomas from Battersea.

"How do you do, sir?" Harold turned to leave. "If you will come this way, sir." John and Harold walked over to where a rack of men's suits were displayed.

"What size do you require?" Harold asked.

"I don't really know. I tried on some jackets in a size forty four, and they were too tight across the shoulders."

"Well, yes," Harold agreed. "It will be better if I measure you first." He got his measuring tape out and proceeded to measure John.

"You could possibly get into a forty six, but a forty eight would likely be more comfortable." Harold started looking through the clothes on the rack. "What color did you have in mind, sir?"

"I think black if you have one."

"Here we are. This is a three piece suit with vest, complete with watch fob and chain. It is very classy. You may go into this room to try it on, sir."

John had got into the pants, when there was a knock on his door.

"Yes?" he responded.

"Sir, I thought you might like a shirt and tie to go with your suit," Harold said. "What color of tie do you prefer?"

"I don't really know, how about a blue one?"

"Excellent choice, sir."

A few minutes later a tap on the door brought Harold in with a white shirt, and a blue tie that John liked.

"Do you need a hat, sir."

"Well, I don't have one. Do you think I should have one?"

"By all means, sir. This quality of suit requires that you should wear a hat. I will return with a couple for you to try." Harold measured John's head, then left.

When he returned he had a top hat, and a bowler hat. He handed the top hat to John, first. John was now dressed, with the neck of his shirt unbuttoned, and the tie draped around his neck. He took the hat and pulled it onto his head, then looked in the full length mirror. Then he stared in the mirror.

"I don't really know that person in the mirror," he told Harold.

"Is the neck too tight for you to button up, sir?" Harold asked.

"I'm not sure. I'm not used to having anything snug around my neck."

"Let me help you with that. If it is too loose, it will cause chafing on your neck and chin." Harold proceeded to button up the offending neck. "I think you are right. I think you could use a size larger. I will get another one, while you remove this one."

"That feels better," John said approvingly when he put the second shirt on. He buttoned up the collar, then hung the tie around his neck.

"Let me show you how to tie it properly," Harold said taking the ends of the tie in both hands. He twisted them a couple of times, then asked,

"Would you mind sitting down on this chair, and watching in the mirror to see how I do it?" John sat down and faced the mirror.

Harold stood behind him and tied the four-in-hand knot. Taking the tie off, he had John do it himself three times, to be satisfied that he would be able to remember how when the time came.

"Now for the hats." Harold adjusted the top hat John had on. "This is the right hat to wear for formal occasions. You can set it at a more jaunty angle like so, or you can wear it straight on, whichever suits you. This one seems to be fitting you correctly. Does it feel too tight?"

"I don't think so. I think if it was any bigger it might blow off in a wind."

"You're right. It suits you immensely, sir. Now I think you should try on the bowler hat. It is more suitable to wear for occasions that are not as formal, but require the well dressed appearance."

John tried on the bowler, with the same experiences as the top hat. It also was added to his pile of selections.

"Now is there anything else, sir." Harold asked.

"Not that I know of." John said after a bit of thought.

"Shoes? socks? under clothing? You don't want to be caught short of things on that particular day."

When they left the store, John wasn't sure whether he had been taken for a ride, or if he had taken good advice. He had bought a complete outfit of clothing from the skin out, and none of it was useful for working the farm with.

"How did you make out Jane?" he asked. "Did you get everything you need?"

"I think I got more than I really need. I am so sorry John. I am costing you so much, and we are not even married yet. Mind you I will be able to use everything I got. Nothing will go to waste," she said sheepishly. "That lady is very nice, but she is an excellent salesman. I bought two dresses to wear to special occasions, as well as two full changes of all underclothing I might need."

"Harold did the same for me. I am sure I will someday use everything, but nothing was overlooked. We won't need to buy clothes for many years," John laughed as he finished.

"Except maybe work clothes," Jane began laughing as she finished.

They headed for the hotel for their dinner. After eating a grand meal of pork roast and potatoes with gravy, accompanied with hot biscuits, topped off with apple pie, they went to the livery stable. Hooking Grace to the buggy, they drove by the clothiers. Jane held the lines while John went into the store. Harold and Ethel helped carry their parcels out so John could pack them in the buggy so they wouldn't fall out. Thanking Harold and Ethel, they were soon on their way home, again.

*   *   *

In Battersea, John had Jane drive around to the back of Andy's place, to his stable. She had been driving for the last several miles, and was obviously enjoying it.

Alighting from the buggy, she gathered up all of her parcels and headed for the house. John proceeded to unhitch and unharness Grace, getting her ready for his trip home. Andy came out as he was ready to mount up and take leave.

"Stay for supper with us, John. There is no hurry for you to go home, is there?" Andy asked. "It is not supper time yet. Maria has it almost ready."

"I guess I can stay," John patted Grace's neck. "I want to ask you if you can keep my clothes here until our wedding day. I am planning on riding Grace in for that and don't want to get my new clothes all covered with horse hair and sweat."

"By all means. I will put them in our bedroom and tell Maria what they are so she won't reveal the contents to Jane."

"Thank you Andy. I really appreciate that."

Grace was stabled in the barn beside Andy's horse.

"Would I have an hour to spare before supper?" John asked Andy.

"We will ask Maria. I am sure you will," Andy replied as he headed for the house.

"The supper will be ready in an hour and a half, or so," Andy informed John. "Are you going on a secret mission, or would I be able to come along."

"As long as you feel free to leave the store, you are most welcome." John sounded happy to have Andy come along. They walked down the streets to the clothiers and entered.

"Good day Mr. Macey," John greeted him. "I have come to pick up that pair of pants I tried on the other day.

"Oh yes. Mr. Thomas. Good, good. Did you get a jacket that fits you?"

"Yes sir, I did. Thank you for your concern."

John paid for the pants, and putting the parcel under his arm, he and Andy turned to leave.

"Good day Mr. Thomas and Mr. Smith. Come again," Mr Macey said.

CHAPTER 20

TO LOVE HONOR AND OBEY

As the men were walking home to the store from the clothier's, John began filling Andy in on plans he and Jane had made: "Sunday, Jane and I are going to the Methodist Church, then after the service we are going to speak to the minister about doing our service on Tuesday. I hope that will not be putting too much of a rush on him."

"That is pretty short notice. Why don't you come to town tomorrow and talk to him in his office? That would allow time to do any adjusting that needs to be done," the groom's attendant suggested.

"That sounds like a good plan. I think I will do that tomorrow. Thanks Andy. I'm glad you are helping me."

"That is what an attendant is supposed to do, brother. I'm just doing my job."

"You make me glad I asked you."

"I'm glad you asked me."

"I'll tell Jane tonight at supper," John finished as they walked up the steps of the store.

"Supper is ready," Maria called as she heard the men enter the store. "No one came while you were away, so I am presuming no one will come while we take time to eat."

When she picked up Freddy to put him in his chair, he began kicking and yelling, "Unca John. Unca John."

John came through the door, looking at the boy with frosty blue eyes. "Freddy. We are all going to sit down to the table. Let's do it."

"Unca John. Unca John." Freddy continued yelling.

"Don't spoil him, Maria. What you do is take him like this" (picking Freddy up roughly) "and set him in his chair, like this."(plop) "There. That solved everything now, didn't it?" John said with a twinkle in his eyes.

Freddy sat in his chair, quietly, no smile on his face, and looked at John in wide-eyed wonderment. He had not seen this side of John, before.

"I've got a good idea." Maria said. "After you are married, you take him home and keep him for six or eight years, until he learns to do what his mother says."

Everyone laughed except Maria. John went to her and put his arm around her. "He'll be different next year, Maria. My, he is like his father. You can lay a lickin' on him after I am gone. I won't be coming around so often after we are married. That should help."

"What do you mean 'he's like his father'?" Andy asked defensively. "I thought he was like his mother."

"You mean sweet and tender?" John asked. "Where do you think his temper came from?" John teased.

"Let's eat," Maria interrupted. They all sat down and Andy asked the blessing of the Lord on their food.

Freddy was much subdued while they ate their meal, and when it was ended, he jumped down from the table and disappeared in the next room. In a few minutes he reappeared carrying the toy wagon. Coming to John, he took him by the hand and led him to the living room. Dropping on his knees he started playing with the wagon, then looking up at John, he placed his hands on his hips and a frown creased his face, as he waited for John to join him on the floor to play with the wagon.

"Don't spoil him, John," Andy said as he entered the room. John just looked at Andy and grinned. When the girls came in from cleaning up after supper, John continued playing with Freddy, while at the same time saying, "Jane, I am going to come to town tomorrow to take you to visit the church minister. Andy thinks we should discuss it with him before Sunday to give him a chance to prepare his service for us."

"Good. That's a good idea." Jane replied. "Maria was saying the same thing, she was. Two heads think better than one, you know, especially since they both have had experience."

"Well, I guess I had better be going home now. I will have to get going early in the morning to get things done. I should be in here about ten o'clock, I guess." John picked up Freddy and hugged him, then kissed him. "Good bye Freddy. I will see you tomorrow."

Setting Freddy down and turning to Jane he took her in his arms while they kissed. "I'll see you tomorrow Jane. Don't run away on me."

"Oh John, you know I was thinking of running away with the man in the moon. I might be gone up on a cloud when you return."

Laughing, John and Andy went out the back for John to get Grace out and leave.

*   *   *

When John arrived home, he found Bell had foaled a lovely bay filly. She had four white feet and legs as well as a wide blaze on her face.

"She is a beauty, Bell. What do you think we should name her?" John asked Bell as he looked the foal over. "Maybe I will ask Jane what we should name her."

*   *   *

Friday morning, taking Ned to ride so Grace could have a rest, he headed for town. Ned was not as comfortable to ride as Grace. He was also considerably slower, however he would get there. *Stop complaining, John,* he thought.

*   *   *

John and Jane walked to the church to see the minister.

"Bell foaled yesterday while I was in town. She has a beautiful bay filly with white markings a lot like her mother, except she has four white feet and legs instead of three," he told Jane.

"What be the name you are giving her?" Jane asked.

"I thought I would let you do that after you move out to the farm."

"How about calling her Fairy? That is a pretty name."

"Yes it is, but I think you should see her before you hang a handle on her. She will grow into a horse as big as Bell, you know. Mind your step on these stairs. I don't want you to fall at this stage of the game."

Entering the church, they were met by Reverend Samuels. "Come into my study where we can talk without interruption," he indicated the door of a lovely room with wood paneling up to the four foot height. The wood was stained dark and varnished to a high gloss. The wall behind the Reverend's chair was lined with book shelves that went almost to the ceiling. Hundreds of books filled the shelves. John idly wondered if he had read them all. When they were seated, John introduced Jane to him, then explained,

"Your Worship, Jane has just arrived in Canada, seeking a husband and a good future. I have got my place improved enough that I think I can support a wife and family, and we seemed to have clicked nicely. We would like to get married next Tuesday if that fits into everyone's plans." John paused to let the minister consider the request.

"Are you both Christians?"

"Yes."

"Do you understand the undertaking you are stepping into?"

"Yes sir, we both do."

"If tragedy should strike your home, are you both mentally prepared to support one another through it to the end?"

"We hadn't thought of that," Jane spoke up, "but I am sure this man would stick by me, and I know I would stay with him. He has the strongest character I have ever met. Even more than my father who is a strong minded Irishman."

There was a pause, for several minutes, after which the minister commented, "So you're Irish, eh? It so happens that I came from Ireland also. What part of the Isle did you hale from?"

For the next ten minutes Jane and Rev. Samuels discussed various things native to Ireland, and the way things were when they left.

"Yes, I'll marry you two," he suddenly broke off the Irish conversation. "Tuesday at two will be fine. If you two and your attendants will stay after the service on Sunday, we can run through the exercises to make you familiar with the way things will progress."

"We will do that." John agreed as he and Jane rose to leave.

✳ ✳ ✳

"You haven't told me yet who you have asked to stand up with you," John remarked as they were walking home.

"I have asked Maria to do the honors. Who have you asked?"

"Andy."

"What about the two children, John?"

"We will have to discuss that with them tonight."

When they entered the store, Andy was waiting on a customer. They went into the living room to wait. When the customer left, Andy joined them and sat down.

"I suppose you and Maria both know you are the ones we have chosen to stand up with us," John opened the conversation.

"No way!!" Andy gasped.

John started to rise up from his chair, "Don't lie to me, you little worm." he threatened.

"I'm not John, honest. **Maria**," he called. "Did you know John asked me to stand up with him?" he asked as she appeared around the corner.

"No. What will we do with the children? Jane has asked me to stand up with her and I have agreed."

"Let's see," Andy frowned a bit, "Who can we get to take care of them that will also be attending the wedding?"

"How about Mary Brown?" Maria asked.

"I think Freddy needs somebody with a stronger attitude. I'm afraid Freddy would cause a commotion with her." Andy predicted.

"How about Hazel and Mac Innesfree and their sons?" John suggested as he settled back onto his chair.

"Hey, they would be great I'll bet," Andy slapped his knee. "I could drive out there tonight. Would you and the baby like to come along?" he asked Maria.

"It would be nice to go for a drive. Could we get a two seater so that Jane and Freddy can also come?"

"Yeah, I'll ask Pete if I can borrow his. Let's get going. The day is wearing away."

"I have to go home, so we can go part way together." John reached for his cap. "I'll walk with you to church on Sunday, Jane."

John helped Andy get his horse hooked to Pete's buggy. "It's lucky he lives next door to you. Saves time when you don't have any to spare."

Everyone was excited to go for a drive, and soon they were all loaded up and waiting on John and Jane to say good-bye. Giving Jane a warm hug and long kiss, he jumped on Ned's back and followed behind the buggy to Innesfree's turnoff. Waving good bye to the buggy load of friends, he took off on a gallop.

✳   ✳   ✳

Saturday morning, after John finished his chores, he went to the field, and cut trees until the sun was dipping behind the hills and trees, and everything was bathed in it's golden rays.

"Such beauty! Jane will love this so much. Only three days left before I will be bringing her here. I think I will borrow Andy's buggy and harness to bring her home. She likes riding in the buggy with Grace. One of the first things I will do after I get all my wedding bills paid, is to take her to select a buggy of some kind for us."

Finishing his chores, and checking all the animals over, he was pleased to find everything going as he hoped they should. The cow appeared to be free of lice, as did Bud. He led them down to water. The others were able to help themselves by going through the passage to the lake John had built for them two years previously.

The cow and Bud both appeared to be more rested, and more interested in life around them. He let the cow loose around the house, until it was time to retire for the night.

* * *

Sunday morning he was up early, and had a bath then dressed in his chore clothes, until after the chores were finished. It was time for breakfast, then time to dress in his better clothes except for his trousers, which he put in a bag. Jumping on Nell's back and picking up his bag he headed for town. Nell was easier to ride than Ned, but still not as comfortable as Grace. Stabling her in Andy's barn and changing his trousers, he went to the house.

"Good morning everyone." he greeted them when he went in.

"Unca John! Unca John!" Freddy yelled when he saw John. Freddy was carrying the toy wagon and wanted John to get down on the floor to play.

"Not today, buddy. We all have to go to church. Are you ready? Where is your good jacket? You have to dress your best for church."

"He won't have it on," Maria called from the bedroom. "He just wants to play with the wagon. You can have him today."

"Oh... Alright, I'll take him part time at least." This big hulk of a man got down to where he could look this little strip of rebellion straight in the fiesty brown eyes. "Freddy, we are going to go and talk to God. We are not taking our wagon to God's house. We are going to walk there. When we come home the wagon will be waiting for us. Now get your jacket on and let's go."

Jane walked into the room as he finished and handed him the jacket. John winked at her, then kissed her lightly. Putting the jacket on Freddy he added, "Jane you can hold Freddy's other hand, and I will hold this one, now we will be on our way. We will meet you folks at church," he spoke over his shoulder as they were leaving.

* * *

At the end of the service, Reverend Samuels announced, "There will be a wedding in this church, on Tuesday at two o'clock for John Thomas and Jane Sleith. It is open to all who wish to attend. Please bring luncheon items."

As they went to the vestibule at the back of the church they were surrounded by people who came to shake John's hand and get introduced to Jane, including Mrs. Waggoner.

"Oh John," she gushed, "I am so happy for you and your lovely fiancé. I wouldn't miss it for the world."

"We will be so glad to have you attend," Jane spoke above Freddy.

" Home! Home!" Freddy was yelling. John picked him up and looked him blue eyes straight into brown eyes, "Freddy, you be quiet, or I won't play with your wagon. Do you understand?"

Freddy put his hands together and pushed them down between him and John. The tantrum was over for now. When the people had all left John dropped Freddy down on the floor and took his hand. Jane took his other hand as they waited for the people to leave for their homes, so they could have the practice Reverend Samuels said he wanted to do with the bridal party.

"You are right about the service. It is more like the style I am used to," Jane reached over and took John's hand. He gave it a little squeeze.

John hung onto Freddy during the rehearsal, to make sure he wouldn't cause a problem.

As they were all walking home, Andy commented, "I think it's going to be a great wedding, even if you do have to carry Freddy while it is being performed."

"Think again, little brother. I'll tell Mrs. Innesfree to sit on his head. That will keep him still and quiet."

Jane and Maria looked at each other, then at the men.

Andy caught the looks. "Don't worry. Mrs. Innesfree wouldn't do that. John is just getting the grooms jitters."

"Since when are you two brothers?" Maria asked.

"Since away back a while ago," Andy answered evasively.

"I'll bet it had something to do with that old table we took out to the farm." Maria said.

"Table?" Jane queried.

"You'll see it." Maria answered.

✳   ✳   ✳

Andy went with John after supper, while John got Nell ready to go home.

"You know little buddy, you almost gave me away there. You better watch what you're saying or you will."

"That wasn't me that called you "little brother." You brought that one on yourself. I think you should tell our women. Once they hear the full story, they won't be so curious, and they sure will never tell anybody. Not anybody, I guarantee it. Those two women have clicked solidly and would not want to do anything to spoil it."

"Just like our mothers did. I guess your right. But I am going to wait until sometime after the wedding."

"That's a plan... That's a good plan," Andy replied as John jumped on Nell's back. "Say is there something wrong with Grace? I notice you have changed riding horses."

"No. I was just giving her a rest. She has been putting quite a few miles under the wheels, and I thought she needed a day or two off." Turning Nell toward the roadway, he said, "I'll see you bright and early Tuesday morning."

As Nell disappeared around the hedge, Andy muttered to himself, "I hope not before sunup."

* * *

Monday, John chopped trees all day. He wasn't taking time to limb them or chop them in shorter lengths. By the time it was chore time, he was feeling less pent-up, and figured he would be able to sleep alright. When he did his chores, he noticed a change in the cow's udder. It wasn't quite so flat and empty looking.

* * *

Tuesday morning, he was up before the sun, feeding the animals. Grace was stabled and fed in her stall. He decided to brush her vigorously before going in for his breakfast.

"I think I will eat slowly, then have a long soaking bath in the tub." He was talking out loud to himself. "I need to kill a few hours before it will be time to go to town. I wouldn't want to get Andy out of bed. He would never let me hear the end of it."

Following his plan he was ready for his bath in fifteen minutes. "I really need a time piece of some kind," he said as he sat in the tub of water. "I must have been in this tub for an hour or so. I think it is time to go. I don't want to be late for my own wedding."

* * *

As he entered the store after putting Grace in Andy's barn, Andy was just coming out of the living quarters, shaking his head.

"How come you're so late John? The sun has been up for an hour."

"Don't be such a smarty pants. It must be mid-morning and you are making excuses for being so late getting up."

"Not at all." Andy pointed to the clock on the wall. It was seven– thirty five.

"Well I suppose I could have gone out and cut down some more trees. I thought about doing that, but was afraid that if I did, I would be late."

"Well, that's alright. I have booked a room at the hotel for you and I to stay in until it is time to go. We will have our breakfast and dinner there before going to the church."

"I've already had my breakfast, before I took a long soaking in the bath tub."

"Alright, let's get our things gathered up and leave. The girls want us to get out of the house until after the wedding. Your parcels are over there by that barrel of flour. I will get mine, and we will be gone after I hang this "closed" sign on the store door."

* * *

The hotel room was plain, but clean. It had the necessary furnishings – two chairs, a table holding a wash bowl and pitcher, towels hanging on the wall beside the wash bowl, a mirror and a bed that was made up. There was a braided mat on the floor on each side of the bed.

The men laid out their things over the chairs, then Andy laid down on the bed.

"Come on John, lie down here for a while before we go for breakfast," Andy coaxed.

"What time is it?" John asked as he submitted to Andy's request.

Andy took out his pocket watch,

"Nine thirty. Let's go over everything in our heads, to see if we have missed anything."

"Starting from the skin, I have underwear, shirt and tie, two pair of pants,—I think I will wear the striped ones, a suit jacket and vest and two hats. Have I missed anything? Oh yes, socks and two pair of shoes. How does that sound?"

"As you were going over your list, I was also tabulating mine. I think we are pretty well prepared as far as clothing is concerned. How about your ring?"

John sat up on the side of the bed and looked at Andy, dismay written all over his face. "Where's the ring? Andy I gave that to you to carefully take care of. Where is it, Andy? Where did you put it?"

"Uh, I put it in the socks I was planning on wearing today. Let me see if I brought the right socks."

Getting up off the bed, he went to his pile of clothes and rummaged through them until he found the socks. He squeezed up and down the folded socks, and finally opened them up over the bed. The elusive ring fell out. John grabbed it.

"I ought to put you down and sit on you, you little runt. You just about gave me heart failure, you know."

"Well, give it to me, and I will look after it for you."

"NO! I will keep it until we go into the church," John told him as he stuffed the ring into his pants pocket. "You're supposed to be helping me, not trying to give me a heart attack. You cluck, you."

"Let's go and have breakfast. We've got a while to wait yet." Andy was grinning as they went down the stairs.

$$* \quad * \quad *$$

They went down stairs again for their dinner, at twelve o'clock. John ordered toast and coffee and toyed with it, while Andy ate a hearty meal of roast pork and apple sauce.

"I don't know how you can stay so little and scrawny when you eat like that," John teased.

"Did you not notice that my father was scrawny, and my mother was little? I got it from both sides. Ricky got the muscular and taller qualities."

"Come on. Quit killing time. Let's go and get dressed and walk over to the church."

"I got two more bites here. I'm not going to pay for them and let them go to waste. Just keep your shirt on. We're not late yet, not for another hour and a half, at least."

John got up and started walking around the dining room, while Andy cleaned up his plate. Then they went to their room together, Andy chattering away about how beautiful the day was becoming.

Entering the room Andy instructed John, "Now put that ring on the table by the wash bowl, so we won't lose it again."

John reluctantly complied.

They were almost finished dressing. John had finished tying and retying his tie until he was satisfied with the results. He picked up his top hat and placed it on his head at a jaunty angle.

"Wow, I don't know this stranger. Are you the John that was giving me such a hard time a little while ago? Black suit coat with grey striped pants, blue tie on a white shirt, shiny black shoes, watch fob and chain. You just look like a million dollars John. You look wonderful. I didn't bring my hat. Should I run home and get it? I want to look like I am close to your equal,

They walked out of the hotel at twenty five after one, arriving at the church by quarter to two.

you know."

"No...You can wear my bowler."

"It will be too big," Andy protested.

"We'll stuff it with paper to make it fit."

Andy put the bowler on, and found it was close to a fit. A little paper inside the hat sweat band solved the problem. They walked out of the hotel at twenty five after one, arriving at the church by quarter to two.

The Innesfree family came, with Hazel carrying Andy's baby. Mac and the two boys had charge of the wide-eyed, silent Freddy. Andy had steered John down the street when he saw them coming, so Freddy wouldn't see John. As the Innesfree family went in the church, Andy looked down the street and saw the women coming. Turning John around, they entered the church vestibule. Andy kept a close watch at the door for the arrival of the women.

"Have you got the ring, little brother?"

Andy pulled the ring out of his pocket and showed John. At that moment the minister came out of his office.

"Wear your hats to the front of the church. When you get there, remove your hats. John pass your hat to Andy to keep until you are out of the church again. Now, you two follow me, John in front of Andy."

They entered the church and walked to the front. The inner door was closed behind them. The organist was playing softly. John removed his hat and passed it to Andy, then turned to watch for the girls to arrive.

There was a rustling sound, then the door opened and Maria, - beautiful Maria, entered. Another rustle of crisp dresses, then, there she was following Maria!

John's blue eyes widened and his mouth fell open. There stood a beautiful chestnut haired lady, with wavy hair that ended in a group of ringlets that hung over her left shoulder. They were tied with a blue bow that matched her dress. The blue linen skirt was straight in front with pleats all around the sides and back, draping gracefully to the floor. She had on a white silk blouse with ruffles from the frilled, stand-up collar, down the front to the waist.

The jacket was also blue linen matching the skirt, and had a snug fitted waist, with gathers at the back waist line. The leg-o-mutton sleeves had white ruffles protruding at the cuffs to look like the sleeves of the blouse. Dainty white lace trimmed the ruffles and the bottom hem of the jacket. Jane was carrying a bible tied with a long ribbon of white. Jane's beautiful emerald green eyes were shining like sun shining on diamonds. Her lovely soft red lips were pursed in a nervous enchanting smile. There was an aura of enchanting beauty about the whole picture of her as she entered the church.

Andy nudged John with his elbow, "Shut your mouth, John," he whispered, "You're gonna catch some flies if you don't."

Andy was grinning broadly, as he also looked at the two beautiful women who were approaching them.

Jane passed her bible to Maria, then looking John straight in his blue eyes, she put her hand in his and they turned toward Reverend Samuels. He was also smiling, and veiling admiring glances at the two beautiful women.

Finally John tore his eyes away from Jane as Reverend Samuels started the ceremony, "Dearly beloved, on this day in the eighteen hundred and twenty seventh year of our Lord, Jesus Christ, we are gathered in the sight of God, to join together this man and this woman in Holy Matrimony. Do you, John take this woman Jane to be your lawfully wedded wife, to love, honor, and cherish from this day forth so long as you both shall live?"

"I do."

"Do you Jane take this man John to be your lawfully wedded husband, to love, honor and obey, from this day forth, so long as you both shall live?"

"I do."

John and Jane then turned to face each other, and taking hold of hands, took this pledge, led by Reverend Samuels.

"I John, promise to remain steadfast in my love for you Jane, through sickness and health, richer or poorer, and forsaking all others will keep myself only unto thee, until death do us part. This, in the sight of God, is my pledge to you."

"I Jane, promise to remain steadfast in my love for you John, through sickness and health, richer or poorer, and forsaking all others, will keep myself only unto thee, until death us do part. This, in the sight of God, is my pledge to you."

"Could we now have the ring?" Reverend Samuels asked. Andy produced the ring. Reverend Samuels took the ring on his Bible, blessed it then passed it to John. Carefully taking the ring, he placed it on Jane's left hand, third finger, then held her hands and stared steadily into her beautiful green eyes.

Reverend Samuels continued, "I now pronounce you man and wife. You may now kiss the bride." John was looking at Jane and didn't hear anything being said.

"John you may kiss the bride...JOHN."

"Oh yessir? What did you say?" he whispered. A ripple of laughter went through the church.

"YOU MAY KISS THE BRIDE."

Reverend Samuels was unsuccessful in wiping the grin off of his face.

John took Jane tenderly in his arms and gently gave her a long kiss.

Andy tapped him on the shoulder. "Come up for air, John," he whispered.

Everyone in the church applauded loudly. Tears were running down Jane's face, and also Maria was wiping tears from her eyes.

"I think you are mine," John said, still holding Jane. The organist began playing the recessional.

"John, let's go." Jane pushed on John's chest. "We've done all we can do here. Let's go outside into some fresh air."

John put Jane's hand around his arm, and patted her fingers with his free hand, as they walked slowly down the isle to the door.

Stepping outside, John came to a sudden stop. Andy passed him his hat, and put the bowler on his own head.

Bill Shakleton was sitting on the seat of a three deck wagon, pulled by a huge pair of Clydesdale horses, across the entrance of the church.

"Andy, I can't ask a beautiful, highly dressed lady to ride in that thing. Get rid of it."

"**Bill**," Andy called. "**John says he won't take his bride in your rig. He says he would rather walk the six miles to his farm. I guess you might as well leave**." he looked at John's distraught face.

Grinning broadly, Bill started his team up and drove away, revealing on the other side of them, the dark chestnut body of Grace with her silver mane and tail flowing in the breeze, looking like a million dollars. She was dressed in new harness and hooked to a brand new carriage. Jacob Innesfree was standing at her head, holding her as the wagon pulled out of the way.

"Now if you think this is not good enough John, we can look around for something else." Andy had an innocent look on his face.

Everyone had emerged from the church, and were clapping and laughing, saying "Go for it, John. Go for it."

Andy helped Jane and then John into the passenger seats. Next he helped Maria get up on the driver's seat. He followed her and picked up the lines. Taking them on an extended drive around town, going down about every street there was in Battersea, he ended it back at the church.

When they arrived, there were several tables of planks on saw horses lined up in front of the church, and they were all loaded down with food.

"Now this is your wedding cake," Mrs. Waggoner said after Andy had helped them out of the carriage, "You two come around here and cut it together, the way you are going to work together from now on."

Andy and Maria flanked John and Jane as they went around the table, and moved in to stand on either side of their charges. As John and Jane finished cutting the cake, Andy leaned over toward John.

"You're rattled John."

"No, I'm not. I've got everything under control."

"Do you remember the vows you have just made to her?"

"Of course I do."

"Alright what are they?"

"I promised her I would love, honor and obey her."

"I hope you do." Andy started to giggle. Everyone else was laughing. John looked at them quizzickly.

"John," Jane laughed, "Those are the promises I made. I think you promised to love, honor and cherish me. Right?"

"And I will," John said as the color was rising in his face. "Next week I will remember the whole ceremony."

"I know John. I know," she patted his arm, her green eyes sparkling.

Mac Innesfree stepped up beside them, and announced, "The buggy and harness are a wedding gift from the whole district and then some. All the people who know you chipped in to get them for you."

John looked at Mac in amazement, then at the crowd that was standing around, expectantly. He swallowed twice, then tried to express his feelings. "Thank you. Thank you. How can I ever thank you enough. Jane and I are so grateful for everything you have done for us." John wiped his eyes.

"You have all made me feel so welcome since my arrival," Jane spoke loudly for everyone to hear. "I know God has been directing our lives, and has chosen the best community in the world for us to live in. Thank you for everything you have done for us - and for John before I arrived." Applause broke out wildly, along with several whistles.

"Come and get it," Mrs. Waggoner said, and started Jane and John filling their plates, followed by Maria and Andy, then the rest of the folks waiting.

✳   ✳   ✳

When the celebrating was finished, Andy and Maria took their charges by the arms, and escorted them to the carriage. Andy and Maria again took the driver's seat, and drove to the hotel where they picked up all of John and Andy's things from their room.

Their next stop was the store. Helping John and Jane out of the carriage, they took Andy's things into the store, while Maria and Jane were bringing out Jane's things and loading them into the carriage. When the transfers were completed, Maria and Andy helped John and Jane into the drivers seat. Andy did a deep bow, and Maria did a curtsey.

"Good bye our dear friends," Andy said. "Please come and visit us soon."

"Yes," Maria said, "We will miss you."

"We will be back," both John and Jane chorused. "Thank you so much for a great day to remember," John added.

CHAPTER 21

THE HONEYMOON

The dim light of evening was enshrouding everything when they entered the farm yard, Jane looked around,

"Oh, John it is beautiful!" she exclaimed, "The house is so big. It is beautiful. I love it."

"You don't think it is too rough and tough looking?" John asked.

"No. I love it."

"Thank goodness. I have been afraid you would think I was bringing you to a shack in the sticks." John got down from the carriage seat. Helping Jane down, he smiled as he invited her, "Come with me. I think Grace would like to see what she has been hauling around." They stood in front of Grace, while she smelled them, then they patted her.

"Good horse," John complimented her. Taking Jane by the hand he went toward the house. Stopping outside the door, he instructed her, "Just wait here a minute, darling." Opening the door he looked around inside to make sure everything was alright, then coming back to where Jane was waiting, he took her in his arms, and kissed her a long tender caress. Reaching down he picked her up and started for the door. His foot went sideways into a hollow made by a tree root. Losing his balance he was mortified knowing he was falling. Twisting his body so that he would fall on his back he landed with Jane on top of him. She gave an audible gasp, and he grunted from the rough landing. Jane started laughing. John looked at her, then he too started laughing.

She turned to face him, and putting her arms around his neck, she cried,

"Oh John, I love you," she passionately gave him a kiss fully on his mouth.

"I don't know how you could feel that way after I nearly threw you on the ground," he said as he got to his feet. Taking Jane's hand, he assisted her to her feet then putting his arms around her proceeded to pick her up again.

She started to protest, but stopped realizing it is a man's pride to carry his bride across their threshold for their first entry into his home – his life, so she put her arms around his neck while he carried her in.

"Welcome home, Mrs. John Thomas," he said as he set her down. He sealed it with a long tender kiss.

Turning to matters at hand, he lit a lamp, then took her on a tour of the house, ending back in the kitchen.

"I bought this stove the day I went to Kingston to meet the train. Mac Innesfree came with me to bring in a load of wood for me, so he brought this stove home for me, and one the same for his wife. Mac got some help to set his stove up, then they all came over here and set up my stove. I haven't been home much since, so haven't yet lighted it. I thought you would like to be the one to light it the first time."

"Oh John, I would love to have the honors. Thank you for being so thoughtful."

"There is some food here, and dishes here. If you want to put together something to eat while I bring the luggage in and put Grace away, I could eat before I do the chores. It will likely take me an hour to do the chores.

✳   ✳   ✳

John got his chores done up in jig time after supper. To his surprise when he entered the house, Jane was sitting at the table writing on a sheet of paper by the light of the lamp.

"I thought you would have been in bed after the long hours you have been putting in since your arrival. Are you not feeling tired, my dear?" he asked her.

"Yes John, I am tired. I just wanted to wait on you. That's all. I thought I would write to my folks to tell them of my experiences. They will be wondering what has happened to me, they will." She folded the paper and rose to her feet. Putting her arms around his neck she looked into his eyes. He put his arms around her, and pulled her close smelling her sweet perfumed hair and feeling the warmth of her body against his.

"Jane I love you so much," he whispered ecstatically. For several minutes they embraced and kissed, feeling their love for each other growing more and more.

"I think we had better get some sleep, my darling. We both need to catch up on some rest." John took her by the hand to the bedroom. "If you need more covers, let me know. I will be in this room across the hall."

Jane looked at the room, then gazed in wonderment into John's face.

"Right you are John," she muttered in a low voice, "I'll be sure to let yu' know."

John went into the other room, where he arranged some hide robes into a bed. Climbing in he lay on his back for a time, thinking about his beautiful wife, and his good fortune in finding one so compatible to him and his way of life. Soon he rolled over on his side, and fell asleep.

It was nearing sunrise time when John was awakened from his sleep by his shoulder being shaken. Turning to see what was happening, he saw Jane looking at him.

"Jane!" he exclaimed. "Is there something wrong?"

"Yes John. There is somethin' verrry wrong."

"Are you cold? I've got more covers I can put on your bed. Would that be what you would like?"

"No."

"What do you want, then?"

"I slept for a while I did, then I woke up and have been thinking."

John's heart sunk with fear of what she was going to say next. "Are you homesick Jane? Do you want to go back home to Ireland?"

"I am home, here. My bed is too big and empty. Could you come and help me fill it up?" she said as she took his hand. "I want you in bed with me. I would like to have some children, and we can't have children if we don't sleep together."

"I didn't think you would be ready to have a stranger in your bed, yet."

"I don't want a stranger in my bed. I think I know enough about you to have you in my bed. John, I love you I do, and have taken an oath in the sight of God, to love honor and obey you. Did you not do the same?"

"Almost. My oath was to love honor and cherish you. Remember?" he teased her as he rose to his feet, and went with her to the bedroom.

That early morning their marriage was consummated amid delirious happiness.

*　*　*

The following Sunday, Maria and Andy had Jane and John stay with them for lunch. During the course of the visit, Jane asked Maria and Andy to come to their farm for lunch and supper the following Sunday.

"Great!" Andy exclaimed.

"We would be delighted," Maria echoed. "Is there anything we can bring?"

"No, we have everything we will need, we do," Jane assured her. "Just come out prepaarred to enjoy yourselves, and have a nice relaxing afternoon."

*　*　*

While John and Jane were going home from church, they began planning the forthcoming visit with Maria and Andy.

"Let's have a picnic down by the lake," Jane spoke with excitement.

"Sounds great. Do you also want a fire there?" John responded.

"In the evening when it is starting to get cool would be great. If the weather stays nice it would be so beautiful by the lake."

"I will bring in a rack load of branches from the spruce trees I am going to be trimming up this week. They will make a nice fire, and I am going to be burning them anyway, to clear the area for pulling the stumps. You could also roast potatoes in the edge of the fire, if you plan ahead." John told her how to prepare and cook the potatoes for roasting.

"If we start the fire tomorrow and keep it burning, I could wrap a venison roast, and it could be cooked in the same fire. It would have to be put in the bed of coals on Saturday to be cooked by Sunday evening. The potatoes can be put in the coals Sunday after we get home from church," John finished.

"That sounds great. What will I be able to do to help?"

"Could you keep the fire stoked, if I bring the fuel in for it?"

"Surrrely John. I could do that. I could."

✳   ✳   ✳

The week progressed as planned, with a deep bed of coals by Saturday morning. Jane watched as John placed the wrapped and muddied roast deep in the fire bed. They both threw more fuel on the fire, and watched as the flames shot up high, spitting and snapping sparks around. They watched until they were sure there was no danger of an unwanted fire starting, then they went back to other preparations. After unloading more fire wood, John took the rack to the house where he and Jane loaded two saw horses and six planks on it, plus six big logs he had cut flat at the right height to sit on. Placing them near the fire, they soon had a table ready, with benches to sit on.

Sunday after the service, Jane took Freddy by the hand.

"You bring out some clothes for him. John and I are going to take him with us," she informed Maria.

Jane kept Freddy with her in the house, while John dipped the potatoes in mud and placed them in the bed of coal, then heaped more wood on the fire. When he came back to the house, he met Andy and Maria and baby Elizabeth as they were coming into the yard.

"Welcome to our humble home," John greeted them as they pulled up to the house. Jane and Freddy came out to help carry their things in.

"John, can you and Andy wait until we get Freddy's clothes changed? He wants to come with you two."

"Alright. There's no hurry for Andy to unhitch."

When Freddy came out, Jane was behind him. "Dinner is ready." she announced.

"Alright. We won't be long."

✳   ✳   ✳

John and Andy and Freddy went out to the barn after eating. John showed his guests his horses and the cow. They looked at them and talked about their future for quite a while, then they all went to the field where John had trees laying down, some limbed up and others with their branches still on. Freddy was having trouble walking through the rubble among them so John picked him up and carried him while they walked across to the fields where the crops were growing.

After looking at the wheat and then the oats, they headed back to the house. "Maria, you gotta see where we are going to have supper," Andy enthusiastically announced when they entered the house. "Gracious John, you sure have made improvements in here since the last time I was in it."

"Isn't it lovely?" Maria cheerfully exclaimed.

"The credit all goes to Jane," John modestly stated. "It is she who has found a better place for things, and is putting drapes over the cupboards to cover up their cluttered appearance. It sure makes an improvement, doesn't it?"

"I'll say," Andy was busy admiring the material of the drapes. "Did you bring this material from Ireland, Jane?"

"Yes. M' mother thought I should bring some material with me. She thought there might not be such a thing in this far away country."

"Well, we have some here in this country, but not as nice as this is," Andy finished. "Let's go to where supper is cooking."

"So that's why you don't have your stove going," Maria remarked to Jane as she picked up Elizabeth. John took Freddy by the hand as they all headed toward the lake. "Oh isn't this beautiful!" Maria exclaimed. "The lake is so blue, and the trees are so green, what are those birds over there?"

"Mostly ducks," John informed her. "There are a few loon, and some cormorants. Down there along the shore is a Blue Heron busy fishing for his family."

"You must love it here," Andy intimated.

"Yes. Listen to the birds in the trees, they serenade me all the time, even when I am cutting down their forest. There's a great variety of them."

Everyone was sitting down to the table, when Andy exclaimed, "Boy have we got a story to tell you girls!!" he looked at John who had suddenly fallen quiet, "You wonder why John and I call each other 'brother'. That is because we practically are. John's parents got on a boat at New Hope, Pennsylvania, and sailed to New York where my parents got on the same boat. They sailed out onto the high seas, where the Captain married them. They had almost a double ceremony. My folks stood up for his folks and then they reversed for my parents wedding. My father had bought a piece of land that had a lot of very tall trees on it," Andy continued, "My father asked John's father if he would be interested in working for him. Within a year it became a partnership. For several years they cut trees and sold them for flag-poles or building logs. They built two houses with a garden between them, and life was good, until John's father had an accident in the bush and got killed." Andy looked at John.

Raising his eyes from the table, John continued the story, "My mother used to go to father's grave after church every Sunday, until the day he stood beside her. Putting his arm around her he told her to go back to her parent's home, and put us two boys in an apprenticeship program. He said we would be alright."

Taking a deep almost sobbing breath, John continued, "The only one where we were able to get into that kind of program in Woodstock, was with a not nice person. Nothing that Hosea my brother, and I could do pleased him. Hosea threatened to run away, even though the penalty is a terrible beating or hanging. Hosea was going to go anyway. We had a year and a half left of the apprenticeship, which was to be followed by three years employment with pay, to the same person." John brushed his hand across his eyes as the memories resurfaced. "I made a plan for him and me to leave after the deliveries in the evening, and meet by a big tree near the Bernard Brook. We were to wait for up to an hour on the other to arrive. Should the other not arrive, the first one was to go on alone. Hosea didn't show up." John put his hands over his eyes and sat silently for a few minutes.

"I had decided I wanted to get into a store," Andy chipped in. "Running that kind of business appealed to me. There was no place in Woodstock, Vermont to do such a thing, nor in any of the nearby towns, so I decided to get on the boat and look elsewhere. I eventually ended up in Battersea. John, how did you ever get across the St Lawrence River?"

"With the good grace of God." John was now ready to continue. "It was early summer when I left Woodstock. On the way I fell off a cliff in the dark. When I regained consciousness, several hours had passed. I made my way through some shrubbery and undergrowth to the shore of a lake. While I was standing there wondering how I was going to get across, two Indians came out of the bush, carrying a canoe." John looked at Jane to see what her reaction was to this unbelievable tale he was telling. She looked stunned. "After looking me over and deciding I wasn't worth bothering with, they set their boat in the water and left, at the same time the Sheriff's dog was coming through the bushes. The Indians came back, picked me up, and brought me with them. We went through many miles of hiking across land, paddling lakes and rivers, then the St. Lawrence River, to just south of Kingston, where they turned me loose."

"That's where life got easier, eh, John?" Andy goaded him to continue the story.

"Not quite," John looked at Andy. "I didn't know too much about wilderness survival, even after spending a couple of months with the Indians. I tried to make a bed, but couldn't break the branches off the trees, so I kept walking all night, hoping to be going in a westerly direction," he paused to rub his forehead. "When morning came I found a growth of bushes loaded with black berries. I started eating them, when I heard a grunt from the other side of them. I looked under and saw a bear looking at me. I started running as fast as I could, and went through some shrubbery, then some trees, and turned just before I stepped over another cliff. The bear was hot on my heels, and being unable to turn so fast, swiped at me as she was going over the cliff. While I was getting my wind, two cubs came running and squealing out of the bush, and soon went over the cliff to be with their mother." John wiped sweat from his forehead. Reliving the memory for him was real. "When the bear and her cubs left, I saw I was at the edge of a hay meadow that had stacks in it. I figured out how I could get down without falling, and went to the nearest stack. The sun was hot, so I made a bed from the hay and covered myself up so I wouldn't sunburn again. I was sleeping when I thought the bear bit my leg. I jumped up to run away, but was blocked by a team of horses and a rack. I turned to go the other way and came face to face with a huge bearded monster, who was holding a pitch fork ready to jab me. I turned and ran between the horse and stack. I tripped and everything went black."

"The poor man. I'll bet he was as terrified as you were," Andy commented.

"Yeah he was. When I woke up, a stranger was coming at me, and I jumped up to escape, and fell on the floor with bedding piled up on top of me. J.L. Hodgson had found me, and had taken me to his home, where I stayed for the next year and a half. It was his wife Ann who was trying to look after me, that scared me the last time."

"Now that you have successfully escaped and have lived here for this length of time," Jane remarked, "you have all your fears behind you, and life is full of freedom for you. I am so happy for you, John."

"Not quite, Jane. This is the reason Andy and I have brought you girls to my farm to explain my story to you. If anyone reports me to the sheriff's office as being a runaway apprentice, they can take me back to Woodstock to give me the punishment they feel I deserve – likely hanging – as long as I live. There is usually a pretty substantial reward offered for the capture of a runaway apprentice. They are treated the same as slaves."

"End of story. Let's eat," Andy stood up to get the food. John went to help him while the girls set the dishes out on the table. They sat down and got Freddy under control, then John asked a blessing from God on their food, and their lives.

"It's not quite the end of the story." John commented when they had started eating. "Andy had arrived in Battersea two years before I did. He left Woodstock before Hosea and I ran away so didn't know anything about that part. The last time we saw each other, Andy would have been about eleven and I was thirteen. Neither one of us had beards, nor had we even reached maturity. I walked in the store to ask the owner if he would stake me while I got started on my farm. He kept looking at me, but finally said he would. I had to sign notes when I took things out of the store, and after he looked at my signature he figured out who I was, but kept it under his hat for a long while. Finally when I went in to buy a gun, he told me who he was. That's the end of the story between him and me." The girls were sitting in stunned silence.

"You both were alone in a strange world and couldn't even talk to each other,... until John went to buy a gun. How cruel life is sometimes," Maria contemplated.

"Now you girls promise on your Bible," Andy admonished, "that you are not going to let any of this privileged information enter into any of your gossiping conversations with anybody but each other, not even our children as long as John is alive, understand? Then only when you are out here at the farm, Get it? You never know when some nosey busybody will be eves-dropping on you in the store. Comprehend?"

"Yes Andy. We understand. Your story is as good as in a vault John." Maria vowed. Jane shook her head in agreement. The two girls clasped hands in an oath.

✱ ✱ ✱

When Jane and John were going to bed that night, Jane wrapped her arms around his neck, and began crying on his shoulder,

"John, my darling John, I am so sure now, that God has a special plan for us in the future. Now I can understand not only your attachment to Andy, but also your attachment to J.L. and Ann. It was God's wish that you should fall into such good hands. I love you so much John Thomas."

Jane wiped her eyes as she thoughtfully pulled the covers up over herself, "John, I thought I had a very hard and heartbreaking experience when I left Ireland and my family. Hearing what you have gone through to get here makes me realize mine was as easy as pie compared to what you went through. It took a lot of something I don't have, for you to have survived. I love you so much and am so happy to be your wife."

CHAPTER 22

NEW ARRIVALS

The cow was developing a large udder, and John could tell her time of calving was close, so he locked her in the corral and kept her on dry feed, to prevent her from becoming sick after calving. Jane named her Buttercup, because the light yellow around her eyes looked like the petals around a black center of a flower. She was a nice gentle animal, very easy to work with.

The week following the picnic, Buttercup dropped a black heifer calf with an abundance of white on both sides of her body. She also had four white legs up to her body.

"That calf is definitely not sired by the bull I brought back," John declared. Jane named her Icecream. She also named Bell's filly Bonnie. "Fairy doesn't suit her at all, at all."

John brought the calf home from J.L.'s after Buttercup had calved, as she had more than enough milk for both calves and the household needs. Ralph had been calling the calf Sunflower, which stuck. John later brought Big Red the bull home with him for a month and a half, then returned him to J.L. until next year. Big Red was starting to fill out with muscling and even some fat in places.

By Christmas time Jane knew she was expecting, and told John.

* * *

The next year – 1828 – Jane went into labor during one night. John stayed by her helping her in any way he could, except for the hour and a half it took him in the morning, to jump on Grace and ride into Battersea to get Dr. Black, then return home again at top speed. In the afternoon Jane gave birth to a sweet little bundle of joy – a girl they named Eliza. John proceeded to spoil her and cuddle her as soon as she was born.

That year John also built a chicken house, and brought home thirty- five hens and two roosters, from the Kingston market. He also built a smoke house and cured some fish and deer meat in it before storing the meat in the root cellar. Helping Jane with the garden cut into his time usually spent in the fields cutting trees and pulling roots. He got only three acres ready for cropping.

There were no foals in 1828, only Buttercup had a calf. It was a bull calf, and was dark red. After New years, Andy and Mac came to help John butcher it. The meat could be kept frozen until March or so, which would give Andy and John a good supply of fresh meat all winter.

*   *   *

Buttercup had another red bull calf in the late spring of 1829, before the grass had started to grow. John hoped there would be no worry about her becoming sick with the problem after calving that many heavy milkers seem to have. Many of the good producing cows had been lost with this problem. John turned the calf into a steer with intentions of keeping him a year before butchering him.

Daisy had a filly and Darky had a colt, both in late June. They were both dark Chestnuts with lighter manes and tails. When Mac Innesfree heard they had arrived, he and his whole family came over to see them. They had a great visit with Jane and John. Before they left for home, Mac told John he wanted to buy Darky's colt at weaning time. Jane named them Rosebud for Daisy's filly, and Major for the colt.

*   *   *

During the spring of 1830 when Jane went into labor with her second child, John again rode Grace into town for Dr. Black, then home again to stay and care for Jane. Nearing supper time she gave birth to a strong healthy boy, while John was getting supper for Eliza and himself. Jane named the baby John jr, for his father, partly because what little bit of hair he had appeared to be blonde and curly. Part of the reason for his name being John was because Jane stated, "I want him to grrroow up biiig and strrrronnng like his father."

John was ecstatic and cared for him and played with him and Eliza every minute he could be in the house.

*   *   *

Bud was now five years old. John was using him just about every time he harnessed horses. Bud was a little taller than Grace, as well as being a little heavier in the bone. Together with Grace, they made a great road team. When he was teamed with any of the other horses, he could pull as much as them, and had more endurance under working conditions. His second crop of foals had arrived for John, two this year, one each from Daisy and Darky.

Not only had Bud grown into a very useful horse, he was also very handsome, with an excellent conformation, topped off with his flaxen mane and tail. John was well pleased with him.

* * *

This was the year that John's cow herd started to grow. Buttercup produced a heifer calf Jane named Tina. Sunflower and Icecream both produced their first calves– both bulls. John said they would both be turned into steers for meat purposes, so they didn't get named.

J.L. and John were talking at the store one day about farming progress and changes needed.

"Ralph is taking a big interest in the farm, and I think I will let him take over. He says it is time to move Big Red and replace him."

"Has he got a replacement picked out?" John asked.

"He has been looking around and has spotted one he likes. He says the owner would be willing to trade, flat across," J.L. informed John.

"Tell him to go ahead and make the trade. He knows cattle well enough, I don't think I need to butt in," John replied.

"He told me he wants you to come with him to make the deal."

"Oh. Well I could do that. What day does he want to do that?" John asked.

"How about day after tomorrow? That would be Thursday."

"Alright. We'll be over Thursday morning."

* * *

Jane wrapped her baby and taking Eliza, joined John on the trip to Hodgson's. She visited with Ann while the men went on their trip to exchange bulls. John had brought Ned and Coal on the carriage, for a reason he was unable to explain to Jane. However when they got to the farmer's place, the man took a big interest in John's team. His name was Harold Jeffries. He said his herd of about a dozen cows were Brown Swiss. They looked like they were good milk producers. They had a very docile temperment. He had used his bull as long as he could and was looking for one of good milking strain, as he supplied fresh milk around Kingston. The deal was made, and as they were getting ready to return to J.L.'s, Harold Jeffries asked John if he was interested in selling his team. John and he discussed a deal for a while, then agreed on a price, and a place and day to meet to complete the deal.

* * *

Late spring of 1831, Walt Isaacs, the traveling salesman drove into the yard close to noon, leading four horses. They put three of them in the corral and his driving team in the barn. The fourth horse was a two year old colt, not yet gelded so he was also put in the barn.

"I'm not needing any more horses, Walt, Would you stay for dinner? Jane will have it ready shortly."

"Thank you so much," Walt graciously accepted the offer.

* * *

The men went to the corral to look at the horses, after dinner. Two mature mares were thick-set chunky work type horses. One was a bay with black mane and tail, a star on the forehead and one white hind, to above the ankle. She was lame in a front foot.

The other was a red roan with red mane and tail. A narrow stripe adorned her face, with both hind legs white half way to the hocks. She was lame on a hind leg. John looked at them for a long time. He liked the conformation of both of them, but their lameness rendered both of them useless for anything other than raising foals. Their value would be very low.

"Are you taking the two mares to the wolf and bear hunters?" John queried.

"Yup. They got lots o' bait on their bones. I should be able t' git fifteen 'r twenty dollars each for them."

"What are the other two you are trailing with you?" John went into the corral, and began examining the teeth of the horses. He estimated the two big mares were ten and twelve years old, but he kept the information to himself.

"The one we put in the barn has bin running with a bunch of range horses. He is pretty badly chewed up." Walt explained as he bit off a chew of tobacco. "He is two or three years old. It is pretty hard to tell his age, as he ha'nt grown properly. I think he is three, and has bin outcast by the range stud," Walt told John as he followed him around from one horse to the next.

"This little filly is part pony, and will make a good kids horse. She is just two years old." As Walt was speaking the filly put her ears back and kicked at John as he approached her. He grabbed her halter and shook her head until she put her ears up. He then examined her teeth.

Entering the barn, John went in the stall by the colt, who immediately flew back and had a good pull on the halter. John took his jacket off and flapped it in the face of the colt until he stopped pulling and lunged forward to the manger. He then took his halter and examined the colt's teeth.

"He is three years old," John told Walt. "If you take him to J.L. Hodgson's he can geld him for you. He would be a lot less trouble after that. The filly is a two year old, and has a dirty disposition. She should not be sold for a kid's pony prospect. How much do you want for the two crippled mares?"

"Forty dollars. They are a good solid pair of mares."

"Look Walt, I will cancel the charges for feeding your horses, and give you twenty five dollars for the pair. Take it or leave it."

Walt started getting his team ready to hook up. He spat on the ground as he drove his team toward the buggy. John went in the stall by the colt. He had his head up and ears forward, but didn't fly back. Walt watched from the doorway while John untied the colt and brought him out. He tied the colt to the back of the buggy, then went to the corral to bring out the other three horses. Walt came over as John caught the two big mares. After resting, both mares were so lame they hardly put the sore foot to the ground.

"Just leave them here, John. I will accept thirty dollars for them. Just bring the filly."

"No," John sounded positive. "My offer is twenty five or keep them, Walt."

"Alright. You drive a hard bargain. Leave them here. I'll take your offer. Just bring the filly."

John went to the house to get the money to close the deal.

✳   ✳   ✳

Jane and John took Eliza and John jr. to go and visit J.L. and Ann Hodgson one Tuesday, about a week later.

"I bought two mature mares from Walt Isaacs a couple of weeks ago. They are both pretty good looking horses, but they both are lame. One is lame on the front foot and the other is lame on a hind," John explained to J.L. "I was wondering if you knew of any magic potion that I might apply to make them sound again, or at least serviceably sound. I want to raise foals from them, and don't like to see them limping around so much."

"We're going to town on Thursday. We could drive out and have a look at them." J.L. adjusted his cap. "Come into the barn and see what I got from the same man."

J.L. showed John the same two horses Walt had when he left John's place. John began to laugh. "Does that colt pull back on his halter?"

"No. He is nervous but stays up in the stall and keeps an eye on us. Ralph decided he wanted to work with them, so I traded two of my older horses for them. Why does thee ask?" J.L. queried.

"When they were at my place the colt pulled back and I slapped him in the face with my coat until he came up in the stall. I wasn't sure he would be cured. I'm glad he learned that lesson. I thought the filly was going to be a dirty critter, and I didn't want to be bothered with her. I wish you all the luck with her Ralph. I hope she turns out good for you."

"Thanks be to thee John," Ralph spoke gratefully.

*　*　*

Thursday when J.L. examined John's two horses, he pushed his cap back on his head.

"Oh oh. I'm afraid the bay may have navicular disease. There is no help for that. The roan has a jack spavin. If thee takes the time and patience to look after it, thee can kill it in about three weeks, and she will then be serviceably sound. She won't be lame, but she will have a bone lump on the face of her hock."

"What do I do?"

"Well mix some pine tar, bear grease, turpentine and Wint-o-green into a soft paste, then rub a very small amount on that lump until the friction turns warm in thy hand. Do that twice a day for four days, then rub on some plain bear grease, and leave it for three days. Repeat the procedure for three weeks. Leave her off work for an extra week, just to make sure it is not strained again."

"Great J.L. I thought you would know of a cure." John proceeded to put the two mares out to pasture.

"Hold on there a minute, son. Let me have a closer look at that bay's foot." J.L. lifted the foot up and started digging in it with his jackknife. After digging and trimming out a lot of excess insole, his knife hit on something hard. "Oh ho," he exclaimed, "What have we here?"

As he was digging at the hard object, the mare started pulling her foot away from him. "It is hurting her. Thee will have to twitch her. I can't hold her foot."

J.L. told John how to make and apply a twitch, then he picked up the foot again to start digging and trimming more. Finally a stone popped out, followed by a lot of stinking puss.

"Can thee get me some alcohol disinfectant?"

"Ralph, could you go to the house and ask Jane to get you the alcohol?" John was still holding the twitch and didn't want to let it go while J.L. was holding her foot.

Ralph ran to the house, and was shortly back with a bottle. J.L. poured some of the liquid into the hole he had made.

"That stone has been in there so long the foot had grown around it. I am amazed she hadn't died from poison a long time ago," J.L. said as he continued pouring a little liquid into the hole, then watch the puss being washed out. Finally it got to the place it was washing blood out.

"There, that seems to be clean, now," J.L. said as he set the foot down. "Put in all the pine tar you can, then finish filling the hole with the mixture you will make for the jack spavin. Just let her out in the pasture with the others. She will likely be better there than in the barn or the corral. I think thee should check it every day if thee can, for a few days at least until it closes up. There is a pretty big hole there, right through the insole of the foot. Keep the hole filled with the pine tar and the mix to keep out infection until the hole closes up."

"I'm not going to let her go down to the lake for a drink until it is healed up, if she lives that long," John speculated. He turned her out in the pasture, where she limped a few steps, then just stood with her sore foot out in front of her.

The men went to the house where the women had a hot meal ready.

*   *   *

A traveling salesman drove into the yard in 1832. He drove a thin horse on a covered democrat full of pots and pans, dishes and cutlery, some spices and flavorings, and anything useful in the house. Jane who was expecting another baby in a few weeks, bought two pots and a pan plus some cutlery. When John came in from the field for dinner, he found the salesman still in the yard, preparing to leave.

"John, ask him to stay for dinner. I couldn't take him to the barn to put his horse away," Jane spoke as she was going to the house to put dinner on the table. She took John Jr. by the hand, as she turned to four year old Eliza.

"Come on Eliza, let's get dinner ready." The three of them left.

*   *   *

Two weeks later Jane gave birth to another boy they named Fredrick.

That year John had three cows drop calves, and five horses had foals. He had decided to raise some foals from Grace before she got too old to reproduce. This year she had a dark chestnut colt Jane named Dude.

"I'm going to take some horses and a load of wood to the Kingston Market on Wednesday," John said to Jane in Mid July. "Do you want to go to the Market, or go and visit with Ann Hodgson?"

"I think I would like to visit Maria, I would. I don't feel a trip to the market, then spending the day looking around would be good. Of course that all depends on what Maria is doing, it does. I just don't feel up to a long trip on the wagon, John."

"That's fine. Do you want to take Grace on the carriage?"

"Yes. I would like that. Then I can leave in the afternoon instead of the early mornin', I can."

"Dude can go with you so Grace won't give you any trouble. Andy can help you when you get there."

"Good. I can do that, I can."

In the morning, John put Shadow and Ben in the barn. He harnessed the two black Clydesdales to pull the wagon by the wood pile, where he loaded it to be ready to leave early in the morning. Turning the team out for the night, so they wouldn't get manure stains on their white trim during the night, he went to the house to help Jane get things ready to go.

*   *   *

When daylight was coming, John went out and put Shadow, Ben, Daisy, Daphne and Grace with Dude in the barn. Harnessing Shadow and Ben, he hooked them to the wagon, then tied Daisy and Daphne on behind. He went into the house to say goodbye to Jane, who was still in bed. Bending over to kiss her, she turned her face toward him.

"You don't mind me not going with you, do you John?"

"No. Sweetheart I want what is best for you. I thought maybe you would want to get away from the farm for a change. I didn't think of you using Grace to go to visit Maria. I think it is a great idea." He put his arms around her shoulders and raised her up to kiss her in a warm embrace, then left.

✷ ✷ ✷

Stopping at J.L.'s he found Ralph and J.L. were about ready to leave for the Kingston Market with their week's farm produce.

"Thee are selling the two greys? I didn't think thee would part with them, or I would have bought them." J.L. was scratching their necks and rubbing their faces.

"Well, I'm getting too many horses, and these two are starting to get a little long in the tooth. Daisy is nine this year and Daphne is two years younger. If you want to buy them, you can. You can also come to my place and pick out some younger ones if you so wish."

"Let's see how thee makes out at the Market. I just may come to thy place and pick up some."

✷ ✷ ✷

John's team of greys were still showing quite a bit of color on their sides and legs, so were attractive to potential buyers as young horses. They sold within an hour after John arrived. The two Clydesdales sold less than a half hour later. When J.L. walked up the Market alley, he came to John.

"How did thee fare?" he asked.

"The greys sold first, then later the Clydesdales sold. I'm sorry, J.L. My original plan was to sell the Clydes. When a man was interested in the greys, I thought if I put a tall price on them, he would buy the Clydes. He never looked at the Clydes, and he never hesitated at my price, because right behind him was another man who was looking at the greys. It was one of those times when I didn't bring enough horses with me. Could I tie my wagon on behind yours to take it as far as your place?"

"Yeah, by all means. When would thou be ready to leave for home?" J.L. asked.

"Whenever you are. I have done more than I really intended to do here."

CHAPTER 23

WELCOME NEW NEIGHBORS

Mac Innesfree drove into the yard in the early spring of 1833. He was driving his team of hot-blood mares.

"God's blessing to you this day, John. What think thee of this pair of drivers?" he greeted John.

"They are a pretty handsome pair of roadsters, Mac." John was looking them over carefully. "What do you have in mind?"

"I thought I would like to raise foals from them for next year." Mac adjusted his cap. "Jacob is getting married this year. He has been working with the two foals we bought from thee, and has a handy dandy team of draught horses. They are four years old now, and he thinks they are the best in the country."

"I'm glad he likes them. Bud has been producing some pretty good horses, mostly dual purpose, but they are as tough as nails, and good lookers, too," John said as he began helping Mac unhitch the team.

"Well, I thought I would like to buy four more from thee to set Jacob up in farming with. He is taking the two at home, so that would give him six. That should be a good start for horses. Dost thou have four to sell?"

"I believe so. Are you going to pick them out, or are you going to bring him over here to choose them himself?"

"Show me what thee has for sale. I will decide after I see them."

After stabling the team, John went to the corral gate and whistled. The herd of horses all came in on the run, and entered the corral. John closed the gate, then threw a few oat sheaves in various places around the corral. Getting an armful of halters and shanks from the barn, he began tying horses to the fence until he had eight of them tied up. He then opened the gate and drove the rest out, throwing some of the sheaves over the fence for them. He rearranged the remaining horses until he had four matched teams tied at intervals around the corral fence.

"There! That is what I have for sale. These two Clydes are both Bell's produce. Bonnie is sired by that stallion that was owned by Ken Brisby. She is six years old. Scotty is sired by Bud and is two years. They should match pretty well when Scotty matures."

"These two blacks are Darky who is ten, and Nell who is nine. They still have ten or twelve years work left in them. Darky is Maud's foal, and Nell is from Mandy. She is the only black foal Mandy had. They are raising a pair of foals, but are not rebred. They are a great pair of horses. I will keep the mares until the foals are ready to wean, as I want to keep the foals."

"These two chestnut geldings are Buck who is three years old this year. He is a full brother to Rosebud who you bought as a weanling. His mate is Ace who is a two year old out of Nell, Mandy's daughter. When they mature I think they will make a perfectly matched pair."

"These two chestnut fillies are both three years old. Queen whose dam is Darky, and Princess whose dam is Nell. They are going well as are all of those three years and over. The two year olds are started and showing a lot of promise."

Mac was looking them all over critically. Finally he turned to John,

"Can you keep them all in while I go home and get Jacob? I think I will let him pick the ones he wants."

"Sure," John responded, "I will put them in the barn out of the sun."

Mac and John hooked Mac's team to the buggy and he left in a cloud of dust.

"I think it is going to rain," John mused out loud to the horses as he was stabling them. When he came out of the barn after putting the last pair away he was greeted by a familiar team and democrat driving in the yard.

"God's greetings to you son," J.L. called. He drove up by the house yard gate and stopped. Ann and Elizabeth got out. Jane came to the door.

"Come in. Oh do come in," she invited, "I was about to make a cup of tea." The two women accepted her warm invitation.

"I think the men have business to discuss in the barn," Ann informed Jane. Herding her two children back into the house, Jane looked at Ann.

"It has been a busy day for John today."

* * *

"Has thee been having a horse show?" J.L. asked.

"Well, sort of," John said picking up a sheaf of oats for J.L.'s team. "Jacob Innesfree is getting married, and Mac wants to buy a field hitch of horses for him to start out with. He has gone home to get Jacob and should be back soon."

"God told me I should get over here to pick out the team of thine that I wanted. It looks like I was almost too late. Tell me what thee has here."

"Let's take them out and tie them in the corral, so you can see them better," John offered.

"First take out Darky and Nell. I want to see if they are as good as Daisy and Daphne." J.L. and Ralph followed the two horses out, talking between themselves.

"Now, turn them around and bring them toward us," J.L. instructed. When they reached John, he stopped the team, and waited for further instructions.

"What is thy opinion, Ralph? Is this what thee desires?" J.L. asked his son.

"Yes father, if John guarantees them to be sound, they are as good as the greys," sixteen year old Ralph replied.

"I'll guarantee them to be sound when they leave my yard. I couldn't extend a guarantee any further. You will have to take a chance on what happens to them after they leave my yard," speaking in his business tones, John looked at Ralph, then J.L.

"That is only fair, John. That is a good guarantee," J.L. spoke to Ralph as much as to John.

Mac and Jacob Innesfree drove into the yard just then.

"We'll take these two," J.L. said when he saw them.

"Would thee be buying the horses I had my eyes on, J.L.?" Mac queried.

"First with the cash is the chooser," J.L. replied.

"Now don't you two friends get scrapping over horses," John cautioned when he realized there was some concern in Mac's voice. "I've got lots more horses for you to choose from. They are younger than these but they will soon grow up."

"Thee're right," Mac admitted. Extending a hand to J.L. he went on, "I want to apologize for my remarks."

John took the two mares into the barn. Mac and Jacob unhooked their team and brought them into the barn. When they got in the barn, John was in the process of taking the chestnut fillies out to tie on the fence. Mac left Jacob to tie the team in a stall, while he took the chestnut geldings out. Jacob came out and he and Mac were looking the four chestnuts over, while John went in to bring out the team of Clydes. John and J.L. then stood in the barn doorway while the other two men looked over the six horses.

"How has the pair of cripples come along?" J.L. asked John.

"Fine," John replied as he stepped to the corral gate and whistled. All the horses in the pasture came up to the gate on the trot. John gave them a few oat sheaves for their reward, then he, Ralph and J.L. went in among them looking them all over.

"It is God's blessing on thee the way those two mares have come sound, again," J.L. remarked. "I really didn't think either one of them would get that good. Thee must be congratulated."

"Most of that credit goes to you J.L." John lifted his cap and brushed his hair with his hand. "I could never have got those results without your knowledge and help."

"John," Mac called, "Can thee come here for a few minutes. Jacob would like to see these horses moving."

"Would you like to harness them and take them for a drive?"

"That would be a good idea. Yes. We will do that. We will use our harness and democrat."

After driving one team, they changed the harness to another team to drive them around, then back to the corral, to harness the third team.

"Where are thy cattle, John?" Mac asked.

"I built a pasture west and south of the house yard to the road. I then run it west along the road to the end of my property. That is the cow pasture. It doesn't work well to have horses and cows run in a small pasture together. Cows can't graze after the horses have eaten, and the young horses run and chase the cows too much. They are coming in now to see what they are missing."

All the men went to the pasture to look at the cows. It was getting late in the afternoon and their udders were starting to look full. John threw them a few oat sheaves. Mac and Jacob looked at them for a while, then moved toward the gate. John followed.

"I think I want the four chestnut horses," Jacob confirmed his decision.

"Good," John said, then a price was settled on.

"I'll pay for Jacob's horses, as that is my wedding gift to him," Mac offered. "I also want to take the Clydes for myself. I am needing some younger stock."

"John?" Jacob turned toward him. "Dost thou have any of thy cattle for sale? I like the looks of them and would like to get a couple for milk cows."

"Yes, I will sell as many as you want, Jacob. When do you want them?"

"After we have a place to keep them. Father has bought the piece of land north of yours," Jacob indicated the road that went through John's place and on out to the north along the lake shore.

"Oh, you are going to be our next door neighbors." John smiled. "That's great Jacob. When is your wedding to be?"

"I think the circuit official will be around to do weddings in January. That will give me the whole summer to get a place ready," Jacob responded.

"I will come over and help you cut and trim trees for your barn and house. You just call in here when you are going so we can go together. Are you starting to cut tomorrow?" John could feel the old excitement rising in anticipation of the project.

"Yes, father and I thought we would. We would like to use the horses we are buying from thee to do the work."

"I think we will ask J.L. Hodgson to help with the building, the same for us as he did for thee, John. I like the work he did." Mac stuffed his hands in his pockets and looked at John.

"You couldn't get a better engineer, Mac. I think he is great," John sounded excited.

* * *

Summer seemed to go by too fast. John was making a trip to Kingston market on Wednesdays, to sell butter and cheese that Jane made during the week. He bought a democrat to make these trips with, so Jane would have the carriage. Twice during the summer he brought home two chunky mares, one pair were a chestnut and a black and the other pair were a bay and a roan. He thought they were being sold at bargain prices, and he would be able to raise foals from Bud with them.

John got his own farm work done, as well as spending many hours over at Jacob's place cutting trees. Many neighbors and Friends from their congregation were out helping as well, and by fall, after the crops were brought in, there was a building bee for a week. They built both the house and the barn, in such a way they could be added to in the future.

The weddings were in February, and Mac asked John to drive the newly weds around town with his team and carriage. John had Harry Potts make runners to bolt onto the wheels of the carriage to slide over the snow. There were three couples married, and they all piled into the carriage for the trip around town.

* * *

Jacob and his bride Maryann moved into the house following the weddings. Jacob and John had kept a fire burning in the fireplace for a week to have the house warm for the arrival of the bride. With much help from the Friends and neighbors, their place was very well furnished.

The year was now 1834. Jane had a baby girl that summer. John insisted on her being named Jane after her mother, as John jr. was named after him.

"We will call her Janie," Jane agreed.

Maryann had a baby late that fall. Jane took some baby clothes over for Maryann to use.

"It is so wonderful having a neighbor so close," she confided to Maryann. "You have no idea how lonely it gets when your nearest neighbor is an hour away. You just don't go to visit very often, so you don't."

"I hope you will be able to come often to help me with the baby. My mother is too far away to help me," Maryann said.

CHAPTER 24

NEW ADDITIONS

Jane went to Jacob's place on Wednesday's when John was gone to Kingston. Hooking Grace to the carriage, and loading all the children became easier, the more often she did it. Eliza was put in charge of the baby, then three year old Freddy was set on the seat and given the lines to hold, while five year old John jr. helped with hooking Grace to the buggy. Jane felt a sense of freedom, and was quite proud of the way her children pitched in to help.

During the year of 1835, John would bring home horses he was able to buy at a reasonable price, as well as occasionally some cattle, most of whom he planned on running on pasture until they got some flesh on them, to make suitable animals to butcher. He often sold meat around Battersea, and at the Kingston market. This year was becoming one of his better years, financially.

During the afternoon in early August, as John was coming to the house, he scanned the sky and noticed a dark cloud coming rapidly toward them. It had white edges and a white streak on one side. Hurrying into the house, he announced, "There's a pretty wicked looking storm coming. I think we should all take cover until it passes. We will go to the root cellar."

The wind was getting up, so they all hurried to the root cellar. They took one of the storm lanterns with them. The wind began to howl as the rain started pouring down in torrents. It was making a terrible noise on the roof of the root cellar, then it got noisier, sounding like it was using hammers to pound the roof. The door was threatening to come open, until John went to it and putting his shoulder against it braced his feet and held it shut.

Suddenly everything went quiet outside. When John opened the door golf-ball sized hail was banked up against it and fell in over his feet. It was still raining lightly. The boys brought the shovel up from the potato bin and began shoveling the hail out of the cellar. John went outside and looked around. He came running back in as the rain began getting harder. By the time he got the door shut, it was hailing again with the golf-ball sized stones, just as bad as before. John braced himself against the door and held it until the second onslaught of hail was over. No one was talking until John turned to his family, "The roof on the house and the barn are still mostly in their place, but they both are smashed to kindling wood," he told them, "Let's go and see how deep the hail stones and water is in the buildings."

They used shovels and pails to clean out the house, then John left the women and boys to finish cleaning the house up, while he went out to examine the barn. Fortunately all the animals were outside, except trembling Bud who was standing with his back hunched up. John wasn't sure if it was from fear or the damp cold. He turned him out in the corral. Going to the house he announced, "The barn's a mess. I am going out to see how the crops are."

John's first view of the fields was devastating. The crops were so hammered down that the fields looked like they had been deeply disked. As he worked his way to the north and west, he found the damage was less severe and by the time he got half way down the field there was actually still crop to be later harvested. At the very out end of the fields there didn't appear to be any hail damage, but the rain and wind had flattened the grain severely.

When he arrived back at the house, Jane asked, "Is there any crop left, John?"

"Well," he replied, "Any surface plants in the garden are gone. What is under ground may be alright. I guess we will find out when we dig them. As for the field crops, it appears the hail went in a narrow strip along the lake shore, stripping branches off of many trees, cultivating the grain fields until they don't look like they were growing one of the better crops I have ever produced. However, the further north I went, the less hail damage was done, until about half way down the field the hail ran out, and the rest of the damage was done by rain and wind." John hesitated while he picked up Janie, "We won't have any wheat to sell this fall, and our oat crop will barely be enough to winter the livestock through that we have. I will likely have to sell some stock, or trade them for feed or something. We are very fortunate to have enough resources to get through to next year's harvest if we are very careful and work things right. God has given us a challenge that is not impossible to meet. God is good to us," John finished his statement as he put his arm around Jane who had come to him and put her arm around his waist. The children all came and put their arms around whoever they could reach. While they were standing thus, John offered a prayer of thanks to our Heavenly Father for saving as much of the crop as He did.

✳   ✳   ✳

John took eight loads of logs to Mike McMurty to get them sawn into one inch lumber to reroof the house and barn. When he and Jane told the people at church about the hail damage, they soon found out that the men started planning on the day they could come to help put the roof back on the two buildings. The designated day was the following Monday. Many of the farmers brought a bag or two of oats from their abundant crop, as they didn't get hailed, and the wind and rain damage was minimal.

John sold two teams of horses, plus eight loads of wood at the Kingston market which made it possible for him to get through the winter safely. He bought two loads of hay, one from J.L.Hodgson and one from another man closer to his home. He traded a good milk cow for each one of these loads of hay.

John planned on picking up seed grain at the Kingston market next spring to put his crop in with, thus leaving all the grain he had been able to harvest, to feed to the stock.

*   *   *

John was out collecting sap from the trees in the early spring of 1836, when Eliza came running out to him to tell him a man with a whole bunch of horses was in the yard.

"There is?" John was surprised, "They don't usually come around this early in the year."

"He said it is unusual, but he came across a desperate situation. He said his name is Walt," eight year old Eliza informed John.

"Alright, let's go in. Do you want to ride Tony?"

"Yeah, can I.?"

"Sure. I'm going to ride Jerry. I am going to leave them coupled together."

*   *   *

Walt was walking around a group of horses that were skin and bones, when John and Eliza entered the yard. The new horses were tied head to tail, and standing with their heads down in a dejected manner. They were a mix of breeds, from Shires to Percherons and everything in between.

"They're so thin you can't tell anything about them." Walt informed John. "The man who owned them got hailed out a hunert percent last summer and run out of feed during the winter, even though he was rationin' it out all winter. I felt they deserved a chance, and right away thought of you."

John was looking at their teeth, then feeling down their legs and lifting their feet.

"The man had a hunert and eighty five acres at one time, but lost it all but twenty acres through a loan he wasn't able to pay off," Walt continued. "He kept two horses. He figured they would be enough to work twenty acres with."

"They would have to be in better shape than these," John prophesied. "Did you give him enough money to feed them?"

"Yeah, but it will take all summer fer them tu get in shape tu do it."

John had been examining them for lice as he went along.

"Well," he said when he had finished looking them over, "there are seven mares and five geldings. They are lousy, and likely full of parasites. It is going to take a week of treatment and care before they will be in a suitable condition to turn out in my pasture. They are all eight years or older, so their age is against them on top of all their other troubles."

"Will yu give me ten dollars each for them?" Walt started to deal.

"Not in this lifetime, Walt. You wouldn't pay half of that for them yourself. How many of them do you guarantee will still be alive in the morning, after the stressful trip they have just finished?"

"Well how about eight dollars each?" Walt ignored John's question.

"How about one dollar each, Walt?"

"The halters they're wearin' are worth more'n that."

"I didn't think so," John countered.

"How about five dollars each?" Walt continued.

"Walt if you will stay this afternoon and help me wash them all good with disinfectant, I will give you five dollars. If you don't stay and help I will give you one dollar each and no more." The positive tone of John's voice told Walt that was his bottom line offer.

"Alright John, I will stay and help wash them. We will do my team too, won't we?"

"Yeah, you can do your team, too, after we are finished doing these." John began untying some of the horses.

"If you want to stay over night you can sleep in the barn loft, and tomorrow we will put up a fence around the buggy shed area out to the road. I could use some help doing that. It would only take the two of us a couple of hours to set it up."

"That sounds like a fair deal. I'll do it," Walt conceded, knowing staying would also include some good meals.

"I think I will bring the rack out of the shed and put some sheaves on it," thoughtfully John scratched his head, then replaced his cap before heading for his team. "If I put it back in the shed, and we tie them around it until we get the fence up, that will give them shelter from the weather. I don't want to have them in my corral or pasture before we get them cleaned up some."

*   *   *

When John went out the next morning to check on the skinny horses, he found one of the geldings had died. Calling his team in woke Walt up.

"One of the geldings has died. You can take some more oat sheaves to the rest of those horses," he told Walt, "While I dig a hole out back of the barn to drop him in. I will bring the team to get him out of the way of the others."

"Y'u still gonna pay me f'r him? He was still alive when we made the deal."

"Yes Walt. I'll pay you for him, as long as you keep on helping me finish this job you brought on me with these horses."

*   *   *

Later in the spring Jane gave birth to another boy to the delight of both parents.

"Look how much help you will be getting with your farm work John," she told her beaming husband. "I would like to name him Micheal, I would. He is such a sturdy little angel. He will grow into a strong powerful man, just like his father, he will."

"He has beautiful dark hair, just like his mother," John countered as he cradled the baby in his hands, swinging him gently back and forth. "I think Micheal is a fine name for him."

"You are getting a pretty good family here," Dr. Black noted as he was getting ready to leave. "Good bye, Jane. We will see you soon. Take care of yourself now," he cautioned her.

"I'll see that she does." John promised the Doctor. "Eliza, Johnny and Freddy are all able to help a lot already, so Jane doesn't have to do as many things for herself when I am in the field."

*   *   *

Summer of 1837 brought a bloom out on the lot of skinny horses he had bought last year. They had gained weight rapidly after the treatments he and Walt had done to them. Now he was able to see where the quality was.

With seven year old Johnny accompanying him while he worked around the yard, he no longer was alone. Talking to Johnny as he worked, he paired two bay mares that both looked like they had some Shire in them, and another pair of mares that were roans with heavy feathering. He also paired two of the geldings that seemed to lean toward Percheron breeding, and two geldings that were chunky roans with heavy feathering. Three oddball mares were one sorrel, one bay, and one black, being more clean legged with less feathering, they were more attractive. John decided to keep them as he liked their conformation and color, and breed them to Bud. The others he and Johnny took to Kingston market at the rate of one team a week, and because they were in top condition, they sold easily for good prices.

*   *   *

Walt made a later than usual trip with horses to sell. He had six horses trailing, and a stranger riding with him. John was busy getting his binder ready to take to the field. The crop was ready to harvest, and was looking good. He was anxious to get the cutting started.

"That's quite a string of horses you got there, Walt," John greeted him. "Did you buy somebody out dry?" Johnny and five year old Freddy were both with John today, and were looking the horses over with their father.

"These just arrived on a boat to Kingston from down south. This is the fella who brought them up. John I'd like you to meet Henry McBain." The men shook hands. "Henry wants me to show him where he can sell them," Walt explained.

"My father buys horses." Freddy piped up.

"Quiet Fred." Johnny put his hand over Freddy's mouth. "Let father do the talking if you don't want to go behind the barn for a spankin'."

"Well, tell me what you got here, Henry." John looked at his sons, then wiped a grin off his face. He was already looking at their teeth and examining their legs. "They look like a bunch of riding horses, or maybe carriage horses."

"They are purebred Morgans," Henry began. "They are among the toughest, hardiest working, strongest pulling, riding horses you could find."

"You mean they are horses who can do everything, except be race horses?" Disbelief was tingeing John's voice.

"The little stallion who is the foundation of the breed, ran a match race against a conditioned Thoroughbred, and beat it in a half mile race," Henry continued. "They are such an amazing breed of horses, they are in high demand in America. The foundation sire stamps his progeny with his characteristics and abilities. You can see it in these six horses."

"Why, then, did you have to go to the expense of shipping them up here to Canada?" John asked suspiciously. "Were you not able to get sale for them in America?"

"I could have, but I thought I would like to see them spread around," Henry responded, "I wanted to see Canada, besides everything else."

"I want to see you ride the ones I may be interested in," John told him. He then pointed out two mares. Henry untied one of them, and with only the halter shank in his hand, jumped on the mares back and rode her around the yard, neck reining one way, and straight steering the other. He then brought her back to the buggy. Dropping off her back, he handed the shank to Johnny, while he took the other mare and did the same thing, this time handing the shank to Freddy.

"They're pacers," John remarked. "First time I have seen pacers."

"They have been accepted into the Morgan registry, but they are descending from the Narragansett Pacers, and are second generation direct male line descendants of the Justin Morgan horse. It gives them a gait that is easy to ride, and fast on the road," Henry finished.

"What are you asking for them?" John asked, realizing he had not seen this quality of horse before. *They are even better than Grace and Bud. They are even better than the offspring of Grace and Bud,* he mused to himself. Watching the way they responded to Johnny and Freddy, who were leading them around, John was impressed with their disposition.

"Five hundred dollars for the team you picked out," Henry quoted. "They may be with foal. There was a long yearling Morgan colt running with them when I got them. The papers will also include a certificate of breeding in case they are."

"They are only two year olds. Aren't they too young to be raising foals?" John queried.

"Well, yes, hopefully they didn't catch," Henry agreed, "I just got the breeding certificate in case they did. You never know."

Walt was watching proceedings with a knowing grin on his face.

"I'll take them. John told Henry pulling his wallet out of his pocket. Walt's mouth fell open and the grin was gone. He got out of the buggy and began looking the two mares over more carefully.

When the deal was finished, Henry asked John if he knew of anybody else who would be in the market for a horse or two.

"The rest that are left are all geldings. They'll make great driving horses," he said, but John was already aware of that.

"Jacob Innesfree might be interested in a driver. You could also talk to his father Mac," John informed the two men. Thanking him for the sale, and further information, the two men left. John turned around to get the horses in time to see the two boys had managed to get on their backs, and were riding them around the yard as Henry had done.

* * *

Jane was expecting another baby this year of 1838 – her sixth child. So was Jacob Innesfree's wife, Maryann. This would be their fourth.

John's two Morgan mares both were obviously with foal. The two boys had taken possession of them, and spent many hours riding them around. John insisted they use bridles on them, which they did most of the time. John also had eight mares besides, who dropped foals in June and July. The Morgans dropped their foals in August, a filly and a colt.

* * *

"This baby is different John," Jane said one evening as they were going to bed.

"In what way?" John asked

"The kicking. It usually happens up here, but this one has movement mostly down here, she pointed to mid way down her stomach and to the left side. "There are no sharp kicks, just big lumps moving," she explained.

John got a concerned expression on his face, and looked at her for several seconds.

"Jane, I think you should go into town and talk to Dr. Black. Tell him everything you have just told me. See what he has to say. I'll go over to Innesfree's first thing in the morning, to ask Hazel if she can come to stay with the youngsters. If she can't, I will stay with them while you go. You must be getting close to your time of having it."

"Not for a couple of months yet, as far as I can figure out."

Holding Jane in his arms as they were talking, he now brushed her hair back in caressing strokes.

"Let's put the problem in God's hands, and get some sleep. Heavenly Father, please care for our baby and help us to bring him into Your world alive, that he may be able to do Your work on this earth. Please put your hand on Jane and bring her through this forth coming trial, so that she may raise our babies as You want them to be. In the name of our most Holy, Jesus

Christ. Amen."

"Thank You Heavenly Father. Thank you John. I think your plan is right. We will put it into the Father's hands." Jane turned over and settled down.

✳   ✳   ✳

John was up before the sun to check his animals and make sure they had enough feed and water for the day. Everything seemed to be fine, so he got Bud in the barn, then milked the cows before he went to the house for his own breakfast. Jane was still sleeping, but Eliza was up and preparing breakfast for everyone.

"Good morning sweetheart. How's my littlest house keeper making out?"

"Fine father. The boys are dressing and will soon be out here," she replied.

"Mother is not feeling well this morning, so I am going to see if Hazel Innesfree can come and stay with you children while I take mother in to see the doctor. I will be leaving as soon as I eat."

John jr. and Micheal came into the kitchen, followed by Janie, and then Jane. John was eating a bowl of cracked wheat porridge with milk, accompanied with a couple of slices of buttered bread.

"Jane, could you have the bible reading with the children, while I get on the road?"

"Yes, of course, dear," she agreed as she reached for the bible in the cupboard. John left as she started the reading.

✳   ✳   ✳

John hooked Bud to the carriage and went to Innesfrees.

"Of course I'll come," Hazel declared. "Harriet dear, thee take over and make the butter and the meals. I don't know when I'll be back as I will stay there at Thomas' as long as I'm needed. Thou're quite capable of running things for me while I'm gone. Now, there's a good girl. Thee young'uns remember thee are under the watchful eye of our Heavenly Father, and He expects thee to be obedient to thy superiors, RIGHT?"

"Right momma," they chorused.

Hazel went to her bedroom, and a few minutes later came out with a carpetbag stuffed.

"Alright John, give me a ride in thy fancy buggy," she tittered as she got into the carriage. She waved and threw kisses to the children as they left.

Bud took them home in a hurry, where they stopped at the house. John tied the lines to the buggy post, then went in the house with Hazel.

"Hello everyone," Hazel called. "Jane tell me what you want done and I will do it for you."

"Thank you so much, Hazel," Jane said as she was putting on her coat. "Eliza knows everything I want done. You and her can work things out, or she can help you." Jane hugged each of the children and kissed the girls and the small boys, then scuffling the heads of the two older boys she left with John.

✳   ✳   ✳

Dr. Black listened to Jane's description of her suspicions, then instructed her to lay on his medical table and bare her stomach.

"Dr. Black, it is not that I don't trust you, but I would rather have John in here with me while this is done."

"Good enough. John will you come in here please?" the doctor said as he held the door open for John. "Your wife wants you here by her side for this next examination."

John took Jane's hand while the doctor began examining the baby. After five minutes of feeling every part of it, he looked at Jane, then at John.

"This child is planning on arriving wrong end first," he remarked. "That is not good."

"Now what?" John asked.

"I think I can turn it, if it is not too big for the space it has to maneuver in." As he finished speaking, the doctor was pressing one hand on Jane's upper abdomen, pulling toward himself, and the other on her lower abdomen pushing away. Five minutes went by, then ten. Finally, when his hands had changed locations until they were in almost the reverse positions, Dr. Black stopped. "There," he said, "If you had waited much longer, I wouldn't have been able to have turned that baby. It is a big strong baby for having two months to go yet."

The two men went to the outer room while Jane rearranged her clothes.

"If Jane had gone into labor with the baby in the position it was in, there are strong possibilities she would not have survived, nor would the baby," Dr. Black told John. "Many women have died trying to deliver a backwards baby. It is very fortunate Jane noticed something was not normal."

Jane had not yet come out, so the doctor tapped on the door, and opening it started talking to her. "Are you alright, Jane?"

"Yes, Dr. Black. I just felt like I wanted to rest for a while. Is that alright?"

"Yes my dear, take all the time you want to. John and I will be right out here talking, if you should want anything."

Half an hour later, Jane came out, then she and John left. In the buggy Jane said, "John, can we go to the store for a while. I would like to talk with Maria."

"Why of course, Jane. I would enjoy a visit with Andy."

* * *

"Maria I have a feeling that something bad or terrible is going to happen. This feeling came to me last night when I thought something was wrong with my baby."

"Are you having sickness or pains? What gives you this idea, Jane?"

"No, I am not having sickness, other than the baby was not laying right. That was not making me sick. No. It is a premonition of something to come."

"You are not having any premature labor, or any other kinds of pains?"

"No. It is nothing I can put my finger on. You have eight children now, have you ever had any premonitions about trouble, with any of your births?" Jane could not get over the feeling of doom.

"Not really. Just the dread of the labor pains. Andy has always stayed with me during the deliveries. Without him by my side I might have had a whole different attitude. He said his father always stayed with his mother, and he feels it is his place to do the same. He says he wants to stay with me. Let's have a cup of tea. Maybe that will help settle you down." Maria rose to put the kettle on as she was speaking. Poking her head through the door to the store where the men were visiting, she asked, "Would the men-folk of this house care to join us women-folk in a cup of tea and crumpets?"

"John has always stayed with me during my deliveries, too." Jane brushed the wrinkle out of her skirt. "He said his father did that, and he feels it is the thing he wants to do. He feels a woman needs all the support a man can give her."

Jane helped Maria make sandwiches for the whole family, then put a bowl of cookies on the table, while Maria was making tea for the adults, and pouring milk for the youngsters.

"Andy, would you call the children in for dinner?" Maria spoke over her shoulder as she was getting plates to set around the table. Jane set the cups of milk on, and they were soon all eating.

After the dinner dishes were done, Jane said she was feeling better. She thought it was time to go home. "Thank you so much for being my sister when I needed one." she wrapped her arms around Maria and gave her a big hug.

"That's what sisters are for, Jane. I am yours any time, and very thankful to have you for mine."

*   *   *

Seven weeks later Jane woke up around three o'clock in the night, with a nagging strong pain. She turned over and massaged the painful area until it went away. By the time John had awakened to get up, she had been through several of them.

"John."

"Yes Jane. What can I do for you?"

"Tell Dr. Black this is the day. There is no big hurry. The pains are not severe yet, and are still a long way apart."

"Will I have time to do the chores before I leave?"

"Yes. Take all the milk to Smiths. They can use it. I will get the youngsters ready to go with you. The two girls and Micheal are to stay with Maria. The two older boys are to go to Innesfrees. Hazel said she would be glad to look after all of them, but I think the baby will be better with Maria. The two girls can help Maria look after him, as well as her own family."

*   *   *

John had the chores done, the children delivered, and was back home by ten o'clock. He and Bud were both sweating profusely.

"How are things going with you, sweetheart?" he asked Jane. She was busy sweeping the floor.

"Alright so far, I am." she responded, "I just thought this floor was too dirty to have company come in to."

John stoked the fire, then started pumping water to fill the reservoir at the back of the stove, then the copper boiler which he put on the front. When he had the fire under control, he went out and brought in a couple of arms full of wood, to fill the wood box.

Jane was down on her hands and knees, scrubbing the wooden floor of the kitchen.

"How are you feeling, Jane?" concern showed in his voice, although he had been through these exercises before, and knew they were just her way of passing time. He knew no harm was being done.

"I'm fine. I'm just finished this part, and will start the living room as soon as I change the water in my bucket."

"I think the living room is clean enough to eat off of. Didn't you scrub it day before yesterday?"

"Well, yes, I did."

"Well how about you having a nice warm bath and putting on some clean clothes.?

"Yes, I would like that."

"I'll pour the water for you, while you are getting ready for it."

"Alright. I'll be there in a minute." she rose to her feet and left to put the bucket away outside.

John was getting her bath ready when she came back in. Going to their bedroom, she prepared herself, by tying her hair up on the top of her head, then wrapping a towel around herself, she went to the bathroom. John went in with her, to make sure she didn't slip and fall while getting in the tub.

"Just stay there and relax as long as you want to Jane. I'm sure the soaking in the water will be good for you." He went out and closed the door. Going to the cupboards he got some bread, and cheese for his dinner. He knew it would be just as well for Jane not to eat until she felt hungry, which usually would be after the baby would be delivered.

It was almost two in the afternoon when there was a loud groan from the bathroom.

"Is it time for you to get out of the water Jane?" he asked on entering the bathroom.

"Yes. That was no pre-runner. I think that was the first of the delivery contractions. I think I would be better to go to bed now."

Dr. Black drove into the yard about three in the afternoon, and John went out to help him put the team in the barn.

"Labor has started earnestly, now. Jane has spent a couple of hours resting in the bathtub of water, but is now in bed - willingly."

"Good for you John. The less stress the mothers have to contend with, the easier the birth will be." Dr. Black turned and headed for the house, leaving John to finish looking after the horses.

Jane was in the midst of another contraction when the doctor entered the house. He stuck his head into the bedroom doorway, "Hello Jane. Are you about ready to deliver that precious bundle of joy?"

"Getting close doctor, I am," she said, trying to be cheerful.

"I will wash up, then I will be right with you. Just hold everything until I come back." he added as he left for the bathroom.

John came in after the doctor had gone back to the bedroom. Going to the bathroom, he also washed up. Picking up an armful of towels he headed for the bedroom. Jane was having another contraction that the doctor was monitoring very closely.

It was about five o'clock when the baby put in an appearance. The head was delivered, then the baby seemed to be stalled, and it was thirty minutes before the birth was completed. The placenta came with the baby. Doctor Black picked up the baby and found the umbilical cord was wrapped around the left leg. Without a word Dr. Black unwound it, then cut and tied it off, completing the delivery.

"I was concerned that something like that might happen," he told John as he was washing up in the bathroom. "Turning a baby before birth can cause that kind of problem, but if I am prepared for it I can usually save the baby. Sometimes the cord gets wrapped around the neck, and I have lost a couple from that. If the baby is not turned the mother may die from not being able to deliver. Then you lose them both, so it is a gamble to be taken."

"Praise God, you were able to save them both for me, and the rest of our family." John spoke from the bottom of his heart, and Dr. Black knew it. Going back in to see how Jane was, the doctor asked her what the name for this boy was going to be.

"We have discussed the name for a boy at great lengths and have decided to call him Hosea," Jane announced.

John was gathering up the soiled towels and bedding, and put them in the laundry tub. "Yes," he said, "Hosea," as he was taking the tub to the kitchen where he had the boiler full of warm water to cover them with. "I am going to get Hazel Innesfree and the boys tomorrow. She said to leave the washing to soak until she gets here, and she will wash it up. She is such a great neighbor to have," John spoke softly.

"Yes." Dr. Black said. "She is great. Now Jane, you stay in bed until I come out tomorrow morning. I want to be here when you get up. I want to make sure everything is going right. That is all I can do now. John if I may have my horses, please." The two men left the house. Jane cuddled her baby close, and closed her eyes.

CHAPTER 25

BLESSED TRAVELING SALESMAN!

An abundance of snow fell during the winter, requiring a great deal of shoveling pathways, and water holes. The cold weather, which preceded it put a heavy cover of ice on the lake, so that when the neighborhood men had their ice harvesting bee in December, the blocks were thick and quickly filled the sleighs to the top. Many of the men had an ice cistern in their root cellar, as John had, but many of them piled their ice blocks on the north side of buildings to prevent the sun from melting them. The heavy snowfall helped keep the sun off of them longer.

"Come along boys," John would say to John jr. and Freddy, "Let's go and get some snow shoveled so we can get our chores done. Eliza, there is a nice pile of snow just outside the house door that you and Janie can carry in to fill the ice barrel with. That will help clear out the doorway as well as making wonderful soft water to do the washing with, or bathing and washing your beautiful hair."

By the spring of 1839, everyone including John and Jane, were glad to see the snow melting and running off to the lake. When the foals and calves started arriving, the boys were out watching for cows or mares that appeared like they were in labor. They were getting good at it, and would inform John when there was one to watch.

John jr. and Freddy also had the two year olds broke to ride and drive without a vehicle, by the time spring came.

"Father can we hook Bess and Archie to the light bob-sleigh today to drive them around?" they asked John while there was still snow on the ground.

"You can if you will take me for a ride with you. I don't really want the sleigh wrapped around a tree somewhere."

"That won't happen, father. They are well broke."

"Jane is there anything you want from town?" John asked when he entered the house.

"Not today," Jane replied, "but you can take the rest of us over to visit with Maryann this afternoon."

"Alright we can do that. This morning we are going into Battersea. We should be back by noon."

* * *

Every day, as long as there was enough snow, the three of them took a team of two year olds for a drive – one pair in the morning and another pair in the afternoon – until they had all been driven on the sleigh at least twice, by the time the snow was gone. The boys had made their father proud of how well they had trained the crop of two year olds.

Walt Isaacs drove into the yard on his semi-annual visit, and saw the boys driving a pair of two year olds, doing odd jobs around the yard.

"Say, that's quite a pair of horsemen you have there. When did you let them take over the work with those colts?" Walt was watching the boys, admiringly.

"You're asking the wrong question, Walt. They haven't let me take over the driving of them yet."

"Those boys aren't very old yet, are they?"

"John jr. will be nine this year, and Freddy is two years younger."

"Well, I'll be.....Are yu in the market f'r more horses? I got some dandy work horses here."

The conversation continued until it was dinner time, and John must ask him in. After dinner, Walt left without making a sale.

* * *

The winter following had much less snow. The boys worked with two year olds again, and got all ten of them driving on the light bob-sleigh by spring. They were using the two original Morgan mares to work the youngsters with, and were very proud of their Morgans.

It was now 1840, Eliza was twelve, John jr. was ten, Freddy was eight, Jane turned six, Micheal had his fourth birthday, and the baby Hosea was two, six children in all.

It was a glorious spring with warm sunshine that made the garden spring up rapidly. Jacob Innesfree's wife was expecting in June, and was having problems with being sick, and having to take to her bed often. Jane was not expecting this year, and spent a great deal of time working in the garden, and caring for her family.

Jacob drove into the yard one day, and went to the house.

"Would you be able to spare Eliza to come and help Maryann," he asked, "until after the baby is born and she is able to look after things herself?"

"Why surely," Jane responded, "I would be happy to spare her to help as long as she is needed there. Eliza is quite capable of making good meals, and caring for the other youngsters, she is. She will be a big help for Maryann. I pray that Maryann and the forthcoming baby will be healthy, Jacob, I do."

Eliza came out of the girl's bedroom with the carpet bag packed full. Jane hugged her then kissed her. "Do your best Eliza. Maryann needs help, not another child to look after."

"I will mother, I promise I will work hard for her." Eliza gave her mother a hug, then went out and got into Jacob's buggy. Jane watched them leave. *They grow up so fast.* She mused to herself.

Three days after Eliza's departure, Janey pestered her mother all morning to let her go and help Eliza at Jacob's place. Wanting to do more to help Maryann, Jane finally gave in, on the promise from Janey that she would help with the work and not play around. While Janey went to pack, Jane went to the door and called the two boys, who were driving their Morgan mares on the democrat.

"Will you two take Janey over to Jacob's place? She wants to go and help over there, and I think it will be a good idea for a few days," she told the boys.

"Sure. We can do that," Freddy replied with an attitude of adult authority.

Janey came out and got into the democrat, and Jane watched them drive out to the yard entrance. As they turned to go down the road to the north, a traveling salesman with two horses behind his buggy turned into the yard. John came out of the barn and met him when the he was half way across the yard.

"My name's Frank McGraw." he said as he spat on the ground. "How are you today?" he coughed a couple of times.

"I'm fine...fine. My name is John Thomas. What can I do for you?"

"Well, I wuz won'erin' if yu'd be interested in buying these two fine specimens of Clydesdale yearlin's? Look at the dandy feet n' legs they have under them. They are going to grow into a fine matched pair of upstandin' horses." he coughed and spat on the ground.

John moved around to give the colts a close examination. "When was the last time they had anything to eat?" John asked. "It's hard to see much good in them when they are so gaunted up."

"Well, it's bin a while since they've bin fed. I'm trying t' git into Battersea to meet a friend there."

"That's still six miles away. Maybe you should put them in the corral and I'll feed them. They can eat while we go to the house for dinner. Jane has it ready."

John had an uncomfortable feeling about this man, but he was not about to turn him away hungry. They put the driving horse in the barn and the two colts in the corral. John threw a couple of sheaves in for the colts while Frank took one in for his driving horse.

As they were going to the house, the boys returned and John helped them unhitch their horses, then he took Frank to the house.

"This is Frank McGraw, Jane. Could you put another place on the table for him."

"Why surely." Jane said as she went to the cupboard for the necessary dishes.

The two men went to the bathroom to wash up. As they were sitting down to the table the boys came in. They waited while the boys cleaned up and sat down to the table, then John asked a blessing on the food.

"Where's Janey?" John asked.

"We took her over to Jacob's to help Eliza." John jr. proudly responded.

During the meal, Frank coughed a couple of times. John got him outside as soon as they were finished eating. They went to the corral and looked at the two sad specimens of horseflesh.

John figured most of their problem was starvation. He offered Frank twenty five dollars for the pair. Frank accepted without quibbling, so they got the buggy horse out and hooked to the buggy. Frank coughed again. John noticed he also staggered a couple of times. Frank reached under the buggy seat and pulled out a bottle, tipped it to his mouth and took a couple of swallows. He then got into the buggy with difficulty and drove out of the yard. A feeling of relief swept over John as he watched Frank leave.

* * *

It was just after dinner a little more than a week later, John was preparing to leave for Jacobs to see how things were doing over there. Janie had not yet returned, and John and Jane were concerned that she might be more nuisance than help. John planned on bringing her home.

He opened the door in response to a knock and saw Dr. Black standing there.

"Hello Dr. Black. What brings you here? We're not expecting another baby yet, and everyone is in good health, -- well except for a cold the three oldest boys have picked up. Nothing to worry about, I don't think."

Dr. Black gestured for John to come out, then when the door was closed, he asked, "Did you have a traveling horse salesman stop here about a week ago?"

"Why yes. I bought a pair of colts from him. He had come just at noon, so we put his horse in the barn and the colts in the corral, to feed them. I took him into the house and he had dinner with us...Why?" John looked at Dr. Black in wonderment.

"Did he appear to be sick, or have any health problems that you noticed?" Dr. Black asked without answering John's question.

John lost his smile and stroked his beard, then replied, "He was doing quite a bit of coughing and spitting, and as we were hooking his horse, he staggered a bit. Then he pulled a bottle out from under the seat of the buggy and took a couple of swigs. I thought he was having a hangover and was working toward another." Looking up at the doctor, he continued, "That wasn't it,.... was it?" John was beginning to feel alarm rising in his chest.

"A day and a half after he arrived at my office, he died." Dr. Black was speaking softly as though that would lighten the blow. "All the symptoms I could see pointed to Diphtheria. I took some samples of his blood and saliva to Kingston to a man there who is studying things under a microscope. He is quite sure it is Diphtheria. The first symptoms seem to be a cold with a high fever. I am so terribly sorry for you and Jane, John."

Suddenly John was fully aware of the grave situation he and his family were in.

"Oh dear God! What have I done to my family?" Feeling the need to sit down he went to the bench at the side of the house. Placing his face in his hands he cried out, "Dr. Black, what can we do now?" desperation shaking his huge body.

"Well John, for starters, I am posting your place with "QUARANTINE" posters. No one is to leave or come in until we are absolutely sure it is all cleared up, and you have disinfected your whole house and all it's contents. Frank McGraw gave me the names of the people he has been in contact with since he took sick, and I am afraid there is going to be an epidemic of Diphtheria throughout the country."

"Was Jacob Innesfree on that list?" John was almost afraid to ask.

"No."

"Oh thank God. Could you go by their place and ask them to keep Eliza and Janie until we are out of Quarantine? They are over there helping Maryann until she is able to take care of things herself."

"Yeah I'll do that. I was going over there anyway to check on Maryann's progress. She should be delivering any day, now."

"I'll be back again in a few days to see how things are going, but I won't come into your house."

As he was untying his horse and getting into the buggy, John asked,

"What can we do when they take sick?"

Dr. Black covered his eyes with his free hand, then looking at John, said, "The only thing I can tell you, is to keep the fever down as low as possible at all times. Put wet, cold compresses on their heads. Put their hands and feet in cool water- not cold- to bring the fever down. Hang a wet blanket on their doorway to try to prevent the ones who are not sick, from catching the disease. I don't know what else to tell you. Maybe you will be able to think of something yourselves. I don't know. I don't know." he sounded depressed. Clapping his horse with the lines he left. John watched him post the sign at the gateway, then turn around and drive through the yard and to the north to Jacob Innesfree's place, disappearing behind the trees. John in shock, turned toward the house. With a heavy heart he opened the door and went in.

"Jane, where are the boys?" he asked.

"They are in bed. That cold is really knocking them off of their feet. Hosea is outside playing over by the swings." Jane stopped talking and took a deep look at John. "What was Dr. Black wanting, John?"

"Come outside with me, Jane. I have something to tell you," he put his arm around her as they headed for the door. Jane looked back at the room the three boys were in, then went out with John. They sat down on the door-step. John held·her while he told her all that Dr. Black had told him. Jane covered her ears and jumped up, screaming,

"Stop! Stop! I can't take any more."

John got up and put his arms around her.

"Jane, listen to me. We've got to keep cool heads, and fight this thing with everything we can. You must help me…. Please help me Jane."

She was sobbing hysterically. John held her and waited. He could think of nothing more to say, —until he remembered the girls. "Frank McGraw was not over to Jacob Innesfree's place. Dr. Black is going by their place to check on Maryann and to tell them of our plight. He is going to ask them to keep the two girls until we are cleared of the quarantine, and it is safe for them to come home."

"Thank God." Jane raised her face to John's. "I wouldn't want them brought home into this." She straightened up, pulled her dress straight, and they both went back into the house. Jane sat at the end of the table deep in thought. Finally, raising her eyes and straightening her shoulders, she turned to John, saying with conviction, "John, we are going to fight this with everything we can think of. First I want you to go to the root cellar and bring in garlic bulbs and onions. Is there still a chicken out there?"

"I think there are two." John replied.

"Good. Bring one of them in," Jane instructed. "I am going to put a large kettle on to boil to create steam, and I will cook the chicken at the same time. I will also make some mustard plasters for them." she was on her feet and rushing to follow her own plans.

Remembering what Dr. Black had suggested, John told Jane, then went to the root cellar. His heart was feeling a little lighter with the hope that Jane had generated. When he returned to the house, he began peeling onions.

"Chew garlic," Jane instructed, "and don't stop until this is all over. We will try to get the boys to chew garlic, too, if we can. We will have to tell them what the sickness is so they will understand why this is so necessary."

Jane put mustard plasters on the boy's chests for ten minutes, then turned them over and put them on their backs for another ten minutes.

John jr. was very flushed and very legarthic. Cold compresses were on their heads and John kept wringing them out of cold water, changing the applications as soon as they began to lose their coolness. Jane got a pan of cool water and immersed John jr.'s feet in it, then another pan of cool water that John held John jr.'s hands in. Half an hour later they could see evidence of the temperature being lowered. John jr. looked at his parents in a much more relaxed way.

Jane and John worked all night on the boys, keeping cold compresses on their heads, and cooling their feet and hands when the temperatures seemed to be getting too high. Jane put Hosea to bed in the bed she and John used, and he fell asleep almost as soon as Jane had finished singing to him.

In the morning as the sun was rising, John jr. looked at his parents and smiled, then closing his eyes, he stopped breathing.

Jane and John went into the kitchen. Jane fell into John's arms, sobbing hysterically. John held her tightly for several minutes. John spoke in a husky voice, "We can't keep him here. We must commit him to burial. I am going to take him out and lay him on the bench outside of the door, while I go out to prepare a place for him." with aching heart he released Jane. Going to the bedroom, he picked up the limp body of his son. Carrying him out of the house with struggling breath to keep back the sobs of his breaking heart, he laid the body on the bench, then left for the garden.

As Jane was going back to the sick room, she heard Hosea coming out of the bedroom. She swept him up in her arms, and chatting with him, dressed him and fed him his breakfast. Checking on the boys, she changed the cold packs, then went back to Hosea, who had finished his breakfast. Jane took him outside where they sat on the doorstep for a while. When Hosea ran off to the swings, Jane went back to the boy's room and changed the cold packs.

Half an hour later John came back. He stood looking at the body which was now cleaned up and dressed in clean overalls and shirt, along with clean socks and his boots that he was so proud of. Jane came out of the house wiping tears from her face, she wordlessly went to John jr's head and kissed him on the forehead.

"I have this sheet to wrap him in. It will make him easier to carry." she said as she shook the sheet open to help John wrap the body. Tenderly picking John jr. up, he carried him out in the direction of the garden. With tears flowing down her face, Jane watched to make sure Hosea didn't follow John to the garden.

Jane fed the boys small amounts of the chicken and onion soup, to moisten their mouths, and to give them a little nourishment for strength to fight off the disease.

Freddy was not responding well, so Jane concentrated on him harder – cooling his hands and feet. The boys were perspiring so much their bedding was damp. When John came in he helped change the bedding. John then took charge of caring for the boys while Jane set up the laundry tub outside, and scrubbed the bedding. Hanging it on the lines, she returned by noon to help John. Hosea came in with her.

"Is there anything you need help with, John?" Jane asked.

"No everything is about the same," John replied.

"Alright then, I am going to feed Hosea out by the swings." she whispered as she guided Hosea to the kitchen.

"Good. You go ahead," John replied.

Taking a large bowl of soup and a couple of slices of bread, Jane took Hosea by the hand and they went out to the swings. She and Hosea ate together, then played for a while. When Hosea became engrossed in swinging, Jane went back into the house.

Looking in on the boys, she looked at John. He just looked at Freddy and shook his head. They both began immersing his feet and hands in cool water, until his body temperature came down again.

Just before supper time, Freddy lapsed into unconsciousness, and in spite of everything Jane and John could do, he died as the sun was sinking behind the trees to the west.

John laid Freddy's body on the bench before going out to dig a grave for him, while Jane went out to get Hosea to put him to bed. He was not by the swings. Search as much as she could, Jane could not find him.

"John," she called in the darkness toward the garden.

"Hello."

"I can't find Hosea anywhere. I have to go back and tend to Micheal. I can't leave him any longer."

"Alright. I will look for Hosea right now."

An hour later John came in. "I can't find Hosea anywhere. I can't see to bury Freddy now. I didn't even have the hole finished. I will have to do those things in the morning, including milking the cows and feeding the horses. Jane you go to bed for a couple of hours, and I will care for Micheal, then you can get up and care for him while I get a couple of hours sleep. Don't worry about Hosea. He has likely crawled into some sheltered place and is sleeping.

"Poor wee tykie. Poor wee tykie. Father in Heaven, please take care of my baby." Jane spoke softly as she was changing Micheal's cold compresses before going to bed.

*   *   *

As soon as there was enough daylight in the morning, John went to the grave sight and finished digging it. At the same time, Jane was washing Freddy and dressing him in clean overalls, shirt, socks and boots that were also his pride and joy. She was talking and singing to him the whole time.

John arrived as she was finished, and the two of them wrapped another sheet around his body. As gently and tenderly as he had lain John jr., John laid Freddy to rest. When the burial was completed, he set out to look for Hosea, searching beyond the yard, while at the same time doing some of the chores.

Taking Bud down to the lake for his morning drink, Bud began snorting and not wanting to go to the water's edge. John tied him to a tree and went to see what was bothering him. When he got to the water's edge his heart almost stopped and John cried out with a breaking voice at the sight of Hosea floating face down ten feet out in the water.

"Oh dear Father, please don't take all of our sons. Please Father have mercy on us." Unable to stifle the sobs, John waded out and pulled the body of his baby son up onto the shore. He realized he had been dead for many hours. With tears streaming down his face and beard, he picked up the tiny form and carried him past the snorting Bud, up toward the house. He laid him on the bench outside the door, and went in to tell Jane...*Jane!...How can I tell Jane! This is our baby, Father! We can't lose him, too!* Please have mercy on us sinners! He brushed his sleeve across his eyes and face then stepped into the house. Jane was just coming out of Micheal's bedroom. John looked at her and stifled another sob. Jane looked at John,

"You're as wet as though you have been in the lake." she stated. "What happened?"

"I found Hosea." his voice was bereft of life itself. "He was in the lake and had been there for many hours – all night I'd say. He's outside on the bench," John waited for the hysterical scream that he knew would come as Jane rushed past him to see her baby. With breaking heart John followed her. When she had finished hugging, kissing and rocking the wet lifeless form, and was ready to lay him down, John took her into his arms. They both wept on each other.

Half an hour later, Jane said, "I've got to look after Micheal. Don't take Hosea away just yet." she let go of John and entered the house.

"I'll go and dig a grave for him," John said as he turned toward the garden.

✳   ✳   ✳

When John came back for the baby, he opened the door,
"Is it alright to take Hosea, now?"
"Yes. He is ready to go home now."
When John went to pick Hosea up, he saw the baby had his hands and face washed and dried, and was wearing clean clothes. Jane came to the door to say good bye to him. "I gave him a sponge bath before putting on the clean clothes." she spoke simply and matter of factly. "I have a warm blanket to wrap him in." she reached inside the door as she spoke, bringing out the blanket.

They worked together to get the blanket wrapped around the tiny body to suit Jane's desires. Then John picked up his son's little body to walk to the garden. Jane kissed the lifeless form again, then caressing his hair, she turned, sobbing and went into the house. John took Hosea to his resting place by the other two boys.

✳   ✳   ✳

When John entered the house, Jane had a cup of hot ginger tea waiting for him on the table. She came out of the bedroom, her face was stony blank as she faced John.

"Micheal is losing ground, John." Dropping to her knees, her face now torn with agony, she cried,
"Please God, have mercy!"
John gently pulled her to her feet and held her close while they both suffered in silence.

"Have a cup of ginger tea with me, and chew garlic, Jane. I don't want you to take the Diphtheria, too. I am trying hard to ward it off. Please do the same. You are so precious to me. I don't want to lose you, too."
Jane looked deep into John's eyes.
"You're right." she said, "I wouldn't want to live without you by my side. You have been so wonderful through all of our years together. I want it to last

a long, long time, yet."

Sitting down to the table, she joined John in a cup of hot ginger tea.

* * *

That night Jane and John stayed in Micheal's room, as they had been doing since the boys started being sick, taking turns sleeping in the rocking chair, changing the cold compresses on his head. Toward morning Micheal started having trouble breathing, and died as nighttime darkness was giving way to a beautiful sky that announced the arrival of the sun.

When Micheal was no longer breathing, without a word, John got up and took the body out to the bench, then left for the garden. An hour later he returned and picked up Micheal's little four year old body. He took hold of the blanket Jane was holding to wrap the body in, and the two of them worked together to wrap the body as gently and perfectly as they had the others. Turning to Jane who was starting to enter the house, he said in a stifled voice,

"Come with me Jane."

Picking up a shawl she went with him to the foot of the garden where it met with the orchard. John laid the body lovingly in the grave, and straightening up he took Jane in his arms. Closing his eyes, he almost whispered into the hair on the top of her head,

"Thank you Father for giving us the pleasure of having these four boys in our lives." He stopped and swallowed hard a couple of times before continuing on in a cracking voice, "We don't understand why You need them more than we do at this time, but since we are not able to see into the future, as You do, we will trust You to do what is right for us," he stopped again and breathed deeply, holding Jane tightly, then swallowing again, he continued, louder now,

"We would dearly love to have some sons, but whatever You have in store for us, we thank You and Bless You for providing so abundantly for us. In the name of Jesus Christ, our dear Lord and Saviour. Amen."

John then released Jane, and picking up the shovel, filled in the fourth grave. When he had finished, he and Jane sat down on the trunk of a very large tree that had fallen nearby. John put his arms around Jane's shoulders and they sat there for a long while, tears streaming down Jane's face, John with an expression of total loss masking his broken heart; sobbing occasionally uncontrollably.

Finally John said with a husky voice,

"God will be good to us. We have each other, and we have been blessed with so many good friends, wonderful land, abundant crops, good quality livestock, and don't forget, God saved our daughters for us. We still have Eliza and Janie." Taking a deep breath, he continued, "We must now get the place cleaned up so we can bring the girls home."

Jane broke her silence at last. "Yes, we must get ready to bring the girls home."

John continued, "We will start tomorrow. Today we will rest and praise God for all the good things we have."

Together they went to the barn and caught up on the chores. When everything was taken care of, they went back down to the garden and sat on the tree trunk, until the evening sun was playing games in the tree tops. Rising they went, John to do the evening chores, and Jane to the house to prepare a hot nourishing meal for the two of them.

* * *

In the following two weeks Jane and John burned everything from the boy's room. The feather tick caused some problems as the feathers either wanted to fly away, or would make a clump that would turn to a black cinder on the outside and unburned feathers on the inside. They required constant working to break the clumps open and straw covering to prevent the feathers from scattering, but the task was finally accomplished.

Jane scrubbed all their own clothing and bedding, and hung them out on the line for a few days to let the sun disinfect them.

Next they both took pails of water with disinfectant in that John used to delouse the animals, making a strong solution, and using scrub brushes, they scrubbed the ceilings, walls and floors of the whole house, plus the cupboards and all the furniture that was left after the boy's room had been cleaned out.

When everything had been cleaned up to the best of their ability, Jane and John each had a bath with disinfectant in the bathwater. They then dressed in some of the freshly washed and disinfected clothes. Jane was going to wash what they were wearing, but John said, "I think we should burn these things. They are not worth taking a chance on." so onto the bonfire they went.

The following morning, John got a hot fire going in the stove, and also in the fireplace. He kept stoking them until there was a hot bed of coals in each place. He then sprinkled three handsful of sulphur in the fireplace, then a couple of handsful on the surface of the almost red hot stove. The burning sulphur made beautiful blue, green, yellow, red and some other colors of flames that John had never seen before. The odor was stifling so he went outside and closed the door as quickly as he could get there. It was mid-morning when this was completed. They did not go back into the house for several hours, giving the pungent fumes of the burning sulphur plenty of time to penetrate and disinfect every nook and cranny that may have been missed in the house.

While they were doing the chores and tidying up the yard, Dr. Black drove in.

"Hello John and Jane," he greeted them, "How are things progressing with you folks?"

"If you have the time, tie your horse up and sit down here with us, and we will tell you." John waved his hand toward the hitching rail.

* * *

By the time John and Jane had finished telling him their experiences, Dr. Black was as heart broken as they were, for he loved those children as though they were his own.

"You two have certainly had more than your share of hardships. I sincerely hope and pray that you are at the end of them. From what you have told me you have done to clean up, I feel quite sure you are clean and free from the disease. I am going to lift your quarantine."

"When do you think it will be safe to bring the girls home?" John asked, almost afraid of what the reply might be.

"Oh, once the quarantine is lifted there will be no danger of contagion. I couldn't afford to lift it if there was going to be the slightest danger. It is alright to bring them home any time now. There certainly have been a lot of deaths from the diphtheria. It is a very sad situation throughout the whole country. I am hoping it has run it's course, and will not affect anyone else. By the way, the horse and buggy belonging to Frank McGraw are at the livery stable, and are for sale to pay the bill against them."

"Waaaal, I don't know if I am interested in anything belonging to him. I got enough trouble from him just driving into my yard." John drawled his words as he scratched his bare head.

"Just thought I'd mention it. Well, I had best get going. I may have another caller waiting for me."

John went with him to his buggy and untied the horse for him.

"By the way," John asked, "What day is this?"

"Oh, I think this is Wednesday," the doctor said after rubbing his forehead.

"Thanks," John almost mumbled. He thought for a few seconds then, "If you go by Jacob Innesfree's place, would you tell them we will be over in a couple of days for the girls if they are free to leave."

"Sure will," Dr. Black lifted his lines, "I was going over there to see how they are getting along with the new baby and all. Well, so long, and all the best to you folks from here on in," he called as he was driving away.

"I guess it is about four or more hours since I put the sulphur on the fires," John said as he and Jane watched the doctor drive away. "I am going to open the door to let the fumes out. By the looks of the chimney, I would guess the fires are out, and the stove will be cold."

"I will have to wax it, so I will. It will be looking like some old thing from the junk yard if I don't." John was glad to hear Jane taking an interest in the things she was so proud of before. He opened the house door, and holding his breath, picked up the milk pails, and the two of them went to the barn. When the chores were finished, they went to the house where John started a fire in the stove, then went to the root cellar for something to cook for their supper. Jane got some clean bedding and made their bed, and then made the girl's bed. John brought in a loaf of bread, a large chunk of cheese and some potatoes, a bowl of butter and a jug of cream. From the garden he brought carrots, peas, a turnip and some green onions.

"These potatoes have some Irish blood flowing in their veins," he told Jane. "They are descendants of the ones you brought from Ireland with you."

"They should be much the better then," Jane said with a smile. John was glad to see her able to smile so soon. He took her in his arms and kissed her.

"Jane, you are my Bell of Ireland. You are such an amazing person. I love you like I have never loved you before." He brushed her hair back from her face and kissed her again.

"I love you John. You are the strongest person I have ever known. I am so thankful that God brought us together. If I don't get something ready to eat, we are both going to pass out from starvation."

* * *

Friday John and Jane went to Jacob Innesfree's. Jacob and Maryann met them at the door.

"Come in." Jacob invited.

"Not for another week or so Jacob, not when you have a new baby. We don't want to take any chances. Dr. Black says it's alright for the girls to come home, though. If Maryann is still needing them we can wait a while longer."

"We would love to see your baby and visit with you for a while," Jane smiled, "but we would feel more comfortable to wait for another week. Thank you so much for asking," she knew this was the right thing to do.

"Dr. Black told us what has happened at your place, and I can manage alright now," Maryann said as she put her arms around the shoulders of the two girls. "They surely are an efficient pair of girls. I will miss them. You girls be sure to come back whenever you can."

"We will," the girls both chorused.

"We told the girls that you had diphtheria at your place, but that is all we've said," Jacob told John while he was putting the carpet bag of clothing in the carriage.

"Thank you, Jacob," John said as he started the horses.

"No, no. It is us who are thanking you for letting the girls come over. They both have been a tremendous help for Maryann."

"Thank you. Thank you," Jane called as they drove out of the yard.

They had no sooner got on the road than Eliza asked, "Where is Johnny? I thought the boys would be coming to get us."

Thus started the heart breaking journey for home. By the time they had reached home the girls were somewhat consoled, but as soon as they got into the house, they both broke down again. The four of them all stood holding each other, the women folk all sobbing.

Jane slept with the girls that night. The next morning they all went down together, to visit the graves of the boys. They stood for several minutes in thought, tears running down their faces, and the occasional sobbing. John then said a prayer of thanks to God, and they slowly walked back to the house. He had a cup of coffee, then got up and went out to his shop.

For the next several days, John spent all his spare time in the shop. Jane wondered what he was doing, but left him to his privacy. She knew somehow, that what he was doing was helping him through his grief.

On Sunday they went to church. Everyone was offering sympathy to most of the rest of the congregation for the terrible losses they had suffered. Andy and Maria had lost three of their children, Freddy and two that were younger than Elizabeth.

"We kept the youngsters separated as much as possible, and Dr. Black thinks that is why we didn't lose more, or all of them. We fed them every kind of medicinal product we had on the shelves. He also thought that was part of the reason they didn't take it. My heart goes out to you my little brother." Andy put his arms around John's big shoulders. John embraced Andy tightly.

"Your loss is as great as mine, Andy. Freddy was just beginning to be a big help to you, as John jr. and our Freddy were to us. The loss of them makes such a big hole in the family. Even the younger ones make a terrible hole in the family. It is so hard to pick up the pieces to go on."

Jane and Maria came out on the steps to go home.

"John, we are going to Andy and Maria's place for lunch. Maria and I will walk. You can bring all the children and Andy." Jane and Maria then walked on past the team, toward the store.

The visit with Andy and Maria and family was like a ray of light in a dark tunnel. Everyone was lighter in spirits on their way home.

*   *   *

The summerfallow had lost it's importance, it would get done sometime. John spent most of his time in the shop doing what seemed to be more important. Saturday morning he emerged with some boards under his arm. Taking them to the house, he laid them out on the table.

"Jane and girls, look. I have made head boards for the boys. What do you think of them?"

"Oh, those are wonderful, John," Jane exclaimed. "They are just what those graves need. The boys will be so happy to be remembered this way."

"Come with me while I get them set in," John began picking up the boards, when Jane interrupted,

"John, why don't we invite Jacob and Maryann and family as well as Andy and Maria and family, and anyone else who would like to come, and do it tomorrow afternoon about five o'clock. Don't you think J.L. and Ann and their family would like to come?" Jane suggested, "Jacob could tell them tomorrow at their service, and we could tell our congregation tomorrow. There are many people who would like to be included, you know."

"That's a good idea. You are right, Jane. I'll go over to Jacob's now and tell them what we are planning."

Jane spent the rest of the day, baking a cake and cookies. She had a premonition there would be more people come than what John had in mind. On the way to church, she suggested to John that he should tell the minister to announce it from the pulpit after the service. Jane felt this was a very important occasion and other people would feel the same.

Reverend Samuels had a special service of comfort for all those who had lost family members during the epidemic. He prayed for strength for the remaining people to get their lives back together again, and carry on with Christ in their hearts.

After the last hymn was sung, he made John's announcement, and extended an invitation to those who wished to come out to the farm.

About four o'clock vehicles started arriving. Reverend Samuels and his wife and family all came as well as about thirty other folks from the Methodist church, then came about twenty five folks from the Quaker's meeting, including J.L. and family and Jacob and Mac Innesfree and their families, and also Mike McMurty and family.

All the adults examined the boards and complimented John on an excellent idea. Many men said they were going to do the same for their loved ones they lost.

Jane had a kettle of tea made, and also a kettle of coffee. Many of the women brought sandwiches because that was all they had time to make. About five thirty everyone followed John to the grave sights. He had many hands helping to erect the boards just the way he wanted them, then everyone with hats in hand stood silently while Reverend Samuels said a prayer. When he had finished, John said a prayer of thanks for the privilege of having the boys even for the short time they were here. He praised God for His wisdom, and prayed for goodness and mercy in the future.

He turned toward the house, and everyone followed him. Jane and Maria and Hazel served drinks, while the children served the sandwiches, followed by the cakes and cookies. It was getting dark when the last of them left.

CHAPTER 26

PICKING UP THE PIECES

John came into the house with a different expression on his face. He was ready to carry on, and it showed.

"Mac and Jacob Innesfree are both going to bring plows over tomorrow, to help get my summerfallow done. The crops will be ready to start cutting next week, and we should have the plowing finished by Friday with them helping. What wonderful neighbors God has put us among."

"The girls and I can do all the chores, John, except cleaning the barn out. We can do the milking, and feeding the horses when they are in the field. We can feed the calves and pigs, and chickens, and gather the eggs, can't we girls?" The girls nodded their heads in agreement.

"That sounds great. That will help out so much. I will be able to stay in the field an hour longer morning and again at night if you do that."

Mac Innesfree had a three furrow gang plow that he offered to loan to John. It required a seven horse tandem hitch (three in front and four behind) to pull it in the field.

"Do you have enough horses to pull it, John?" Mac inquired.

"Yes I have lots of horses. I am planning on using one outfit in the morning and another one in the afternoon to speed things up. Yes. I have lots of horses. Everything two years and over is broke to ride and drive, thanks to my boys."

* * *

John started plowing shortly after five in the morning using four horses and his gang plow. He changed horses at noon and plowed until eight at night.

That afternoon Mac Innesfree brought over his three furrow plow with his four horses. He planned on using John's gang plow while John used the three furrow plow.

In the evenings Mac took Grace on the democrat to go home for the nights, then to come back again the next day after his chores were done.

Jacob brought five horses and his gang plow. He used four horses on the gang plow, the fifth to ride home after the days work.

John's first day in the field with the seven horse hitch, went slowly. He had selected the six most athletic, attentive horses to work in the lead of the two hitches. His lead horses had no tongue to guide them, or hold the eveners up off the ground, so when they would start from a rest stop, one or more of them would invariably have a leg outside one of it's traces. John would have to stop the horses and put the offending leg back in it's place. Finally by the evening of the first day the horses were alert enough to the problem, they would stay inside the traces when they were resting. Once that was accomplished the work went much faster.

The first day when the horses were changed at noon, what he had accomplished in the morning had to be learned all over again with the second hitch of horses. After each rest John would check and fix the collars on all the horses, then get the lead team inside their traces. Sometimes while John was walking back to the plow one of the lead team would kick at a fly and set it's foot down on the outside of the trace. The lessons were learned much faster when John didn't notice a leg outside the trace, until he noticed the horse walking oddly. The hair would be getting rubbed off the leg making the leg tender. The horse was glad to get it's leg in the right place again, learning more quickly to stay in the right place.

Friday afternoon the field was finished. The men sat around and talked while the horses rested for half an hour. John thanked them and shook their hands warmly before they each went on their way to their homes. Mac took his three furrow plow and four horses, and Jacob taking his gang plow and five horses.

The next week John started cutting his crops, and everything was back to normal. Jane and the girls continued doing the chores around the barn and yard, giving John more time to work in the fields.

*   *   *

The next year, John sold another ten horses, to keep pace with the ten foals that were born. That year of 1841 brought in good crops, and John got another eight acres of trees cut and the stumps pulled out, which enabled him to increase his acreage under cultivation.

"Let's go to the Quaker's meeting house this weekend." John suggested to Jane one day. "I think it would be nice to visit with J.L. and family. It will also be an experience for the girls to attend their way of worship. We will go over early Sunday morning. I will get up extra early so I can do the milking before we leave."

"That sounds great. A change should be good." Jane replied. "I will get up with you and come out to help with the milking."

"So will I father," Eliza spoke up, "I want to help, too."

* * *

"Oh, it is so good to see thee." Ann exclaimed. We thought thee had forgotten the way here."

"John has been so busy, we haven't really gone anywhere for a long time." Jane explained.

John Ralph came out of the house to help put the team away. J.L. helped the women out of the carriage.

"You can hook your team on the carriage." John told Ralph. "There is room in it for everyone."

"I want to ride with the driver." Eliza cried.

"No. I do." Janie defied her.

"Now, wait a minute." John held up his hand. "There is room for one to ride up there going to the meeting, and the other coming home from the meeting. Eliza will let her younger sister, Janie ride up there first. Remember what the Bible says?" Eliza shook her head in the affirmative. "What does it say?" John asked her.

"That we should do to others like we want them to do for us." Eliza hung her head and proceeded to get into one of the passenger seats.

"That's right, Eliza. I'm glad you remembered." John said with finality.

John Ralph had finished hooking the team, and was watching the family concert with interest.

On the road, J.L. had a big grin on his face.

"Did thee pay attention to how to handle young ones, Ralph?" he teased his son. "Ralph has announced his intentions of marriage for next year." he was speaking to the rest of the company in the carriage. "We are very happy he has made the decision."

"Who is the lucky girl?" John asked Ralph.

"Matilda Makin." Ralph responded, "Thee will likely remember her."

"You mean that skinny little girl that used to step on your toes at the meetings?" John sounded surprised.

"Yes. That is the one." Ralph squirmed a bit. "She stopped stepping on my feet, John. She is a wonderful girl."

"Congratulations, Ralph. I'm happy for you."

"Thou will receive an invitation to the ceremony and the reception."

"Thank you. We will certainly be there." John replied with great pleasure.

"Thank you Ralph." Jane responded, "We most certainly will be there."

✳ ✳ ✳

Early in the spring of 1842, John had driven a team on the democrat into town. He put his team in the livery barn, instead of taking them to Andy's barn. When he left the barn to go across to the clothier's store, he stopped and looked at the various vehicles outside the livery. A two seated buggy caught his attention, and he examined it closely. After he had purchased a pair of overalls from the clothier's, he walked to Andy's store.

"Andy, can you come with me for an hour or so? Can Maria look after the store that long?"

"Just a minute. I'll ask her" he disappeared into the back for several minutes. When he reappeared he was wearing his cap and a jacket. Mrs. Waggoner came in and began looking around.

"What will you have today, Mrs. Waggoner?" Andy asked.

"I need a can of tea, and some brown sugar. Would you also be able to deliver about fifty pounds of flour to my place sometime today or tomorrow? There is no hurry for it, but I will pay for it now."

"Very good. Here's the tea, and I will have the sugar measured out in a minute," Andy told her. When he set the bag of sugar on the counter, he figured up the bill. "I will deliver the flour as soon as I can arrange it," he informed her.

"Thank you Andy," she paid him and left.

"Good day, gentlemen," she said as she closed the door.

✳ ✳ ✳

Maria came into the store to take over while Andy went with John. At the livery stable, John showed Andy the two seated buggy. "This is what you need Andy. You and your family are not getting away from the store enough. If you had this we could take our families to various different things, like the Kingston market once in a while, for instance."

"We could also come out to your farm more often. Is it in good condition?" Andy's interest was aroused.

"I looked it all over and it seems to be in top condition. It could use a washing and cleaning up, as well as greasing the axles, but I think it is sound. Look at these wheels." John shook the wheels. "They seem to be as good as new, and the undercarriage is solid. I think it is good."

"Where is Bill?" Andy was looking around.

"I'll get him, he's likely in the office in the barn." John left and was back with Bill Shakelton in a couple of minutes. Andy and Bill began discussing the buggy, and finally began negotiating a price. When the deal had been made, the men left for the store.

"Maria's not going to have a baby this year?" John asked.

"No. We just haven't had heart for that kind of life since the kids are gone. Things are getting pretty drab around our place."

"Jane and I are having the same problem. I think it is up to us men to do something about it."

"What do you suggest little brother?" Andy looked at John with deep curiosity.

"Well, Ralph Hodgson is getting married this spring sometime, and we're invited to the wedding. How about you and I taking our two nice buggies to the wedding, and dress up in the same suits we wore for my wedding, and drive the married couples around town? I think taking in the wedding will bring back a lot of good memories and heal a lot of wounds. I know it would for me," John finished, looking Andy in the eyes.

"I think you're right. I like the idea, and am gung-ho to do it. Anything that would get us past this stalemate we seem to be in would be a good move."

"Another thing that came to my mind, your horses are getting along in years. How would you like to buy a team of geldings out of Grace and sired by Bud?" John looked at Andy to catch his reaction to this suggestion.

A grin creased Andy's beard as he looked at John, "I knew there was something more to this than just getting me to buy a buggy," he replied.

"No, really Andy, I'm serious. I didn't do this to drum up business. I just think you need a good team of horses for yourself. Honest Andy. This is not a scheme. Trust me. I will just give you the team for old times sake, if that will make you feel better."

"There I like that deal better," Andy said with a big grin all over his face. "Shake my hand on it, brother."

They shook hands, and now John was grinning. That was what he wanted to do from the start of the deal, but didn't know how he would get Andy to accept it.

"Alright, now we've got things set for the wedding, right?"

"Yup," Andy said as they entered the store.

* * *

The place was full when John, Jane and family entered the meeting house. Andy, Maria and family came in right behind them. They all stood along the back wall. There were five couples standing across the front of the group of people. The girls were dressed in simple white, floor length dresses, the same style and length that the women wore every day. Their hair appeared to be done up in buns on the back of their heads, and were covered by a wide brimmed bonnet, the same color as their dresses. The bonnets were tied under their chins.

The men they were standing with were dressed in their suits they normally wore to their weekly meetings. The service was read from the bible, followed by the oaths the couples took. It was very deep and very meaningful. The service that followed was based on the reading of Paul's letter to the Ephesians, Chapter 5 and Chapter 6. He also read James, Chapter 2. The service ended with the Minister's words: "What God hath joined together, let not man put asunder."

As soon as the service was over, John and Andy went outside, and untying their teams, drove them to the front of the building. The bridal couples came out and three couples got into John's carriage, while the other two got into Andy's buggy. The men drove them around for half an hour, ending at the Meeting House where there was a feast of celebration prepared by the women from the service. John and Andy stayed for part of the feasting, then loaded up their families and headed for home.

John had some of Andy's children with his children, so Janie was riding in Andy's two-seater. Jane was sitting on the driver's seat by John, at his request. They discussed the wedding and the vows, comparing them with the ones they had made. John put his arm around Jane's shoulder and pulling her close to him, spoke of the thoughts he was having,

"Jane, I think it is about time we put our grief behind us, and proceeded to start living again. Do you agree?"

"Yes, I just don't know how to get started."

"How about this?" he dropped his arm to her waist and pulled her over until she was laying across his knees.

"John...John...Stop...You are going to drop me off of the seat."

"Not in this lifetime would I let you drop," he whispered as he bent down and kissed her with his beard and hair covering her face. She stopped struggling and put her arms around his neck. The children were giggling and putting their hands over their mouths. Eliza looked behind to see what Andy and Maria thought of the silliness, but they were wrapped in each others embrace and also kissing. The horses were doing the driving on both rigs.

*   *   *

On one of their many visits to John's farm, Maria suggested, "Let's have Christmas together out here. The children have so much more room for running around, which gives us more time to visit and enjoy the Spirit of Christmas"

"Great idea," Jane clapped her hands. "I love the idea, and I am positive John and Andy will, too. Come out the evening before, so the children can all hang their stockings together. Janie is getting old enough she won't want to hang hers many more years. It will be fun to have the younger children to put on the show for."

Things were back to more the way they used to be, and everyone was happy, and having a joyous time.

*   *   *

The following summer 1843, with John in close attendance, Jane gave birth on May 2, to a strong healthy boy. When he arrived John held him gently in his hands and looked at him with tenderness for a while before passing him to Jane.

"Look Jane, God has blessed us with a beautiful boy. Isn't he everything your heart could desire?"

"I have been praying that God would grant us some sons, and give them life to full manhood." Jane looked at her new son with deep love. "He is so precious, he is. I couldn't bear to lose him," she raised her eyes to John's face. "What will we call him?"

"Well," John spoke slowly, "I haven't dared to think of boys names for our baby. Now that we really have one, I will. Have you got a name in mind Jane?"

"I was thinkin' maybe Henry. What do you think?"

"That sounds good, and goes with Thomas quite nicely." John was looking at the baby again, "We will have him baptized as soon as possible." He was looking thoughtfully at the baby, then he looked at Jane. "We are going to do everything within our knowledge and power to protect this boy. We are going to constantly ask God to spare him for us to raise to manhood."

Henry was taken to church for the first time the following Sunday, and was baptized.

That year Andy and Maria had a boy May 30th, they named Thomas James. Also Ralph and Matilda had a boy July 5th they named John Matthew.

* * *

In the year of our Lord 1845 Ralph and Matilda gave birth to a girl they named Elizabeth Ann. Andy and Maria had another girl born June 14th, they named Hannah Anita. Also on July 8th, Jane gave birth to another boy.

"There John," she said, "we asked for sons to raise, and now our prayers have been answered. Isn't he a precious wee soul?" Jane cooed to the baby. "I thought Georrrge would be a right nice name for him. What do you think?"

"I have been giving a name a lot of thought. Charles Thomas is the name I had come up with. It seems to suit my fancy." John was speaking with pride.

Jane looked at him in thought for a moment, running the name over her lips. "Oh yes, I like that name. So—Charrrles he shall be."

Charles was also baptized on the following Sunday, when he made his debut into the outside world, and his first visit to church.

On their way home from church, Jane turned to John,

"This is ouurrr family now John. This is ourr who--ole family," she was glowing with happiness. "May God give them His grrreatest Blessing!

End of Part 2

LINEAGE RECORDS.

John Lampton Hodgson – born December 1778 in Darlington, Durham, England. Came to Canada. Advertised in a U.S. Quaker magazine for a wife. (When Ann James (Dec. 9, 1775 - ?) arrived in Ontario by train, he looked at her. She said "Well?" He said "I didn't know thee was so old." She said, "Now or never." He said, "Thee'll do. Thee'll do.") {This information supplied curtesy of Muriel (Robinson) Hammond} They were married April 25, 1816 and had a family of two:

1. John Ralph Hodgson – May 1817 – Feb. 18, 1901.
2. Elizabeth Ann Hodgson – December 13, 1819 – November 21, 1899 (died in Michigan)

John Ralph Hodgson (May 1817 – February 18, 1901)and Matilda Makin (1823 in England – Aug. 1, 1899 in Storington County, Ontario) married in 1842 . J.R. cut logs for their home and after the wedding they walked from town to the not-quite-finished house. She sat outside while he made a chair for her to sit on. (Information curtesy of Muriel (Robinson) Hammond. They had a family of nine:

1. John Matthew b. July 5, 1843. He made a business of cheese-making. first in Ontario, then in Manitoba.
2. Elizabeth Ann b. 1845
3. Edwin Watkins b. June 9, 1850, married Sarah A. Webb, January 20, 1875 in Storrington Twp. She was born 1850 and died 1882 in Sunbury. Edwin remarried Hester Shannon on March 27, 1883 in Storrington Twp. On. Hester was the daughter of William Shannon and Elenor McNeely. She was born September 13, 1859 in Sunbury.
4. Emma Jane b. 1852.
5. Alfred H. b. 1852
6. Mary Matilda b. 1856
7. Robert R. b. 1859
8. Ruth Jane b. September 14, 1861
9. William Lewis b. May 10, 1864

The first born of this family – John Matthew Hodgson – married Eliza Spencer Brown, February 18, 1869. They had nine children:

1. Laura M. b. June 1870
2. Lydia May b. December 25, 1871
3. Emma Eliza b. 1873
4. Elwood John b. 1875. died 1962 Brandon, Manitoba.
5. Lindley Robert b. July 14, 1877
6. Annie Albert b. April 6,1884
7. Allan Jay b. April 6, 1884

8. William Henry b. July 27, 1886
9. Mabel Ruth b. 1892

Third child of John Ralph and Matilda Makin was named Edwin Watkins Hodgson. He married Sarah A. Webb January 20, 1875. She died in 1882 in Sunbury. He remarried Hestor Shannon, March 27, 1883. daughter of William Shannon and Ellenor McNeely an Irish couple. They had seven children:

1. Alma Mary b. February 21, 1884. married Thomas Gail Patterson.
2. Matilda (Tillie) Makin b. August 11, 1885 never married.
3. John Ralph b. August 4, 1887 served in the first world war. He was gassed and suffered the effects the rest of his life.
4. Elenor (Ella) b. May 1, 1891 married Peter Bengt Holmgren
5. William Shannon b. August 21, 1894
6. Beatrice Anna b. February 6, 1896 married Samuel Crebbin.
7. Edna Ruth b. February 14, 1900. married Bertram Robinson.

ACKNOWLEDGEMENTS.

I am ever grateful to Uncle Chris Thomas for writing the Thomas family history as he knew it. It is the only recording of the facts of the Thomas life that I know of. His work is to be found in the Hartney History Book – A CENTUARY OF LIVING 1882 – 1982. What a treasure this book is to the families who lived part or all of their lives in or near that small town.

Much of my story is based on the facts to be found in that historical book.

Grateful appreciation to Muriel Hammond, whose mother Edna Robinson was Edna Hodgson. Fortunately for me, Muriel's hobby is collecting and/or assembling her findings in binders. She has a whole bookcase full of these binders. She was gracious enough to supply me with the information that shows the connection between her family and the Thomas family.

Also to my family members – daughter and husband Beverly and Steven Harold for proof reading my finished pieces, to daughter and grand-daughter Helen and Ashley Ross, and also my son Christopher Ross who all had a hand in correcting some of my confusing messes and getting things on my computer straightened up for me.

* * *

The information regarding the terms and sale of land in 1822 was found in the historical book – "Land Policies Of Upper Canada" by Lillian S. Gates. (no longer in print). I was able to borrow it from the University Of Alberta, Rutherford Library, through the Inter Public Library borrowing system.

ABOUT THE AUTHOR

I was born April 20, 1926 in the brick house my grandfather Alfred, had built for his bride in 1902, located five miles south-west of Hartney, Manitoba. In 1928 he moved into his newly built retirement home, three and a half miles north of the home farm, and close to the Souris River. When they moved grandmother took my next sibling – Mary, and myself with her besides her adopted daughter – Marion. During our seven years stay with them, we never missed a Sunday of going to church unless the weather was too formidable.

Grandfather was a dedicated Christian and from his attitude toward life, and with grandmother's coaching, we received our basic Christian education. From grandfather we learned the love of nature and animals, and respect for God. I was born with a love of horses, which started showing itself when I was old enough to open the screen door and escape to the barn.

I married in 1950 and by 1954 realized this marriage was not going to work. I took my three children and two horses and went to work for farmers. I subsequently met Ken Ross in 1957. We married in 1958 and five more children followed. During those years I started writing for my own pleasure, then for organizations I had helped organize, where I became the newsletter editor, and sometimes the secretary.

My era of being able to do the work for horses finally passed, and I went into goats, where I again organized the owners and started writing the newsletter for them.

When I reached the age of having to give up life with the animals, I sold off everything and moved to Edmonton, Alberta to be close to many of my children and their families.

While living in retirement I decided to return to writing, this time stories from my past, which led to writing the fascinating stories I had heard of my ancestors. I am finding it most exhilarating, and wish I had started it much sooner when some of the now deceased people could have given me information from their recollections.

ISBN 141209927-7

9 781412 099271